RAPTURE

THE DEVIL'S GATE MC

USA TODAY BESTSELLING AUTHORS

C.R. JANE
MILA YOUNG

DEDICATION

*To all the readers who look up to the sky and wish for their dreams
on the stars, who love hard, and who never want to grow up...
This book is dedicated to you...*

Love
C.R. and Mila

Trigger Warning

Please Read...

Rapture is a paranormal romance standalone where the heroine ends up with more than one love interest. It may have triggers for some as it has darker themes, blood play, sexual scenes, mention of non-consent, violence, sexual assault, and kidnapping.

JOIN OUR READERS' GROUP

Stay up to date with C.R. Jane by joining her Facebook readers' group, C.R.'s Fated Realm. Ask questions, get first looks at new books/series, and have fun with other book lovers!

Join C.R. Jane's Group

Join Mila Young's Wicked Readers Group to chat directly with Mila and other readers about her books, enter giveaways, and generally just have loads of fun!

Join Mila's Group

RAPTURE

THE DEVIL'S GATE MC

They saved me…only to sacrifice me…

To him.

They call it the Rapture, when the vampire king comes.

And this time, he's come for me.

Just as he's come every ten years for so long, no one can even remember when it all began.

He's the villain in my story, I see that right away.

But when his teeth sink into my skin…something happens.

Something that isn't supposed to.

Instead of draining me like all the others…

He changes me.

Makes me like him.

Now I'm trapped in his kingdom of monsters.

Completely unrecognizable from the girl I once was.

He and his lost boys have changed the rules of the game.

But the more time that passes, the more I realize...I still want to play.

RAPTURE SOUNDTRACK

Welcome To The Black Parade
Chemical Romance

Birdcage
Thomas Lizzara

better off without me
Matt Hansen

Scars
Papa Roach

Lost
Sarah Proctor

Paint It Black
Claudillea

Somebody Else
Ruelle

Just A Girl
Astyria

what doesn't kill me
Kacey Musgraves

Anybody Else
Faouzia, Jonah

Back From The Dead
Besomorph, AViVA

Listen to the Spotify Playlist Here

"To die will be an awfully big adventure." -Peter Pan

PROLOGUE
BEFORE

GWENDOLYN

I'd woken to my parents arguing again, and this time it wasn't just a disagreement. This was a full-on screaming match filled with slamming doors and harsh, cutting words. It left me shaking in bed, convinced they were finally done for good.

My father lost his job at the local fishery port several days ago, and ever since, there'd been no peace in the house. The hushed, worried whispers had grown louder every day, to the point their arguments could be heard clearly through the walls. My mother would try to hide her tears, but I'd walked in on her more than once to find them streaming down her face. It was clear we were in trouble, and I could barely sleep.

Especially when I'd overheard them this morning,

I'd been slipping out of bed in the early hours, trekking up the hill to hunt with my bow and arrow. My father had fashioned it out of oak for me, and he'd worked on it for days before giving it to me on my birthday.

If I caught enough rabbits, I could sell their fur at the markets. And I'd hunt every day if I needed to until Father got another job. Anything to stop the arguing and keep our home.

I spotted a grey-furred rabbit hopping through the field of blue and white flowers and sprinted forward on silent feet behind it. This wasn't my first time hunting. My father always liked to brag that he'd been hunting deer when he was my age. No time like the present to brush up on my skills before I moved on to bigger game.

I glided quickly through the meadow, my hands tightening around the bow and arrow, when the animal paused.

I followed suit, my heart drumming in my chest, imagining the smile on my parents' faces when I showed them what I'd managed.

The animal lifted its nose in the air, sniffing.

Had it caught my scent?

As a wolf shifter, I could easily hunt it in animal form, but then I'd risk losing control and devouring it. I hadn't exactly gained strong dominance over her yet, even if she was an omega, but Father was always telling me that I needed to build my skills both with and without my wolf. To be adaptable, because life was never steady. It could change in a heartbeat.

I understood, and now it was time to make him proud.

I lifted my weapon, straightened my spine, and pointed the bow down as I notched the arrow to the string. Aiming for the rabbit, I tried to steady my breath and arms.

A smoky breeze suddenly got caught in my throat as I inhaled through my nose.

I turned my head toward the village down in the valley, and the sight sank deep inside me, freezing me to my bones.

Fire was engulfing the village.

The sky grew darker with black smoke, brutal amber flames blazing across the huts. It hungrily licked the sky, and people were madly running around to put out the fire with buckets of water.

I gasped out loud, causing the rabbit to scramble madly away from me. But I didn't bother trying to go after it again, not with the sight in front of me.

Sparks of dread flared in my heart.

Dropping the bow and arrow, I turned and ran down the hill. The wind whipped against me, the downward momentum pushing me to go faster. A sob slipped past my throat as the crackle of fire sang on the wind blowing past me.

I ran faster, my sight narrowing to the right of the village where my home was, where I'd last seen my parents.

Howls came from all around me, and terror rose in the back of my throat, a scream pressing forward. Townspeople were already in their wolf forms, scrambling away from the growing inferno.

My foot suddenly caught on a root, and I went flying. The ground came rushing toward me as I smacked into it so hard, all the air swooshed out of my lungs, and I cried out in shock.

Fear tightened in my chest. My parents...they were all I had. "Please be alive, please." I began to sob with terror at what awaited me in the village.

The fire grew worse, and even from my position, I felt its heat on my face, the smoke stinging my nostrils.

With renewed panic, I scrambled to my feet, pushing past the pain in my knees and shoulder that I'd crashed down on.

Our town was ruled by the wolf shifters who lived there, with guards to keep us safe. How did this happen?

More howls came, and the fires raged higher.

Crackling and snapping, sparks flew in every direction.

Leaving the hill behind, I darted frantically to the village while people ran past me, yelling at me to turn around.

I didn't listen to them. I couldn't.

I cut across the pebbled street where the smoke grew thick. My eyes stung, but I covered my nose and mouth with my sleeve and ran madly. Fire roared all around me, flames bursting out of windows, licking the walls, scorching them with burn marks.

People were screaming, most running away. The blaze was giant, towering over the town. Some homes were completely engulfed, others untouched.

I sprinted across the open marketplace where people were rushing in every direction, frantically yelling for help.

Bodies lay in front of some homes, burned to the point where I couldn't recognize them. Smoke curled up from their bodies, and a scream got caught in my throat from seeing them.

I forced myself to look away while tears filled my eyes and smoke assaulted my senses.

I finally came upon my family cottage. A small brown building that was perfect for the three of us. By some miracle, it hadn't caught alight yet. The only reason I could guess was that we were located at the rear of the village, backing onto the woods.

The blaze behind me heightened, the gust of wind lashing at my hair, engulfing me with the stench of smoke. I coughed, the pain like acid on my throat.

But I kept going, rushing past the open front gates, and I burst into the house.

"Mama," I frantically yelled. "Papa!"

I ran into one room and the next, my pulse speeding. Had they escaped?

Outside the window, the neighbors' house glinted orange with the fire.

Darting into the kitchen, I tripped over something. I moved too fast to catch myself and fell forward, landing on my hands and knees. The faint scent of blood found me, and I tasted it on the back of my tongue.

Crying out, I swiftly twisted around to find exactly what I'd fallen over.

"Papa," I cried, fear piercing my chest.

He lay on his back on the tiles in a pool of blood. Wide open eyes, he stared at the ceiling. Blood gushed from his slashed throat. It spilled from him, running down the side of his neck.

My heart struck my ribcage, and I desperately shoved myself back across the floor until my heels hit the iron stove.

Tears rushed down my face, and I curled in on myself, hugging my knees, my head spinning.

My mind screamed to run out of there, but I couldn't move.

I struggled to breathe, unable to call out for help.

Shutting my eyes, I couldn't erase the image of my father savagely killed, torn apart and left to die.

In a flash, the thumping of footsteps resonated somewhere in the house, growing louder as whatever it was moved closer to the kitchen.

I flinched, trying to squeeze myself into the crevice between the stove and wall, wanting to disappear. What if Papa's killers were still in the house?

A figure filled the kitchen doorway and I screamed, tears blurring my vision.

Soft hands were suddenly on my arms, words reaching me. "Hush, Gwendolyn. You can't make a sound."

Eyes widening, I wiped the tears away. "Mama!'" She looked scared, her eyes rimmed red from crying.

I threw myself into her arms, sobbing uncontrollably. She lifted me into her embrace and walked me out of the kitchen.

"Now listen carefully. I need you to do something for me, Gwendolyn. Can you do that?"

I nodded, trying to stifle my tears as she lowered me to my feet. We were in the living area with the fireplace and two couches covered in knitted blankets. She was opening up the cabinet doors where she kept the linen. We didn't own a lot, but she pushed a bed sheet and blanket aside and then looked at me.

"You have to get inside now, Gwen. And don't say a word." Her voice trembled, and she kept glancing over her shoulder.

Straining for breath in the smoke-infused air, I stared at her. "What's happening? Who killed Papa? The fire will be here soon." My words were running fast out of my mouth.

"Please, sweetie. You need to get inside. They're already putting the fires out, but something more dangerous is coming back for us."

"Who?" I choked on my breath, and before I knew it, she'd gotten me to climb into the cabinet that offered me enough space to sit upright.

"Don't make any sounds. Can you do this for me, Darling?" she whispered in a pleading voice just as a loud bang sounded so near, it might have been inside the house.

Mama flinched, her wide, terrified stare glancing to the hallway, and her hands trembled as she gripped the doors.

"I'm scared," I whispered.

"They're here," she mumbled under her breath, then fiddled with the ring on her finger. She took it off and gave it to me. "This is yours now, Gwen. It's our family ring and you must treasure it. It will always remind you of me."

She curled my fingers around the ring, then smiled softly and traced a hand over my cheek. "I love you so much, Gwen. I'll always be with you in your heart, no matter what happens. Please,   remember to always fight for what you want. I love you, my sweet angel. Now, cover your ears."

Without another word, she shut the cabinet doors, and darkness closed in around me. I quickly pushed the ring into the pocket of my pants. But panic engulfed me as my mind raced with who was coming back. The same people who hurt my father?

Thunderous footfalls sounded, and I hugged my knees tightly to my chest.

A sharp screech came from somewhere in the house, and I pressed myself into the corner, shaking.

The floorboards creaked in the hallway, like they always did when anyone heavy walked over them.

Tears rolled down my cheeks, the urge to scream in the back of my throat. But Mama's words blared in my head.

Don't make any sounds.

A crashing of wood splintering came from somewhere nearby, followed by my mother's scream. Glass shattered and I flinched, tears rolling down my face.

Mama! I almost cried out.

Don't make any sounds.

A loud thump came, like something hit the floor, followed by a squelching, wet noise and a thunderous growl.

I trembled, my breathing see-sawing in and out of me, my vision blurred. To stop myself from screaming, I clamped a hand over my mouth and sat there, frozen and terrified, picturing my mother left to die just like my father.

A gurgling came next, and then the pounding footfalls seemed to run through the house.

Something more dangerous is coming back for us.

Shaking, I didn't dare move and remained that way long after the sounds vanished. So much so that I must have passed out, because when I opened my eyes again, the door was being pried open and a man with the kindest eyes I'd ever seen was staring at me.

"Hello there," he soothed. "I'm not going to hurt you."

Even delayed, the shock startled me, and I flinched backward, screaming with dread.

He had strawberry blond hair that was graying at the temples, and somehow, he got me out of the cabinet.

My pulse raced through my veins, my knees so numb from being cramped up that I couldn't stand on my own.

The man held me and smoothed the hair out of my face, studying me with the softest brown eyes. "You're safe now, little one. The fire's been put out. We're searching for survivors."

I blinked at the man I instantly recognized as a shifter by his heavy wolf scent.

"My parents," I gasped, peering over to the hallway where all I saw were bloody drag lines. Remembered horror pounded in my mind, and fresh tears fell from my puffy eyes.

I tried to stand on my own but stumbled, and the man held onto my arms to steady me. "It's only you in the house. I don't know what happened here, but you're not alone anymore." He looked at me with pity in his gaze. "My name's Caleb and I've been helping with the clean-up of this town, rescuing who's left. What's your name?"

Everything was too much, too confusing, and still, my

name slipped past my lips in a whisper, "Gwendolyn. But where's my mama?"

The bridge of his nose pinched. "There's no one else in the house. But you don't have to be alone anymore. I have a large home, and there's always room for one more; you can stay until your mama comes back." Even as the words slipped from his lips, I knew he thought she was dead.

Without warning, he lifted me in his arms and carried me out to the hallway where there was indeed no sign of my mother. Only blood. So much of it was on the floor, and more was splashed on the walls.

I cried, trembling in the man's arms.

A sliver of sunlight caught my eyes once we stepped outside the house, the smoke clearing, and I looked up to the bright sky. It heated my face, and I was certain I heard my mother's whisper in my ear.

I will always be with you in your heart.

"I have a large garden you can play in, and a family who will love to have you there, so you'll never be alone. Okay, Gwendolyn?" Caleb said, distracting me.

I wasn't sure how to respond because I wanted *my* family, not a different one.

Around us, the fires were out. Only wisps of smoke curled from the charred remains that were once homes. Most of the huts were destroyed. Those that remained, like mine, were black on the outside from how close the fire got, but there were maybe only half a dozen of those remaining.

We reached a white SUV by the side of the dirt road where Caleb set me on my feet. I kept staring at my home, at the village that had been obliterated. A few people searching the burned homes in the distance remained, but I didn't recognize them.

Caleb collected a blanket from the backseat, and wrapped it around my shoulders. "We can wait to see if you recognize anyone in the village who might have information about your family."

His words were soft, and every time I looked at him, I saw my father in his kind eyes. He offered me a bottle of water.

I nodded, wiping at my tears. "Okay."

"I won't be long; I have to go speak with my friends." He walked quickly to the others nearby, without waiting for my response. He paused to talk to two females, then soon returned, announcing, "They're going to ask around for your mama."

I nodded, hugging myself with the blanket just as a distraught couple came over to us.

The woman with reddish hair offered me a soft smile and asked for the man's details in case they needed to get hold of me if they found my parents. They gave me pitiful looks after that, and then they left. I didn't know them, but neither of them offered to take me with them.

Caleb turned to me, and I stared at him, too choked up to reply. "Should we head out?" Black soot stained his face and arms from having searched for survivors in their burned homes. He was a kind person, I could see that clearly. He would have gotten along well with my father.

"Yes." The tears fell and my chin trembled.

He opened the back door for me and I slid inside. Before

closing the door, Caleb paused, his lips pinching, and I saw the pain etched in his eyes. "I don't think anything I say can ease your pain from today, but my grandfather once said something to me that has always stayed with me."

I blinked the tears away. "What was it?"

"That sometimes the universe will challenge us. It will take away everything. But every one of us has the power to change our fate. You just have to fight for what you want no matter how much it hurts."

With a small smile, he closed the door and got into the driver's seat, and started the car. But his saying brought back my mother's last words.

Remember to always fight for what you want.

Grief burned through me, and I dropped my face into my hands, crying.

"I'm really sorry this happened to you, Gwendolyn," he murmured. "I heard from friends about your village going up in smoke, and we all came quickly so we could lend a helping hand. But we didn't get here quick enough."

I wanted to say something about this not being his fault, but no words came. As we began to drive away from the village, I stared out my window, up at the sky, watching the ash blowing in the wind like snow.

Ashes of where I'd once belonged, and the life I'd lost.

Forever.

CHAPTER 1

8 YEARS LATER...

GWENDOLYN

"**G**wendolyn!" Sussana's shriek filled the air, rattling through the closet-sized room I slept in, stirring up dust and cobwebs until I couldn't help but sneeze.

My eyes were heavy, my body so tired that even the shrillness of her voice was almost forgettable in my desperation to go back to sleep.

The door was thrown open so hard it banged into the wall behind it. Beyond Sussana's body, I could see rows of boxes lining the hallway.

Right.

Today was moving day. I was so exhausted from packing for most of the night and the last couple of weeks that I'd almost forgotten the big event was here.

Not just moving day. It was the wedding day as well.

For a second, my chest tightened, the air around me growing thick and cloying as I thought of Caleb, the soft-hearted beta who'd saved me all those years ago. He'd been gone for four years now, his death sudden and mysterious.

And everything had been terrible since then.

But I guess I was still alive.

"Have you suddenly gone deaf?" Sussana snapped, her voice dragging me back to the present.

With a deep exhale, I turned towards her, pasting a plastic smile on my lips.

"I'm sorry. I guess I was a little tired after being up so late —" I began, not surprised in the least when she immediately went into a rant about my ungratefulness for putting a roof over my head and food in my belly all these years. I tuned her out because at this point...I had the speech memorized.

As I slid off the mattress on the floor she so graciously allowed me to sleep on, I kept my gaze on her face. Sussana was a pretty woman, there was no doubt about that, with hair the color of rich cream and eyes a sky blue that she could make cry on command. With her tight figure, it was easy to see how poor Caleb had been dragged into her web, marrying her before he could realize the decay that lay inside the pretty package.

He'd been too kind to survive her, I'd always thought. But Alpha Silver would have no such problem. From what I'd seen, they'd be a match made in heaven. Much better than his beta had ever been.

"Are you listening?"

Whoops. I'd zoned out again.

"Yes, ma'am. I'll have everything done in time for the ceremony."

She sniffed, her gaze tracking from the top of my head to my toes. No one had a better talent for making someone feel small than Sussana. It was a gift, really. "Make sure to take a shower and brush your hair for once. I'll not have you embarrassing the Alpha."

Without another word, she stepped back into the hallway and slammed the door, so hard that a spider and a pile of dirt fell from the ceiling.

I shivered and grabbed my shoe, smacking the damn thing before it did something crazy and lunged at me.

Spiders around here were known to do that, in my experience.

I closed my eyes for a second, and I went to my place. The one I always did, where I was with my family, in the town where I'd grown up. I imagined waking up for a Saturday breakfast, and then going on a long walk. I imagined fishing at the lake with my dad. I just…imagined.

The horrible thing was…so much time had passed, that no matter how many times I went through this particular exercise to prepare myself for what was sure to be a terrible day… I was still forgetting their faces. They were more like blurs at this point. All that was left was the memory of the warm feeling I'd always had when they'd hugged me.

But I was sure that would fade away soon as well.

My parents had been found eventually, dead of course, their bodies left in the woods. The fire and their deaths were blamed on marauding thieves who'd eventually been caught when they'd tried to attack a more prepared village. But bringing the murderers to justice hadn't brought my parents back, and I still felt the pain of the loss of my parents like a swift knife in the chest.

Pushing away the self-pity, I threw on the work dress I'd need for this morning's chores, and I darted into the hallway, dread for the day licking at my spine.

Sussana's prized daughters, Dierdra and Persephone, were seated at the table, both of them glaring disdainfully at the egg whites and spinach on their plates. Sussana had put both of them on a very strict diet for the wedding. I, thank goodness, had avoided that fate. Sussana had informed me that I was "already beyond help" and Cook didn't need to waste her talents on me.

So charming.

Dierdra was practically her mother's clone, while Persephone reminded me of Caleb every time I looked at her, with her strawberry blonde hair and warm brown eyes.

Too bad neither of them had inherited his charming personality.

There was no love lost between the three of us. Having to cater to their whims from the moment Caleb died had made sure of that. They'd had the chance to treat me like a living being worthy of respect—even like their sister—and instead, they'd made my life hell.

I hoped they choked on their egg whites.

Persephone's scornful gaze followed me as I walked to the sink and immediately began washing the dishes Cook had stacked up from making the girls' breakfast. If I was lucky, I'd be able to make some toast with her homemade sourdough bread, something completely forbidden to the trolls at the moment.

Persephone and Dierdra were whispering to each other. I overheard the word "rapture" and frowned, wondering if they were both reading the same book or something.

A couple of minutes later, they left, only a few muttered taunts thrown my way, and I could breathe again.

At least for a couple hours more.

Staring out the window, I could see where pack members were setting up the enormous white tent that would hold the reception. We'd all be moving into the Alpha's house in town, but this one apparently had the bigger backyard since we were on the outskirts, so the celebration would be taking place here.

All the important members of the pack would be attending. Which was a shame for them, because their new "Luna" was going to be nothing like their old one.

My thoughts drifted to the Alpha's son, Atlas, my cheeks warming as I pictured his beautiful face in my head. He'd never given me the time of day—but really, why would he? I was below dirt in this pack and he was…everything.

"Better go get ready for the ceremony," Cook murmured under her breath, knocking me gently with her hip to take my place at the sink. Cook couldn't be caught being kind to me in front of Sussana and the girls, but she'd always done her best to show me kindness when they weren't around.

She shoved a piece of the sourdough toast I'd been

longing for into my hand, and I quickly shoved it into my mouth before heading out of the kitchen and to the servant bathroom. The only bathroom I was allowed to use in the place. Usually, there wasn't any hot water left, but at least I knew none of the three devil women would deign to walk in there and give me a hard time.

The servants had all apparently showered, because there was indeed no hot water. I took the quickest shower I could and then hopped out to get dried off and try and make myself presentable.

I stared into the mirror as I brushed my hair, trying to avoid the negative thoughts that crept in every time I saw my reflection.

I was…different.

There was no denying that.

My hair was lavender. And I'd never touched it with dye. I'd just been born out of the womb with light purple hair. It was long, down to my ass. And it drew stares wherever I went.

As if that wasn't enough, my eyes were odd as well. They were a bright amber color, more gold than brown, with flecks of green and yellow in them.

Like I said…I was different.

The rest of me was alright, I guessed. I had a pert nose, upturned slightly at the end. A few freckles dotted my cheeks and nose, but the rest of my skin was smooth and tan. My boobs were fine, I supposed—certainly not huge, but more than a handful.

Not that I went around grabbing them all the time or

anything…

I sighed and jerked my brush through a stubborn knot in my wet hair. It didn't really matter what I looked like; no one in this town was going to touch me with a ten-foot pole, even if they did think I was easy on the eyes.

Sussana had made sure of that.

Speaking of the she-demon, I heard my name shrieked from somewhere in the house. I hastily threw on the pale yellow monstrosity of a dress I was expected to wear today and rushed out of the bathroom.

I found her in her closet, glaring at the poor seamstress who had helped her into her wedding gown.

Why did evil souls have to come in such pretty packages, I wondered as I stared at her in her gorgeous lace gown. Since I'd seen her this morning, she'd had someone come in to do her hair and makeup. She was the picture of a blushing bride, with subtle pink and gold tones to her eyes and her hair done up in an elegant french twist.

The Alpha was going to be so pleased with himself. Which wasn't that hard to accomplish, honestly, since he was always pleased with himself.

There was self-confidence…and then there was him.

"Get in here and polish these shoes," Sussana snapped, kicking the box in front of her and frightening the poor seamstress to death. She dropped the needle and thread she'd been holding, and I watched idly as it unwound across the black carpet.

Keeping my face the picture of indifference, I knelt and grabbed the new shoes—shoes that did not need to be polished in the slightest. I knew, though, that I would spend the next half hour dutifully removing the invisible blemishes and marks that only she could see.

While I went to work on the sparkly white heels, she admired herself in the full-length mirror that hung on the wall in front of her.

"I think I look even better than at my first wedding," she announced with a wicked giggle. I stiffened at the casual mention of her marriage to Caleb. She never mentioned him. If she did, it was only to complain that he'd brought the blight of me upon her.

Anger curdled in my gut at the pleased expression on her face. I'd never be able to prove it, but I swore she'd had something to do with his death. For someone she'd been married to for fifteen years, someone who had treated her like a queen, she'd never shown any sign of mourning. She'd even worn a black veil to the funeral so no one could see her decidedly tear-free eyes. She couldn't even muster up fake tears for the event.

Caleb had deserved so much better than her and what had happened.

"Give those to me," she snapped after she'd finished loving on herself. I handed her the shoes and she inspected them with a frown, probably peeved that she couldn't find anything to yell at me for.

Give it a minute, woman. I'm sure you'll find something, I thought to myself. She finally glanced up, landing on my still-damp hair.

"Go do something...with that...thing on your head," she

hissed before checking her watch. "You're due to start handing drinks to guests in fifteen minutes! I can't believe you would stress me out like this on my wedding day."

Honestly, she was something. My hair would be perfectly fine if she hadn't called me for her shoes.

But of course, I didn't say anything.

I never did.

Not since the night after Caleb's death when she'd dragged me out of the bedroom and into the tiny closet I now resided in.

"Pack your things," she said calmly, a proud glimmer in her gaze as she stared down to where I'd been sobbing quietly into my pillow.

My eyes roved over her face, confused.

"Pack. Your. Things," she repeated, a hint of danger breaking the calm.

I slid off my bed, my insides trembling. I was exhausted from crying and mourning all day. I'd already had everything taken from me. And now Caleb was gone. The one bright spot in my life.

"You're kicking me out?"

She laughed, the cruel sound grating on my ears and my nerves. I'd always known she didn't like me...but this was something else.

This was hate.

"I wish that was possible, you useless girl. But what would the pack think? I may not be able to get rid of you quite yet, but I at least can put you where you belong."

I don't know what got into me then. I knew better than to speak when a snake was poised to strike. Maybe it was the grief that clouded my mind. Maybe it was my complete tiredness of having fate give me the middle finger.

"No." The words leaped out of me.

There was a long moment of silence as her gaze widened, before the black started to overtake the blue. I didn't get a warning before her claws were suddenly lengthened and she was swiping across my chest...

As I walked along the hallway, I trailed my fingertip across the long scar that had never healed, puckering the flesh and serving as a reminder of what the world could do to you if you weren't careful.

Maybe someday I'd get my voice back.

But today was not that day.

———

The girls were going to drive me mad. They were up to something...I was sure of it. Their underhanded whispers, the way their stares lingered on me. There were plenty of other people here to catch their attention, all the eye candy the pack held, in fact.

Which made it all the more suspicious why their focus was completely on me.

The ceremony had been gauche and pretty, but it had gone off without a hitch. Sussana's crocodile tears of joy had been the icing on the cake as she stared lovingly into the Alpha's eyes and promised to love him for the rest of her life.

Or at least until someone bigger and badder came along for her to sink her claws into.

Since Sussana was a shifter, she wouldn't have to worry about losing her beauty to aging for a long, long time.

Pity.

The Alpha better watch his back.

A flash of gold caught my gaze, and I knew without turning my head all the way who it was.

Atlas.

There were beautiful creatures…and then there was him.

A class of his own.

A face that drew stares wherever he was. He'd been a god at our school. Not just for being the Alpha's son, and presumed heir to the pack.

But because of him.

He shined. I didn't know how to explain it.

He had high cheekbones that every girl had to be envious of, and a square jaw that was so perfect it had my ovaries begging for relief.

If that was a thing.

His eyes were an aquamarine color that reminded me of waves caressing a golden beach under a sunset. And, of course, they were outlined by long, black eyelashes that I wished I could steal. His hair and skin were gold. That was the only way to describe them. Like he'd been touched by King Midas himself.

And unlike the other pretty shifters in this town, of which there were many, he didn't seem to be rotten on the inside.

Which may have been a pity, because every time I saw him, I longed for something I'd never have.

There was a minute, early on in the reception, when I'd

been handing out flutes of sparkling, fizzing champagne... when I'd thought he'd been staring at me. I'd been so awkward about it that I'd almost spilled a glass on Ms. Pennyworth's outrageous leopard gown.

It probably would have improved the garish thing, but caused me a whole boatload of other problems.

Someone had cleared their throat behind me, and I'd realized that Chartruse Bennett had been standing behind me, the queen to Atlas's king.

I'd heard that they'd been on again, off again for most of senior year, even though I'd never actually seen him act affectionately towards her in any way in the hallways.

It was incredibly annoying to feel the shock of disappointment fly up my spine.

Of course he hadn't been looking at me.

No one ever looked at me.

I was currently beside the wedding cake, doing my best to avoid staring at Atlas, because I'd been given the delightful task of cutting it into pieces and serving it to the guests in exactly ten minutes. And heaven knows I didn't need to get distracted by his face and end up falling headfirst into the cake or something.

It was quite the specimen—the cake—I'd already made clear that Atlas was as well. It was eight layers tall, with white roses in between each layer and edible crystals and lace all over the outside to coordinate with Sussana's wedding dress. I knew beyond the white frosting was a delicious chocolate ganache that Cook had spent hours perfecting.

Hopefully I could sneak a piece after the festivities were over.

None of the shifters here did things like eat cake. Even with their beyond-average metabolisms, image was everything to these creatures.

I heard a soft rustling beside me, near the cake table, and I glanced over to make sure everything was alright.

Horror.

So thick I could taste it.

As I watched the gorgeous cake begin to fall over, as if in slow motion.

My life literally flashed before my eyes.

Because I was done for.

The cake splattered all over my dress and shoes as it tumbled off the table and onto the floor as every eye in the tent turned my way.

Fuck. Fuck. Fuck.

Tittering laughs trailed off behind me, and I saw Dierdra and Persephone dashing off across the lawn.

Those cows.

Sussana was stalking my way, dragging Alpha Silver behind her, her face the picture of fury.

This was it. She was going to kick me out. I'd be forced out into the wilderness. The nearest pack was hundreds of miles away. I had about as many outside survival skills as a gummy bear.

I would definitely die.

Maybe that would be a good thing.

The thought slipped into my head, but this time, I didn't know if I wanted to push it out.

"What the fuck did you do?" Sussana hissed at me, her false face slipping in the wake of her anger. Her arms were stretched out in front of her like she wanted to strangle me.

"I'm so sorry, Sussana," came Atlas's smooth voice from behind me, not sounding particularly sorry at all.

Wait, what was he apologizing for?

She came to a screeching halt, her mouth hanging open, a little slack-jawed as she was faced with Atlas's brilliance. His father, Alpha Silver, was a handsome man, but his first wife had been a complete stunner, because he could not compete with his son.

I flicked a glance over to Atlas, trying to understand what he was doing, but he ignored my gaze.

Sussana shook her head, like she was forcing her way out of a trance, and glanced back and forth between the two of us.

If I hadn't been scared shitless of what she was going to do, I would definitely have been laughing right now.

Suddenly, it hit her...right about the same time it hit me. He was apologizing for the fallen cake, wasn't he?

"You knocked the cake over?" Her voice was incredulous...and a bit suspicious. I couldn't blame her; I'd never seen Atlas do a single clumsy thing in school, and I'd been watching him...a lot.

Yes, I was fully aware that it bordered on creeper status, but I was sure that the rest of the female—and probably male —population was right there with me.

Alpha Silver had his eyebrows raised, clearly confused as well. I'd never seen him treat his golden son with anything but pride over his accomplishments and how it reflected on his reputation as a parent. I wasn't sure he was buying this story either.

"I, unfortunately, got distracted watching Tatum and Dupree fall into the pond out there, and I stepped right into the table," he explained. "Ahh, there they are now."

We all glanced towards the pond out by the back fence and watched as Tatum and Dupree, two of the single pack members whose idea of a good time was getting completely blacked out, staggered from the pond. They were completely drenched, looking more like wet dogs than anything else.

It was like the stars had aligned. Sussana's face gentled, and all the anger seeped out of her. Because how could she be angry at her new stepson? The stepson she obviously wanted to fuck by the way her gaze tracked over his features.

Gross.

A flash of discontent sparked through my chest at the thought of her sinking her claws into him.

"Mistakes happen," Sussana simpered. "Luckily, Cook has an extra just in case." She gestured to where Cook was already bringing out an identical cake from the back entrance. Sussana popped a cruel glare my way. "We always have to be prepared with Gwendolyn around. Her clumsiness knows no bounds. We all lucked out that she didn't have a hand in this. We'd probably all be wearing cake right now." Her laugh was a pretty tinkle that burned my ear drums.

Atlas still didn't glance my way, but I couldn't help but

notice that his body tensed up at her comment…almost like it upset him.

Well, it sure as hell upset me. Embarrassed me as well.

I wasn't clumsy. I really wasn't. But since things did tend to happen around me…mostly thanks to her terrible daughters, I certainly had that reputation in her eyes.

I took a step backward, wishing I could melt into the gauzy white fabric of the tent. Sussana and Alpha Silver turned back towards their guests, forgetting about me for at least a moment.

But I was still covered in cake, and a few of the guests were staring at me and obviously talking about me as I stood there.

Nausea built up in my throat, like a drain that was plugged. And I couldn't take it anymore. My hand went to the ring I wore on a chain around my throat, the only thing I had left of my mother, and I rubbed the dark purple stone in my fingers, trying to calm myself down.

"Go inside and get changed. I'll handle this." Atlas's voice washed over me from where he was still standing.

But his eyes were on me now. The warmth of them like the sun grazing my skin.

It was the first time he'd ever spoken to me.

And I was absurdly desperate for it not to be the last.

"Go inside?" I choked out.

"To clean off the cake?"

"Oh, right," I mumbled, my face heating up in embarrassment about what a spazz I was.

I'd thought about what I'd say to him if he ever spoke to

me. Practiced it a few times, actually. Sometimes I imagined the conversation with my hand down my pants, but that was a whole different beast.

Words had somehow escaped me now that we were actually speaking.

Exit time.

I moved to rush past him to the house, but hesitated a step away.

"Thank you," I murmured to him, wishing I had better words for the kindness he'd just shown.

And it might have been my imagination, but as I walked away, I could have sworn that he'd responded with... "Always."

CHAPTER 2
GWENDOLYN

Our new house was beautiful. I couldn't deny that. Fitting for an Alpha. Out of all the houses in the pack, this one had been spared no expense. Stained glass windows, and high ceilings. Gold fixtures that gleamed. Wooden floors without a scratch. And so many rooms.

One perk was that I was in a bedroom once again, and not a spider-filled closet of a space. With this many rooms, it would have seemed suspicious if I hadn't been given a bedroom. Even if the Alpha didn't give a damn about me.

Another perk…I wasn't reminded of Caleb everywhere I looked. There were too many memories in the old house. It was nice not to breathe and be forced to remember that he was gone every second.

I hadn't seen Atlas since the night of the wedding. He'd

been sent away for pack business so his father could stay here with his new bride.

I missed him.

I wasn't sure how you could miss someone you didn't even know, but something had happened that night. Something had burned between us. I'd seen it in his gaze, and I really, really liked it. I wanted the chance to discover more of it. To see if the reality of him was as good as the promise.

"The Rapture is in one week. What if he doesn't like her? She's absolutely miserable. He could very well decide she's not enough," my stepmother muttered worriedly from the dining room.

I was standing in the hallway, about to enter, but her words stopped me cold. There was that word again.

Rapture.

There was a menacing fear when she'd said it. Like she was terrified of it. But what was she even talking about? And who wasn't going to be liked?

I walked into the room then, and her words abruptly cut off as she scowled at me.

The Alpha didn't look perturbed to see me there. He gestured me towards the table, placing food on a plate—something he definitely hadn't done before.

"Sit, sit," he said jovially—also something that seemed wrong coming from his mouth. He wasn't a happy-go-lucky kind of guy.

Sussana was sitting there pouting, but she didn't say anything.

What the hell was going on?

I nibbled on a piece of bacon, wondering what I was supposed to do now. I hadn't planned on being allowed to eat. But you had to walk through the dining room to get to the kitchen, which is why I'd entered the room in the first place...to start my chores.

"So you've been with us now for six years?" Alpha Silver asked, his grey gaze feeling like it was barreling into my skin.

Personally, I did not like being watched while eating, but I guess beggars couldn't be choosers.

"Eight," I answered carefully, making sure my voice wasn't at all petulant when I answered, lest he think I was ungrateful to be here.

"Mmmh," he replied, putting a piece of pineapple in his mouth as he chewed thoughtfully. He was about to say something else when I heard the front door open, then shut, followed by the sound of footsteps coming down the hall.

"Son," Alpha Silver growled, and I froze in my seat.

Atlas.

He was back.

Sparks flew up my spine, like just his proximity had the ability to set my skin on fire.

He settled onto the chair next to me and I glanced over at him, willing myself not to fawn...or swoon. Because that could happen.

My fork clattered to the table when I saw the heat in his gaze as we locked eyes, and I quickly forced myself to look away, a blush darkening my cheeks. I didn't dare peek at Sussana. I was just hopeful she wouldn't notice.

Alpha Silver either didn't notice, or he didn't care because he launched right into peppering Atlas with questions about how his trip had gone.

It was odd for him to be discussing pack business in front of me. But I guess he could have forgotten I was here, even though I was seated right next to him. That happened to me sometimes; I would be in a room, and everyone would forget I was there. Like I was just drapery instead of a living being.

"Any news?" Alpha Silver growled. My eyes widened when I heard the unmistakable sound of fear in his voice.

What would someone like him be afraid of?

"There are whispers he's been seen," Atlas answered. His hands were balled into fists, so tightly that his knuckles were turning white as I watched.

"How long?" Sussana choked out, sounding equally afraid. "How long do we have?"

I'd never heard her being afraid of anything. And now, fear was sputtering to life in my chest as well.

"A few days at the most. The Rapture is upon us."

"The Rapture," I repeated slowly, glancing at all three of their solemn faces. "What is that? Why do you all sound so afraid?"

Sussana stiffened in her chair at my question, but my gaze was now locked on the Alpha, who was all of a sudden feigning a relaxed posture. "Mmmh, a story for another time, perhaps," he responded silkily.

Atlas was so tense next to me, I could feel it radiating off of him like it was a tangible thing.

"Don't you have chores to do?" Sussana suddenly snapped, and I nodded slowly, dread thickening in my throat.

This had all been terribly confusing. Being invited to sit for breakfast in the first place, and then every second that had transpired since then.

I stood up quickly from my chair and grabbed my plate before striding to the kitchen. Someone in this blasted place had to slip me some answers.

Because I was beginning to think that I had something to do with the Rapture. And I didn't get the feeling it was going to be a good thing for me.

————

Cook was kneading dough at one of the giant kitchen islands when I strode inside. It was hard to play it cool. I just wanted to grab her shoulders and shake her until I got some answers. How had I lived in this pack and never heard of the Rapture before?

After washing my plate in the sink and putting it away, I walked over and took one of the dough balls, and began to knead.

Cook was silent, as usual, her graying red hair pulled back in a neat bun and her features pensive as she worked.

"Why are you staring at me?" she finally asked, not glancing up at me.

"Sorry, I spaced out for a second," I answered lightly, working the dough with my fingertips. "I was just thinking about the carnival coming into town."

Cook stopped pummeling her dough and glanced up at me, confusion dotting her brow. "Carnival?"

"Yes, you know. The Rapture? I wonder if they'll have apple cider." I prattled on, noting the way her face had blanched of color, but doing my best to keep up my clueless facade.

She slammed her hand down on the counter and I jumped, my words fading away. "Do not say that word," she hissed.

Cook had been a servant for the family long before I'd come into the picture, but I'd never heard her voice like that before. There was an ache there, like the very word had the power to destroy.

"You're not excited about the carnival?" I pressed, knowing I was pushing my luck.

"You stupid girl. It's nothing to do with a carnival, for God's sake. It's when *He* comes!" Her voice trembled and her eyes were wild and crazed.

"Who's *He*?" I barked, allowing my voice to lose the free and easy tone I'd been using to start the conversation.

She took a deep breath, closing her eyes and falling apart in front of me. "No one knows where he comes from, or where he lives. He's shown up at random for centuries, or maybe even longer than that. He takes a sacrifice from our midsts, and then he leaves. It's always the same."

"A sacrifice," I repeated in a whisper, my heart thumping so loudly in my chest it sounded like it was filling the whole room.

"He drains whoever it is. Right there in the town center." The words sliced through the room, and I began to feel a little lightheaded. "I need to go lie down," she announced suddenly, her voice sick and anxious. "Can you—" She gestured to the dough that still needed to be finished and put into the oven for tonight's dinner. She didn't wait to hear my answer, she just stumbled away, like she was going to pass out.

My mind was whirling as I watched her leave. I picked up the dough and worked on shaping it, but I was operating purely on muscle memory; no part of my mind was attached to the task at hand. Who was the "He" she'd been so scared of? And a sacrifice? What was this, the 1700s? You didn't just make sacrifices anymore. I had to be confusing what she said.

Except...

"What if he doesn't like her?" Sussana's words echoed in my head.

Sussana appeared in the doorway just then, and I froze, because Sussana thought kitchens were beneath her, so this was a highly unusual occurrence.

She stood there awkwardly until I turned to throw the bread in the oven. "Alpha Silver and I just wanted to make sure we didn't scare you. The Rapture is nothing to be afraid of. Just a town tradition that makes everyone stressed because it's so much work. But it's really not a big deal."

If they were trying to make me not suspicious, this was the wrong route. Sussana obviously had a much higher opinion of her acting skills than she should.

"What exactly is the town tradition?" I asked, trying to keep my voice light.

She began to play with the ends of her hair. I was half

expecting her to start blowing bubbles in a moment to complete the picture of innocence she had going.

What was strange is that this might have been the most civil conversation I'd had with her since Caleb's death.

Even more suspicious.

"It's just when a more…rambunctious MC comes to visit."

"An MC?"

"A motorcycle club," she snapped, annoyed, before quickly schooling her face once more. She turned to walk out of the kitchen. "Nothing to fear."

I was definitely starting to fear.

———

Thirty minutes later, I was out on the open road. When I'd turned sixteen, Caleb had given me an old beater motorcycle that had turned into my most dearest possession. He knew that sometimes it became too much.

I wished I had the bravery to just keep going.

Maybe someday I would.

The wind beat through my hair as I rounded a bend, getting far too close to the ground as I did so. There was a lookout point a few miles outside of town, and it was my place. It was a ways off the main road, which was nice because it discouraged kids from town from going through the effort to come out there. But the underbrush was low enough I could get there easily on my bike.

Needless to say, I was shocked when I saw Atlas of all people leaning against a tree near the cliff's edge.

He didn't seem surprised to see me.

I waffled for a moment about leaving awkwardly, but in the end, I stayed. And it wasn't for the view.

I slipped off the bike and kicked out the stand before going to sit next to him against the tree.

"Hi, pretty girl," he murmured, glancing over at me.

My cheeks flushed as his breath softly caressed my cheek.

"I'm not sure what's going on," I told him, searching his emerald green eyes for answers.

"Can you feel this?" He grabbed my hand and tingles spread up my skin.

"I—yes," I finally whispered.

"I haven't been able to feel anything but this, for so long it seems like forever."

I cocked my head, still not understanding. There was so much sincerity in his voice, so much…pain.

What did Atlas Silver really know about pain? I knew his mother had passed away when he was fourteen. But the rest of his life seemed to be pretty picturesque…at least on the outside.

He leaned in, so close that our lips were just inches apart. And I was on fire.

"Are you going to let me kiss you?" he murmured.

I realized I'd never wanted anything more.

He must have seen the "yes" in my gaze, because his mouth was all of a sudden brushing against mine. My heart was beating in my ears, a low roar that drowned out everything. Sparks were exploding like fireworks in a midnight sky.

This was everything I'd dreamed about.

After the first brush of our lips, I was desperate for more. I whimpered when he pulled away and then his lips were back, closing over mine, cutting off the sound. His tongue dipped in sweetly, teasing me as I chased him. He explored my mouth, his hands coming to intertwine in my hair, guiding my head right where he wanted.

The longer the kiss went, the harder our kisses became, until the sweet licks were aggressive and deep.

All I could think was that I wanted more. I wanted...it all.

Something was coming, I could feel it in my veins. Whatever this Rapture was, it was going to mean change.

I had been at the whim of everyone for what felt like my whole life, with no end in sight.

Why shouldn't I take something for my own for once?

I shifted until I was sitting in his lap, enjoying the way his eyes widened, the black overtaking the striking green.

"Are you sure, little omega?" he murmured.

"Omega" had always been used as a criticism, a taunt, since I'd come to this pack.

But when he'd just said it...

It was beautiful.

"I want this," I murmured. "I need it."

That must have been enough for him because his lips were crashing against mine as he maneuvered me into place. I was straddling his legs, our chests flush against each other. I could feel his heavy cock nestling against my aching core.

I liked this position. I could stare into his eyes like this, absorb how fucking pretty he was. My breath was coming out in gasps.

"I won't be able to let you go," he warned in between deep, licking kisses that threatened to shatter my soul into pieces.

I just whimpered in response, because being owned by Atlas sounded freaking incredible at the moment. His tongue slid in and out, mimicking the rhythm I wished his cock was doing inside me at that moment. I was a virgin. Obviously. The whole pariah thing hadn't really provided many opportunities for me. And my first heat hadn't arrived to really tempt anyone yet.

But I couldn't wait to change that. His kiss was everything. He was devouring me. Each kiss echoed through my body until the empty ache inside of me was a painful void I was desperate for him to fill.

With his knot.

I sucked eagerly at his tongue as I threaded my fingers through his gold hair, still feeling like this couldn't be real because I'd fucking fantasized about this very thing so many times.

I shifted and rolled my hips on top of his jean-covered cock, mindless with the need for friction. I couldn't remember ever being so desperate. A growl rattled around in his chest as I moved against him.

"Tell me you understand," he warned, as he tilted my chin to make sure I was looking at him.

"I understand, Alpha," I purred, feeling drunk as his warm, cinnamon scent rolled over me in waves. I didn't really understand. But his words were doing something to me. And if it meant I got more of his body and his scent, I was all for it.

My words must have done something for him because as soon as "Alpha" slipped from my tongue, he ripped down the zipper of his jeans and then tore my panties out from under the dress I was wearing. Turned out he was commando.

And he was huge. All this time he'd been packing an anaconda-sized dick down there.

But of course he was huge. Everything about him was designed to torture me and make me want him.

It felt even better to roll over his bare cock with my bare skin. My need felt desperate and crazed. Almost painful in its intensity. And the spike of his apple cider scent.

It was a wonder he wasn't triggering my heat.

As it was, my body was completely prepared to take him, and as he gripped my hips and pushed himself into me, I softened against him, so wet that my pussy made an obscene squelching sound as I sucked him deep inside of me.

He didn't hesitate when he found the evidence of my virginity. A flare of possessive heat spiked through his green gaze as he ripped through it, catching my cry with another deep kiss.

"You're such a good girl. Taking all of me. My perfect little omega."

I moaned at his words, desperately wanting to be his good girl at that moment.

A sweet burnt sugar scent wrapped around me, and I realized I was perfuming.

Shit.

His growl turned feral as he surged up into me until I was finally completely filled, settling right above his hard knot.

"Always knew you'd feel perfect," he murmured. His words floated over me, and I knew there was something about them I should have followed up on, but the need for him to fuck me and fill me was too all-consuming to speak.

"So fucking perfect." He lifted me by the hips until I was sliding off his cock, and then slammed me back down, my loud cry echoing around us. Tears were streaming down my face as he started fucking me with a desperate hunger, each time stretching me to the limit.

It felt so good.

I sipped tiny gulps of his scent, madness trickling at my mind with each taste that I got.

His hand moved between us and his fingertips sharpened into a claw. He used one of the sharp tips to shred the front of my dress so that my breasts were bared to the cool air. As soon as I was exposed, his lips were closed over one of my nipples. Atlas sucked in hard, and it was almost too much as he continued to thrust in and out. My body was alive for the first time, sparks cascading across my skin. Pleasure tore through me as I came violently, a sob ripping through the air.

Atlas's face was determined as his thrusts grew hard.

"Such a good girl. My little omega. Never felt anything so good," he purred, and I cried out as slick drenched his cock.

His thrusts grew harder at the same time as he moaned around my nipple.

I came again, which wasn't a surprise, and his thrusts grew erratic as his teeth sunk into the skin around my nipple.

A moment later, he was filling me with his cum, something I thankfully didn't have to worry about; omegas could only become pregnant when they were in heat, and although I was definitely perfuming, it wouldn't be enough.

"Fuck," he growled, burying his face in my neck and taking deep breaths as he squeezed me close to him. "That was amazing." He was slightly trembling as he held me.

It had been amazing. The best a girl could hope for if she wasn't giving it to the love of her life.

Although, in a different world, if I was a different omega, maybe he could have been.

I was surrounded by his scent, and a little afraid that I was now addicted to it. I'd never been attracted to someone's scent like this before. I was already trying to prepare myself for the letdown when he walked away from me and I couldn't have it anymore.

Atlas pulled his face away and studied me, a small, pleased smile on his lips that was ridiculously sexy, if not mysterious.

What was he thinking?

He withdrew from me then, and a little whimper escaped my mouth. I was sore…but I was also…empty.

I didn't like that feeling, the sensation of no longer being whole. Atlas was never going to be able to be that Alpha for me.

We were too far apart in the social chain. I hadn't heard anything yet, but it was only a matter of time before an omega was pulled from another Alpha's family and given to Atlas to mate.

My bloodline would never be considered good enough for marriage.

Not that I should even be thinking thoughts like that.

He huffed out a growl just then, and I glanced at him, only to see that he was staring at his slick-covered dick, which was also covered in my blood. Before I could say something—apologize?—his lips were crushed against mine once again. That kiss held the promise of something I was too scared to trust.

But I didn't think any other kiss was ever going to match up to it.

"Wish I could keep this image permanently in my mind," he huffed when he pulled away, leaving me a panting, breathless mess.

We were suddenly too close. What I was feeling...it was too much. I launched myself off his lap like his dick had suddenly turned into a bomb.

"Gwendolyn?" he murmured as I turned my back to him and frantically put my clothes back in place. His cum was leaking out of me, and the sensation that I'd loved just a moment ago, suddenly felt like it was killing me from the inside out.

"Just give me a second," I huffed, trying to keep the tremor out of my voice.

He didn't give me a second. Instead, Atlas walked up

right behind me until his chest was pressed against my back, and his arms were wrapped around me.

"Why are you torturing me like this?" I spit out, suddenly furious. I'd wanted sex with someone I was attracted to. And instead, he'd turned it into something I was going to think about constantly.

Something I was going to crave maybe forever.

"I'm not trying to torture you, my Darling," he murmured, nuzzling into my hair and soaking me even more with his mouthwatering scent.

I huffed. The fact that my last name was "Darling" had served as a never-ending source of jokes growing up in the pack. But again, just like he had with "Omega", he somehow made it seem much sweeter than anyone else ever had.

"We should have been doing this a long time ago. I've wanted you—"

I scoffed. "We went to the same school. We've lived in the same town. If you wanted me, you could have had me." I stared off into the sunset, hating how much I was enjoying his touch still.

"I—haven't been in the best place since my mom died. I turned into a fuck boy, and then I just was disgusted with myself. I didn't feel like I deserved you."

Maybe some girls would have said I was stupid for not immediately calling him a liar, but I'd been at his mother's funeral. As the pack Luna, everyone had attended. I remembered him as a beautiful fourteen-year-old, standing in front of his mother's coffin, trying not to cry. I'd only been twelve, but I remembered his pain as clearly as if it had happened yesterday.

"I haven't slept with anyone in two years, trying to stop being such an asshole and someone you might actually like," he murmured.

Shock flooded my system. Girls were constantly all over his balls. If that was true…that was honestly a bit impressive.

Although it still didn't explain why I hadn't known that he knew I existed until the night of the wedding.

He must have sensed my continued hesitation because he pulled me in closer. "I know that the scar right above your lip is when you crashed your bike against the stone wall beside your house on the way to school."

As if his words held magic, the scar above my lip began tingling.

I hadn't told anyone what happened to me that day on my ride. Sussana was just mad that I'd gotten blood all over my clothes.

He continued on.

"I know that you're an amazing writer, and in English last year, you wrote about your parents dying. You convinced your teacher to not share it with the class even though she wanted to. I know that you hate chicken but you force yourself to eat it because you don't want to offend Cook. I know you sneak out on Fridays and give out food to the Manchester family. I know you hide how brightly you shine, because you don't like attention…" He spun me around and tilted my chin so I was staring up at him, his emerald eyes shining with emotion. "I see you, little omega. I've always seen you. And I think…you might be the only person in this world that actually sees me."

The emotions were too much then, and I ripped myself from his grasp and raced towards my bike, kicking it into gear and speeding away as my heartbeats raced away with it.

I couldn't help but glance back. It was like there was a rope tied to me and I had no choice.

Atlas was staring at me as I rode away.

And there was no missing the promise in his eyes.

I just hated that I actually wanted him to keep that promise…

CHAPTER 3
GWENDOLYN

The end was coming, but I was finding it hard to care.
Because of him.
Atlas.

He'd been on my mind constantly since that afternoon, filling my dreams and giving me hope a brighter future existed for someone like me.

As murmurs about the Rapture filled the streets of the town, I forgot to be afraid.

Atlas was all I thought about.

He would find me in the kitchen and *take* me on the counter.

He would sneak into my bedroom and hold me close.

Any time I was in the room, his eyes would follow me.

We'd drifted past love, right into obsession. And I couldn't get enough.

———

Atlas

I stared at the paper in my hands, struggling to understand what it said.

It was my birth certificate.

I'd gone to grab it from where I knew Dad stored important papers, needing it for a program I was applying to...

And now I was wishing that I'd never seen it.

Even though it explained so much.

It explained the beatings, the disappointment, and the practiced abuse. It explained the harsh words and the hate in his eyes every time he looked at me and pack members weren't around.

The reason that my father, Alpha Silver, hated me so much...was because I wasn't his son. Evidently, my mother had stepped out on him with a rival Alpha. I vaguely recognized the name scrawled in my mother's handwriting on the certificate.

Landry Johansen.

I hadn't felt myself sinking to the floor, but now that I was there, I was grateful because I didn't think my legs could support me at the moment. It was hard to fathom the secret I held in my hands. It was also hard to imagine my mother having the balls to sneak behind my father's back.

My mother had been weak. My father hid his particular brand of evil behind a mask, and she'd gone along with it. I didn't blame her for it. It was just a fact of life. Growing up, she'd let him beat me to avoid it happening to her.

Life hadn't really changed after she'd passed because by that point, she'd been just a shadow. A pretty, quiet shadow that made my father—Alpha Silver—look good. In a way, I was glad she was gone, because it felt like maybe she was free now. And what she'd been doing as the Luna of this pack wasn't living—it was dying.

And it was selfish of me, but I was glad I didn't have to watch it anymore.

I was so distracted staring at the certificate and wondering what it meant that I completely missed the scent of my father coming in from the hallway.

"What the fuck are you doing?" he barked, causing me to jump out of my skin as he lunged toward me and ripped the certificate out of my hands. I dashed to my feet, the adrenaline spike I always got from his presence giving my limbs life once again.

I didn't take a step back, though; I knew better than that.

The one thing my father—fuck, I wasn't sure what to call him at this point—hated most, was any sign of weakness, especially in his heir apparent. It was probably why he got along so well with his new wife; she was an impenetrable void, evil inside just like he was.

"I guess it makes sense," I answered, proud of how steady my voice was. "You're always an asshole, but you've always been a bigger asshole to me."

He growled, the sound of it trying to batter at my knees and force me to the ground. Thank fuck I'd finally grown strong enough to not bow anymore. His coppery scent assaulted my nostrils as he continued to push his dominance onto me.

"You owe me everything. I kept you and your pathetic excuse of a mother when I should have thrown you both into the streets. I've given you a future, a pack. And you've been nothing but a motherfucking thorn in my side since the moment you came into existence."

It shouldn't have stung when he said those things, not after everything he'd done.

But that was the shit thing about having emotions—sometimes they couldn't be controlled. Especially when you'd worked your ass off your whole life, trying to earn a monster's love. Only to find out you were never going to get it.

"Mmh," I mused. "She may have been pathetic, but at least she had better sense than to have a child with you."

It was honestly like an alien had taken over my body, and by the flare of his nostrils and the flash in his gaze, he thought so too. I'd never dared to talk to him like this before, with so much disrespect. But evidently, finding out the truth had broken down my barriers.

It wasn't a surprise when his clawed hand tore at my chest.

It was a surprise when I swung back.

But letting him get that first strike was my downfall. He went so deep that the blood began to pour out of me, and even though I punched him back every time, eventually the blood loss became too much and the room began to spin.

I crashed into a bookshelf and a shower of hard books rained down on me, pounding into my already aching body.

"You insufferable fool. I made you, and I can easily take everything away."

His features were more wolf than human then, and I knew if I looked in a mirror, I would see the same thing in my reflection.

I struck out with my claws, grinning crazily when I struck his shoulder and blood sprayed out. He roared before assaulting me with a flurry of claws and fists. With the way the world was fading around me, every hit felt like being pounded by concrete bricks.

He finally knocked me to the ground, and I laughed as blood continued to seep out of my wounds. My father stared down at me in disgust before spitting on me. "Get yourself fucking cleaned up. I own you, boy. And I'm not going to let you forget it."

Alpha Silver stalked from the room without a glance back, leaving me possibly bleeding to death on the cold, wood floor.

A second later, a sound caught my attention, and I thought he'd come back for more.

But no, there she was, like a burst of sunshine on a cloudy day…Gwendolyn. Her eyes held a terrified glint as her gaze danced over my injuries, and then she was rushing to my side with a small squeak.

Her delicious scent passed over me, and I already felt better just being in her presence.

I half wondered if I'd actually bled out and was dead in heaven. Because that's what life felt like now that I'd finally made her mine.

Or at least I was finally taking steps to make her mine.

"Atlas," she whispered. Her hands hovered over one of my wounds and a tear slipped down her cheek as she stared down at me in horror.

"Don't—cry," I choked out, lifting my hand feebly to try and touch her smooth skin. The world was spinning around me, and the outline of her perfect features was going in and out of focus.

"Hold on," Gwendolyn murmured before springing to her feet and racing out of the room.

I groaned as I tried to move, feeling my body trying to heal. If I survived this, it was going to take a minute to get better, even with supernatural healing abilities.

There was a flurry of movement in the doorway; Gwendolyn was back with a bucket and some rags in her hand.

She sank to her knees next to me once again and tore the rag into strips, before tossing them into the bucket. "It's water with salenia root. It will help you heal faster, and it should numb you at least a little along the way." She pulled one of the now purple-hued rags from the bucket and wrung it out before carefully placing it on one of my bigger cuts where my father's claws had gotten me almost all the way to the bone. I hissed as the cool fabric was placed on my wound, but immediately started to feel some relief.

I'd heard of salenia root before, maybe in school, but I

wouldn't have been able to tell you what it was for. This girl was incredible.

Her hands were shaking as she worked, and I watched her, unable to drag my gaze away from her face. That's how it had always been since the moment I'd seen her. I wasn't sure how she—and everyone else—had missed the fact that I'd been obsessed with Gwendolyn for years.

"How much did you hear?" I asked, hating the lick of shame churning in my gut because she'd watched him beat me like that. She paused, her hands hovering over the bucket.

"Enough that you should hate me for not running in and trying to stop him," she answered in a thick voice.

I scoffed at that, the slight jarring movement sending shockwaves of pain radiating across my skin.

"Right. Like he wouldn't have then torn you apart. That wouldn't have helped either of us," I told her soothingly.

She inhaled a shaky breath, reaching back into the bucket for another rag. I was lying in a puddle of blood, but my head was getting clearer and clearer as my body worked to heal and she gave me some pain relief.

"Has he—has he done that before?" she stuttered out.

A tendril of her unique colored hair had slipped into her face, and my insides ached for a reason other than the pain—she was by far the most gorgeous creature I'd ever seen in my life. She was the most gorgeous creature I would ever see in my life.

Sometimes it hurt to look at her, because I was so afraid of what life would be like if she ever decided to leave me.

I weighed my answer—I didn't want to appear weak in

front of her. One of the things an alpha prized was being able to defend and take care of his omega.

I didn't want to come off as weak, but I also didn't want to lie to her.

"Often," I grunted as I tried once again to sit up, but this time succeeded.

Her lower lip quivered, and I resisted the urge to capture it with my teeth. Not sure I was capable of that, or even how sexy that would be considering my current state.

"Why did he do it today?" she asked as she pulled one of the blood-soaked rags off one of my cuts and dipped it back into the bucket. Apparently she hadn't been here for quite all of it.

"Today I found out that I'm not actually his son," I replied calmly.

She dropped the rag she was holding and almost tipped over the bucket in her shock.

"I—I wasn't expecting that," she finally muttered, her small pink tongue flicking out and licking the bottom of her lower lip briefly. A move that was far more alluring than it should have been.

"Mmmh. Me neither." A dark chuckle slipped from my mouth, the sound jarring and slightly hysterical to my ears.

"Makes sense, though. You're so much better than him," she said angrily as she applied one last strip on my wound.

I reached out and grabbed her hand before she could slip away from me. "Thank you," I told her, brushing a kiss across the top of her hand.

A faint blush appeared on her cheeks. "I would do anything for you," she admitted shyly.

My wolf sat up and outright howled inside of me. "Not just for helping me, little omega. But for seeing me."

It was something I'd said to her before, and I knew that she still didn't get it. But the fact of the matter was, no one had ever seen me. The real me. They'd seen the Alpha's son, the playboy, the popular kid. They'd never seen through the facade that I put out to the world, and if they had, they wouldn't have stuck around.

From the moment I'd locked eyes with her at my mother's funeral—a moment I was sure she didn't remember, but that had jumpstarted my world—I felt like she not only saw me, but she liked what she saw. The good. The bad. The ugly.

I loved that about her.

Hell. I loved her.

It was on the tip of my tongue at every moment, but there were moments where it still felt like she was a flight risk, and I could lose her if I said something so extreme.

I leaned in and brushed my lips against hers, wishing I was better just so I could be inside her once again.

"Let's get you up," she whispered, and I nodded, knowing it would only be worse for me if Alpha Silver walked in and still found me on the ground. Another sign of weakness he couldn't handle.

Gwendolyn helped me to my feet, and I couldn't help but pull her in for one more searing kiss even though it made every cell in my body hurt. As I stared down at her, in awe of the emotions swirling in her pretty eyes, I made a vow that she was going to be mine. And we were going to get away from here.

After the Rapture, everyone was going to be far less on edge. The vamps would come, they'd leave, and then so would we.

Just a few more days...

CHAPTER 4

GWENDOLYN

The sky was an overcast, almost green color as I headed out to the garden to grab some peppers for dinner. Gusts of winds whipped at my hair and I shivered, feeling like eyes were on me. The house had been quiet all day, with no sign of anyone, not even the servants. I would have enjoyed the solitude, but the whispers of the Rapture had only grown louder in recent days. Everything felt off.

Atlas had told me not to worry. His mother had sent him out of town for the last one, but he seemed to think it wasn't as big of a deal as people made it seem. He was sure that things like "sacrifices" were just tall tales, and that it was really just a motorcycle gang stopping through town and scaring people.

But I wasn't so sure.

Speaking of which...hands gripped me around the waist and I instantly recognized Atlas's touch.

I turned in his arms and immediately, his lips were on mine, kissing me deeply, his tongue licking languid strokes against my own. He moaned as I deepened the kiss, and I was immediately ready for more...

Like all great things, I should have known that it was never destined for someone like me.

A shadow fell over us, followed by a deep growl that startled me.

Without warning, Atlas flew backward, abruptly ripped out of my arms, our kiss torn, my insides shattered.

I drew in a breath and screamed.

Atlas' eyes were huge and wide, arms stretching out for me, panic on his face while two enormous Alphas restrained him, one grabbing him around the waist and the other wrenching his arms backward hard, forcing him down to his knees. Atlas thrashed, his jaw clenched, muscles tensing.

It all happened so fast that I didn't have time to think.

"Stop, you're hurting him," I called out just as one of the men drove a fist to his face. Blood spurted outward from his busted nose, and my insides crumbled.

I threw myself at them, but someone else snatched me by my hair and yanked me backward. I cried out, turning at the last second with a snarl in my throat. I expected another guard, but instead, it was Sussana right in my face.

My stomach dropped. She'd caught us. We never should have shown affection out in the open like that. I should have known better.

The expression on her face could have skinned me alive with fury as she snapped, "You're filth. Atlas is your damn brother. Are you even ashamed of what you've done, embarrassing him this way? Embarrassing me?" The question was pointed, weighted with the hatred she'd held for me for as long as I'd known her.

"He's not my real family. Surely you know the difference," I replied raggedly, my heart racing a million miles an hour. "Now, let me go." I yanked from her grip, stumbling right into the arms of another of Alpha Silver's enforcers.

He grabbed me with his meaty hands, hurting me with how hard he squeezed my arms. Sneering, he stared at me with disdain.

I whined, and I kept staring at Atlas, anger burning in his eyes as he thrashed against the men. They dragged him backward, away from me.

"Sussana, you can't do this. Release me now! Leave Gwendolyn alone," he barked. "My father will never accept this."

But Sussana stared at him like he was dirt on her shoes. "I don't need you getting in my way."

Rage bled through me, and I didn't know what came over me, but I bit down onto the enforcer's arm. He groaned, his hold easing just enough for me to slip from his grip.

I ducked and ran toward Atlas, unsure what I could do, but my wolf danced beneath the surface. I was never taught to fight, but the blaze burning within me gave me a sensation of being invincible. What Atlas inspired, I'd never experienced–a sense of belonging and being more than the lowly pack omega.

Since that fateful night at the wedding, he'd been in my heart. Finding someone like him who wanted me the way he did...was like a dream. I was terrified to lose him...I'd already lost so much.

A strong hand snatched the back of my neck, fingers digging into muscles until I cried out with pain, and my knees buckled underneath me.

Atlas was gagged then, to stop his shouting. Metal cuffs snapped around his wrists, attached to chains. I trembled, fighting the man holding onto me, but I failed...of course.

"Why are you doing this?" I hissed at Sussana between clenched teeth. I wasn't one to ever talk back to her, and even now, it went against everything inside me as an omega. I was the one who obeyed and never talked back. That was my position.

The fear pummeling through me, the emotions crowding in my chest, they were making me braver than usual.

She pursed her lips, her eyes darkening. Instead of responding, she turned her head to the men keeping Atlas chained up. "Toss him in the basement cell until my return."

Atlas' eyes grew wider, white anger flaring behind them, and he pulled against his restraints, but with two against one, hauling him by chains, he stood no chance. They practically dragged him across the ground as he fought them. And just as they wrenched him around the corner of the house, his gaze met mine one last time.

Fear painted over his features, consuming all the light and

happiness he usually held in his gaze, and replacing it with abject sorrow and helplessness.

The worry tightening my chest grew, and I couldn't breathe. Every inch of me shivered.

My heart squeezed. "Atlas," I cried out.

Then he was gone.

I turned to Sussana who already walked away from me. "Bring her," she barked at the man holding onto me. And he did just that, still gripping the back of my neck like I was nothing more than a scrawny alley cat.

"Why?" I whispered, as I prepared myself for whatever punishment she had planned for me. There was a reason I never ran away from her family, even after all her abuse. No one wanted an abandoned omega. We were seen by everyone as useless...as weak.

The loud roar of motorcycles cut through her answering silence like an ominous sensation settling into my bones.

"I always thought you were useless," Sussana said silkily, turning and coming towards me. She gripped my chin hard, her fingernails digging into my skin to the point of pain. "For Caleb's sake, I kept you safe, fed you, but you never respected me. You were a blight on our family, preying off of Caleb's soft-heartedness, and now your actions with Atlas? You don't belong with us." Her gaze glowed red with fury.

A dull throb cut through me at her words. "Caleb made me part of the family." I shook with each word, holding myself tall...well, as tall as the guard at my back allowed.

She tightened her jaw. "He's not with us anymore now, is he...he's nothing but a memory, and just like him, you'll be nothing but a memory soon as well, albeit an unpleasant one. The Rapture will make sure of that."

I flinched back. "Wait! What do you mean?" I was shaking, my lungs tightening, making it hard to breathe.

She pushed her perfectly curled strawberry blonde hair from her face, looking radiant, hiding as usual the fact that on the inside, she was nothing but poison.

Her gaze lifted to the man still holding me, and she commanded, "Take her to get changed for the ceremony. We leave in ten minutes. We can't be late."

"Ceremony?" I repeated, hating myself for the fear threaded through my voice.

"Gwendolyn, you stupid girl. Your fate is destined and there's no fighting what's coming for you." She turned abruptly and walked away from us, while the enforcer roughly drew me into the house.

Fate. My mother and Caleb both told me to fight fate and create my own path in life. But what if they'd been wrong? What if all this time, I'd been stupid enough to believe I stood any chance to change my destiny?

I couldn't even concentrate on where I was being hauled as my head swam with confusion.

The Rapture. Ceremony. The MC.

What was going on?

Sussana's maid, Henrietta, waited for me in the main room, scowling. She was a cold woman who looked like she wanted to kick me every time she glanced my way, and there was a reason I kept far from her. But now the guard shoved a hand against my back, and I stumbled towards her.

"Strip," she demanded, already pulling at my clothes roughly.

She ripped the clothes off me, the guard assisting her until I was left with nothing but my bra and underwear. The man's lecherous stare covered me in goosebumps.

Henrietta pushed a dress over my head, which might as well have been a potato sack for how baggy it was, the fabric prickly against my skin. I bristled as she brutally tugged it down over my head and shoulders.

The white dress fell to my knees. It was a simple design with short sleeves and V-neckline, the material feeling thick against me. It was hideous. I might have laughed if I wasn't on the verge of tears with how scared I felt.

I tried to scratch my shoulder where the fabric itched.

"Stop moving. This cloth is best for absorbing blood."

I grimaced, and tears fell as I tried to pull away from her. I wanted to scream with panic, but the guard gripped my shoulders, holding me in place. Henrietta quickly laced a red ribbon around my waist, tying it up at my side with a knot, cinching in the fabric. A bag of a dress was still that, even with a ribbon.

"What's going on?" My words stuck to the roof of my mouth from how dry my throat had gone.

"Shoes off," she demanded, ignoring me. Just as I stepped out of them, the guard seized my wrist and we were flying out of the house and rushing up to the family town car. I'd never been permitted to ride in it, until now, it seemed. The fact that Sussana allowed me to use it was a warning of danger in itself.

Climbing into the back where it smelled like fresh leather, I found it was just the guard and me. Immediately, we drove away from the manor and made a beeline for the open gates at the end of the long driveway. We passed the open land, the trees, the village I'd called home for years.

Icy terror slid over my skin as I stared outside at my familiar surroundings, and an ominous sensation flooded me that maybe this was the last time I'd see them.

"Do you know anything about what happens at the ceremony?" I asked the bald enforcer who wasn't paying me any attention.

He shook his head and continued to sit silently beside me. So much for getting some insight into what I was about to walk into. I'm sure the guy was too scared of Sussana to say anything.

We passed homes and manicured lawns, and it wasn't long before the landscape changed to storefronts. Soon enough, we emerged at the town square. The closer we got, the more my heart raced.

There were people everywhere, crowded in the square, and even in the car, I could practically taste the tension and fear heavy in the air.

Once we stopped, the guard jumped out and he was on my side of the door, opening it. He took me by the arm and pulled me out.

I couldn't seem to catch my breath as everyone started to twist around to stare at me. Their murmurs rose on the breeze, sounding like a cicada's song on a hot summer's night.

Except this was a tune playing a countdown to something horrible for me. I was sure of it now.

Any chances of remaining calm had faded away, and panic was now firmly curled in my chest. I tugged against the enforcer, my bare feet pressing into the hard ground.

"I can't be here. Let me go." I pulled against his grip, needing to get away.

Voices rose around me, the crowds pointing, laughing, feeling pity for me. It was too much, too quickly.

But there was no way to stop the guard who yanked me forward, the masses parting for us. Their pitying gaze was like knives against my skin.

Tears flooded my eyes, and I frantically searched for anyone in the crowd who'd help me. But they all reared back when I reached a hand out to them, pleading.

I was feeling lightheaded as the panic continued to build, like an oncoming storm.

The guard's hand constricted my wrist, and it wasn't long before he launched me into the center of the town square. I fell to the ground, the sharp rock of the cobblestones digging into my palms and knees.

An enormous overhead fabric the color of night encased most of the center. It stole the sunlight where I'd been thrown, while everyone waiting beyond the red rope remained in the light.

I picked myself off the ground, staring out to the townspeople who all huddled behind the red rope. I turned slowly on the spot, watching the people surrounding me, desperate for one pack member willing to help.

Their gazes were sharp with fear, and no one said a word. They only stared at me in terror.

I didn't bother asking what was going on again. Reality pulsed in my thoughts.

I was the sacrifice at this Rapture.

It explained everyone's pitiful and almost relieved expressions. They were all just glad it was me standing here, and not them.

Sussana walked up just then, and studied me from behind the rope, smiling gleefully. Hate for her churned in my chest. I knew with every fiber of my being that she'd been the mastermind behind my current state of affairs.

Fear and adrenaline drummed in my veins, and I was shaking. I had nowhere to run, and I tried to scream, but the sound was stolen as the thunderous roar of motorcycles grew louder as they got closer.

I jerked towards where the sound of the bikes were coming from, a cry falling from my lips.

Others in the crowd screamed out in fright then.

They should try being in my position, I thought.

I turned again, studying all of the people who were offering me as a sacrifice so willingly.

Memories from the past flashed in my mind—Papa's body laying cold and bleeding on the kitchen floor. Mama's screams before she vanished. They were taken from me on a day when I should have died as well.

Maybe this was fate making things right.

Losing my family had been the hardest day of my life, but today perhaps could match it.

Terror grazed the back of my throat, and I tasted bile, almost able to smell the acrid stench of the fires that ripped everything from me eight years ago.

But I soon realized what I smelled was the burning stench of tires from the motorcycles suddenly roaring up the street, coming right toward us.

The MC had arrived.

People yelled in fear, parting frantically as seven huge bikers carved their way through the crowds, coming right for me.

I backpedaled until I hit the rope. Someone shoved a hand into my shoulder, pushing me forward under the shade of the overhead covering.

I stumbled a few steps before righting myself, watching as the MC riders smoothly rode in on their bikes. The townspeople's silence was deafening, but my heartbeat banged so loud, I was certain everyone could hear it.

Their bikes were all black, and they moved like shadows towards me. The obvious leader of the group, was dressed in all black as well, including his helmet. And I couldn't make out any distinguishing features as he rode.

A sudden explosive shot came from one of the other bike engines, and everyone screamed in terror.

The riders continued to move, like death incarnate, towards their sacrifice.

Me.

Cook's words came back to me, flaring loudly through my mind.

It's when He comes!

He takes a sacrifice from our midsts, and then he leaves.

I was the sacrifice about to lose everything. My lips were trembling, but I held in my tears..I didn't run.

Because where would I go?

Their presence seemed to darken the day, sending even the sun behind clouds.

I found myself in the exact center of the town square as the bikes circled, then one by one, they parked around me.

The head rider stopped across from where I stood, dropped his stand, and slid smoothly off his bike.

I knew I should run, scream, or do something, but instead, my feet were frozen on the spot. I was unable to take my gaze off the towering man as he prowled towards me in a tight leather jacket and pants that hugged thick, powerful legs. Despite being completely covered, his clothes did nothing to conceal the sheer size of him.

The rest of his gang remained on their bikes, still wearing their helmets and watching us, an incredibly intimidating sight.

The hairs on my arms lifted as he pulled his helmet off, turning away from me to set it on his bike. Hair the color of raven feathers was my first glimpse of the stranger. It sat messily on his head, like he couldn't be bothered to tame it. Examining the back of him, I was at least relieved to see there were no signs of horns or scales across the back of his neck.

It was stupid the thoughts that crossed my mind when I was about to face my executioner.

He turned toward me then, moving almost sensually… confidently, like he was sure in his ability to control everything around him. Shadows covered his features at first, revealing only his eyes. Two red dots pierced through, so intense they seemed to stare into my soul. I could have sworn I was face to face with the devil, and now I questioned *what* exactly the male was…rather than who.

My breaths caught in my throat while a shiver curled around my spine. I stepped back, my hands pressed tight to my stomach.

He strode towards me, taking long steps, the shadows fading from his face, the breeze lashing the longer hair framing his face.

I was immediately struck by how cruelly beautiful he was. His sharp features only enhanced his simmering danger.

He moved gracefully, his gaze easily sliding down my body. Red eyes were now pale silvery orbs—reminding me of the brightest full moon.

Hunger flashed behind them, and I had no doubt this man was capable of atrocities and reveled in committing them. Everything about him spelled darkness. He was a monster in a beautiful mask. I couldn't even call him tall, dark, and handsome because those words were wasted on him. He was unlike anyone I'd ever seen before. He carried himself with arrogance, with the promise of death if you glanced at him the wrong way. Here was an example of the cruelty of the world that somehow, *he'd* been blessed to be so ridiculously gorgeous…in a rugged, *I'm going to rip your heart out and eat it,* kind of way.

He was a killer, that was clear.

My gaze trailed over his body. There weren't any weapons

on his belt or in his grip. So how was I to be killed?

Towering in front of me, he ran a long fingernail down my cheek before lifting my chin, inspecting me. I felt insignificant under his stare, and wondered for a minute if he would even find me adequate to be sacrificed.

Was there a requirement for that?

I might have laughed at my idiocy if I wasn't hyperventilating, my breathing coming so fast the world tilted off its axis for a split second.

"Are you going to run from me, little omega?" he purred with a mocking voice that cut through the murmuring crowds.

My breaths came quickly, but with the weight of his stare on me, I shook my head.

"That's a shame. I was hoping for a chase." A smile tugged over his full lips, half amused, half annoyed. He glanced around at the mass of people gathered around us, seeming to revel in their fear.

"Something hasn't felt right about today, but you're going to make it all better, aren't you?" He cocked his head, examining me closer.

I didn't move, feeling like the mouse in front of the wolf. Like if I moved that would just make him attack quicker.

"Are you Death?" I asked, finally finding my voice.

He stared at me, and I felt like he was seeing into my soul…and found it lacking.

"Sometimes. But you can call me Pan."

Pan. I ran his name over my mind, thinking it was a rather strange name.

His gaze turned curious, and he took hold of my arm in a strong grip. His touch was icy, and his movements were smooth and powerful, so much so that my mind was racing trying to figure out what kind of creature he was. I'd never seen anything like him.

Pan moved behind me, his chest and groin pressed against my back and ass. I caught his heady scent on the breeze—musky and almost sweet, like raspberries.

He trailed his fingers across my chest, like a taunt, until his arm was across the front of my shoulders, locking me against him. Almost tenderly, he swept my hair from my ear, eliciting goosebumps across my skin. His breath tingled across my neck.

"You're a beautiful little thing. What do they call you?"

"G-Gwendolyn," I whispered.

"Gwendolyn," he repeated, like he was savoring the taste of my name. "Now tell me, *Gwendolyn*...are you a screamer?"

I trembled, close to tears, but I held them back.

His question raced through my mind, as did his chilly breath dancing across my skin. He was holding me...possessively...almost greedily. Like he wanted me.

And for some terrible reason, that was bringing out my own need, blooming between my thighs, and it terrified me.

I desperately fought the unwanted flames licking at my insides, unable to understand how arousal could even be a thought right now.

"N-No." My response came out breathy. I felt trapped and completely helpless. Embarrassed.

I couldn't stand the sight of the onlookers, staring and

waiting with bated breath for my death, so I closed my teary eyes.

"I guess we'll find out very soon, won't we?" he purred.

This was a game for him, wasn't it? He loved to see his victims squirm, to make them cry out. He fed off their fear.

Suddenly, he dragged me off my feet, his tongue lazily drifting down my neck until it was circling my pulse point. Panic shot through me, and I began to thrash, pushing against his arm.

"I've changed my mind about what's going to happen today, little omega. I've decided I'm going to make you mine. And then you'll learn just what it means to be ruled by me."

"And I'll always hate you," I responded in a whispery, shaky voice.

The sharp sting of fangs came fast. He bit down into my neck savagely. I shuddered, the coldness sinking into my veins sending me into a panic.

My scream echoed across the town square.

———

Pan

My teeth sunk into the softness of her unblemished neck, a spark of desire shooting right to my cock. Blood spilled into my mouth, and I greedily swallowed the decadent flavors of sweet berries and honey bursting over my tongue.

I drew it all into my mouth, needing to drain her.

Sipping, licking, I lowered my arm to her stomach, pressing her tighter against me, tempted to completely devour her. I couldn't remember the last time I'd tasted someone so completely delectable, to the point where I'd crawl out of my own skin if it meant getting it in an endless supply.

Wouldn't that give these wolves a shock? Tempting...

Once every ten or so years, we turned up for our honorary collection of a debt owed to me by the Silver family. A debt that could never be repaid if you asked me. It was the only reason I kept returning...to put the fear of death into their family line, because I shouldn't be the only one living with rageful vengeance as my constant companion.

Though, their offering today surprised me.

A thrill of arousal kept bursting through me as I enjoyed the feel of her body against mine, so intense that I'd lost my breath. A vampire like me didn't need air, but around the living, my body drew it in to smell their intentions.

From the moment I'd laid eyes on the delicate creature they'd offered me, I'd been enthralled. Lavender hair I wanted to curl around my hands as I bent her over, and eyes as bright as amber's flame, staring at me, so beautiful in her terror.

Five-foot-six, she was on the thinner side, even with her full breasts. Blazing heat ripped over me as I watched her trembling at my arrival. Pale smooth skin that I couldn't wait to touch...and her scent...fuck, the second I'd inhaled it I wanted her, desperately.

Her maddening beauty awoke something primitive inside me that hadn't reared its head in...well, forever. All I could think was how much I needed to taste her.

It was refreshing to be surprised for a change.

Rarely did I meet anyone who sparked any kind of interest for me.

The gorgeous creature shook in my hold just then, her fingers digging into my arm as I continued to sip at her throat.

I paused for a moment.

Something was very wrong.

Her pulse grew steadily louder in my ears, faster, until I could feel it thumping in my body.

That was the problem–Gwendolyn was still very much alive, her blood flowing into my mouth. By now, she should have collapsed in my arms and passed out from a lack of blood.

One quick bite was all it ever took. Drink and savor my victim with a sharp prick. The toxins in my fangs killed them, ensuring their blood didn't coagulate, allowing me to keep feeding while they died.

So, how in the seven realms of Hell was she still alive?

I stiffened, my gaze narrowing as I held onto her writhing body as she attempted to escape. Somehow, this lavender haired sprite of a girl had managed to deepen my growing fascination with her.

Too bad for her.

Silently aware of the town watching me, the last thing I needed was for them to start rumors that the vampire king was growing soft. I didn't want them doubting I'd come to kill. These sheep couldn't be allowed to grow confident.

What came next—they surprised us in ten years with

wood stakes? Fuck that.

It wasn't acceptable, and rather than let her go, I sunk my fangs deeper into her neck, tearing flesh and drinking her in faster, gulping down as much of her sweet nectar as possible.

Then I could feel her shadow deep inside of my skin...of her soul, preparing for departure. Her fight weakened, mingling with the pleasure surging inside me. My cock was digging into her back as her blood filled me with a savage passion I hadn't felt in centuries.

She groaned weakly, shuddering against me. Her soft, pleading moans were music to my ears, knowing she'd pass this time. I'd drink her dry to ensure she did just that.

Her murmurs finally silenced, and she gradually slumped against me, her heartbeat flatlining.

Gwendolyn had just died in my arms.

Someone once told me death was a gift, and with her death, I'd bestowed Gwendolyn with the greatest gift of all. Eternity.

I held her up with a hand pressed hard to her chest, and slid my fangs out of her neck. With a single thought, I retracted them inside my mouth and licked the last drops of blood off her skin.

Addictive.

The sound of the audience murmuring made my hackles rise, reminding me of their presence. I hated these petty shifters with their airs, hated how they played home as if they were civilized. Far from it. Deep inside, they were primal animals longing to return to the woods. But they'd forgotten the old ways, forgotten who they really were.

The thin veneer of an ability to live harmoniously amongst other supernaturals had been forgone long ago. There were reasons I lived in Darkland, as far as possible from them, why I made it forbidden for anyone to reveal our location. If I had to see them more than once every ten years, I'd have slaughtered every one of these weak dogs by now.

Glancing at my right-hand man, Luke, I lifted my chin. "Take her," I commanded.

He got off the bike and marched toward me, collecting the unconscious girl into his arms. Luke was one of my biggest men, and he had the space on his larger motorcycle to keep her in front of him, especially if he held a hand around her middle.

Without a word, he shoved her up and over his shoulder and made his way back to his bike.

I'd had enough of this worthless town, and I was impatient to find out more about what made Gwendolyn special.

Brusquely, I stepped toward my bike and dragged on my helmet.

It crossed my mind that in the past, I'd drunk my victims to the point of no return and discarded their bodies in the town center. But not Gwendolyn.

She was mine.

Kicking the stand up with my heel, I started the engine, and it roared to life, scaring the onlookers. They recoiled, and I sneered under my helmet, the scent of their fear stinking up the air.

I took off without another thought, needing distance between me and them before I took more than one life today.

CHAPTER 5

GWENDOLYN

Death was chasing me in my dreams, and unbearable darkness was everywhere.

That was all I remembered as I jerked upright in bed with a scream in my lungs and a starved inhale of breath like I'd been suffocating.

Memories flashed of the Rapture, of me forced into the town center, of Atlas taken from me, leaving me broken. And of *Him*.

The vampire king I'd been sacrificed to. The people I'd lived with for eight years, delivering me to my death without a second thought.

I pressed a hand to my neck, grimacing at how tender my flesh felt over the two puncture points right below my ear.

My eyes hurt, and I kept blinking against the vibrant light from the overhead chandelier, trying to stop feeling like I was losing my mind.

Where was I, anyway?

Black stone walls and cathedral-like arched ceilings with wooden beams surrounded me. I was in a four-poster king-sized bed covered in inky black sheets with the headboard luxuriously upholstered.

Thick, black curtains covered the window, revealing nothing outside.

I frantically pushed my legs from under the bed sheet, and my knees gave out the moment I placed my weight on my legs.

My knees struck the wooden floorboards, and I groaned as a strange sensation clawed through my gut. The kind that made me cry out and clutch my stomach. Something was very wrong with me.

Scrambling to my feet, I steadied myself to not fall over again, when a spark of pain tore across my middle, burning and stinging. I held my arms around my stomach, stumbling against the wall, figuring I had to find out where I was. But the growl of agony in me deepened.

Hunger. That was what this felt like. The worst possible hunger pains in the world.

It came again and again in waves and left me screaming, desperate to stop the torture.

What was going on with me?

I swung my gaze to the door, a heavy pounding thudding in my ears.

Frantically, I ran forward and pushed it open, finding myself in a grand hallway that speared outward in two directions. The ornate, gothic architecture continued with lofty ceilings, dark walls bathed in dim lights, and an ominous sensation as though I'd stepped into a crypt. No windows anywhere to gauge my bearings, just hallways that stretched as far as the eye could see.

The need to get out of here drove my legs forward, and yet the never-ending battle of the cruel growling within me deepened.

I had no idea how far I'd gone, but there were other passages I took, mostly left as though I moved in a great circle around whatever this building was. I passed locked doors, every hallway seeming to lead to nowhere.

It was only when I came across someone that I came to a dead stop in the corridor. Every inch of me was alert of each move she made as she emerged from a room, holding onto a bucket and mop.

She had her back to me, wearing a black dress that came to her knees, her vibrant red hair pulled back into a ponytail.

The hairs on my arms lifted, my ears perked, and I could swear I heard the soft patter of her heartbeat.

A hiss fell past my lips, a feral sound I didn't recognize, and tearing my mind from the female was impossible. She set the bucket and mop down, then turned to shut the door, locking it.

Pain stabbed in the pit of my stomach, burning, growling with a need I didn't understand.

My legs were moving before I'd become conscious of it, and the speed I traveled at astonished me. In a flash, I was right behind the woman, inhaling her scent, brutal, hungry thoughts ravaging my mind.

I didn't understand the desperation coming over me, and I swallowed a growl of agony. My ravenous need couldn't be lessened.

The maid shifted to twist around, having sensed me, but I moved fast, my hands driving against her back, and I shoved her against the wall.

I surprised myself with the strength I had–she was at least three inches taller than me–and I easily subdued her, my hands frantically tearing at her dress and hair for skin.

She shrieked, but the darkness invading me came too fast; it slipped into my thoughts like a shadow. I unleashed an anguished growl, my lips peeling back over teeth, and I pressed my mouth to her neck.

Her cries escalated, they came louder, more desperate. Yet I was frantically gnawing my teeth over her flesh, never breaking it. What the fuck was I doing? A part of me knew this wasn't right, but the need within me overpowered any other thoughts.

Frustrated, I yanked my head back, her skin marked with my teeth marks, but I hadn't drawn blood.

Wait…blood? Why did I want that?

Her heartbeat pulsed in my ears, and a vein thumping under her skin called to me, coaxing another growl from my stomach.

The female said something, but I couldn't make it out behind the sound of her flowing blood. It was beautiful and called to me.

Such a strange sensation to feel both starved to the point of agony, and so confused about what to do about it that I wanted to scream.

I suddenly jerked back, the corridors spinning with me just as the woman whipped around, fright splashing over her face.

"Don't do this," she pleaded. "You're not allowed to. There are rules," she cried out, clutching the fabric of her dress at her chest in a panicked reaction.

I didn't know how to respond, didn't understand what was going on with me...or what she was talking about. And I sure didn't want to terrify this poor girl.

But the moment she turned and threw herself down the hallway, something triggered in me.

I hurled myself after her, a maddening need to catch her becoming all consuming.

Chasing her was no effort at all, and I savagely dragged her to the floor. She cried out, pushing a hand to my face, thrashing madly beneath me.

I'd never been strong, but somehow I easily overpowered her again. I straddled her, and no matter how hard I tried to get ahold of the...hunger inside of me.

I failed.

Only the raging pulse of the blood in her veins filled my ears. When I stared down at her as she lay on her back, her eyes stained with tears, I watched the way her skin seemed to almost grow translucent, revealing to me exactly where every blue vein lay.

Her pulse drove me to madness, and I bared my teeth

while she screamed. Her hand jutted out to block me, and I snatched it, latching onto it.

I bit down, tearing skin this time, and exhilaration curled in the pit of my stomach.

A sudden strike to the side of my head came so unexpectedly that I flipped sideways onto the floor, crying out. I blinked at the sight of another maid dropping a mop handle before dragging her friend to her feet.

Then they both ran.

And I lay there, letting the insanity of my hunger swallow me as I fell into a darkness that made no sense.

————

Groaning, I dragged myself up, a splitting ache pulsing across the back of my head where I'd been struck.

I had no idea how long I'd been out of it, but no one had come to find me. And I couldn't help but wonder if this was in fact my Hell made up of endless corridors that left me starved and terrified.

Slowly, I made my way back the way I'd come, and I ended at an alcove that shone from moonlight pouring in from a doorway that led outside.

Passing through the archway, I found myself on an oversized stone balcony. It was nighttime, the stars and moon the only points of light around me. I could faintly make out the craggy outline of mountain peaks underneath the mountains.

From what I could see from the full moon, there were

forests as far as I could see, and further in the distance, the land came to an abrupt, jagged cliff that fell into a pit of darkness. A single, serpentine bridge stretched across the gorge at least fifty feet in length.

On this side of the bridge, the woodland spread outward to more mountains on either side of me.

Directly below the balcony, the area was cleared of trees and filled with what looked like a burned-out bonfire, and logs for seats. It reminded me of a campsite.

Turning around, I peered up at the building...too big to be a manor...it was a castle. But not a castle from a fairytale, more like from a dark dream. I was gasping as I stared up at it, overwhelmed in the face of its enormity. It had dark sandstone walls, and the short towers strangely reminded me of gothic churches with arched stained windows. And then there was the enormous tree that grew out of the middle of the castle, like the building had been constructed around it.

Gigantic, umbrella-like branches with bottle-green leaves reached outward, shading the home from the moonlight.

Thumping footsteps on the stone floor had me turning my attention toward the arched entrance.

A figure emerged from the shadows, and I drew in a sharp, scared breath.

Tall, with broad shoulders, and sinfully attractive, the monster from the town center stepped outside.

Pan, he'd called himself.

Just like the first time I saw him, I was transfixed. Everything about this...vampire was overwhelming.

And that's what he was, right? A vampire? A creature

from a dark nightmare…come to life. Or I guess death. They were undead right?

I couldn't tell if he had me under a spell, or just in a constant panicked state, but my hands were trembling as he walked closer.

Piercing silvery eyes and full lips called to me. They were captivating and enchanting.

Leather pants hugged his powerful legs, and his buttoned-up white shirt was open at his throat, with sleeves rolled up to his elbows. He appeared just as intimidating and beautiful as I remembered.

Messy hair fell around his face, and his mouth was twisted into a grin, the tips of his fangs cushioned on his lower lip.

He was temptation and death all rolled up in a beautiful package. And he looked far too interested in me at the moment.

"You're an unexpected surprise out here," he mused, his voice lighter this time, but still as deadly.

"I'm trying to figure out where I am," I answered cautiously, worried he was going to lunge at me at any moment…and continue his meal. "It's not like you explained anything before turning me into a snack."

A winged creature flew past and I took a step back in surprise. When I glanced again at Pan, he was smirking, clearly amused watching me so out of sorts.

"Where are we? What is this place?"

His gaze slid down my body, then back up as he dragged

the back of his hand across his mouth. Hunger ignited behind his eyes, and it roared within me too, the same one I'd lost control of inside the castle. Where I attacked the poor maid like a raving blood-starved monster.

A dark thought threaded its way through my consciousness...wondering just what I'd become.

"We're in Darkland," he purred his answer, distracting me from my thoughts. "It's a place for all lost things." His predatory eyes grew wilder as he stepped closer.

I retreated, but escape seemed futile, and it wasn't long before I found myself pinned against the railing with this monster leaning in, grabbing hold of it on either side of me.

"Now, isn't this an interesting situation? A hare finding herself caught in the vampire's den. There's only one thing to be done. Do you know what that is?" His voice was cool against my skin, covering me in goosebumps.

"To let the hare go?" I responded lamely...or maybe foolishly since I knew he could crush me without a hair falling out of place.

He leaned in a bit more, and I twisted away from him, but his face was in my hair, inhaling deeply. An animalistic growl rolled over his throat. "He's going to eat the hare. You smell delectable, too delicious to not devour, and I can't stop thinking about how sweet your pussy will taste."

I pulled my shoulders back and drove my hands to his chest, to dislodge him, but he didn't move even an inch.

"Should I have just killed you, Gwendolyn? It's a bit tragic after all that you ended up here, isn't it? Not many do, and the ones who do, don't last long. What about you, pretty girl with lavender hair...do you think you'll last?"

His hands were sidling to my hips, fingers digging into my pelvic bones, keeping me against him. Panic clawed into my chest. I couldn't breathe, yet my words slipped out. "It's my hope that I will."

"Hmm. We'll see."

I was certain that his earlier bite was what led to me going all crazy and attacking the maid. That dark feeling churned inside me again. He was turning me into one of him, wasn't he? Gods, had I already become one? Is that why I tried to bite the maid? And why my stomach hurt from hunger, to the point that I couldn't stand it? Even now it lingered, and just the thought of the maid's blood deepened the ache once more.

I knew little about vampires, and the things running through my head came from fiction, like Bram Stoker's Dracula. Was that even real, and if so, did that mean I had to drink Pan's blood to become a full-fledged bloodsucker? Growing up, I didn't exactly have access to a lot of books, but Cook would slip me some to read when I was alone in my room.

"You've got me here, now. What do you want?" I asked, my hands shaking and pressed against his solid chest.

There was no response. Pan stared at me, and my dread locked into place.

Something cruel shifted behind his silvery eyes, the center of his irises blooming red as I watched. His hold on my arm constricted, and I whined, pushing against him.

"Obedience," he whispered against my cheek. "That's all I

want." The tips of his fangs were suddenly on my neck, grazing over my skin down to my collarbone, his tongue tracing the path. "Why do you smell so delicious, little one?"

Heat shifted inside me, while his hands were tugging at my sack dress.

"Please, let me go," I whispered desperately, all while fighting the urge to not go into a full panic attack, remembering advice Cook had once given me.

Girl, sometimes you've got to fake it until you make it. Don't show them your fear, even if you're terrified on the inside.

Pan pushed my dress up, his icy fingers suddenly on my thighs. "You think you're scared now, little omega. But you have no idea what real fear is yet. I can show you what I can do to a girl like you, if you'd like. Or, if you prefer, I can throw you out into the woods and you can discover for yourself all the other dangerous things out here that want to skin you alive and suck the marrow from your bones."

I whimpered, but anger flashed through me for the first time, making it a bit easier to think through the terror.

Lifting my chin, I chided, "I learned long ago that monsters were real and that they looked like normal people. That they were a lot more terrifying than the fictional creatures we're told live in the dark and in the woods."

His gaze widened with a strange delight as he threaded a hand through my hair. Fisting it at the back of my head, he tipped my head back. "My brave, broken little bunny. You have no idea where you are, do you? But you'll learn soon enough."

He grinned wider, and all I could think was, *oh fuck*, I was dealing with darkness itself.

His cold, stony eyes never left my face, his skin perfect as porcelain, with a beauty that took my breath away. Of course, I shouldn't find anything about him beautiful, and yet it was hard to not be caught in his allure. My cheeks flamed with shame that I found his touch enticing. I'm sure a therapist would have a field day since I was obviously a headcase.

I had to find a way out of this madness.

Was there a way to convince him to let me go? It seemed like a useless endeavor to think I could reason with Pan about anything at this point. Didn't vampires have a thing called thrall, where they could get you to do what they wanted? Maybe that's what he was doing to me, which would at least explain why the pulse between my thighs tingled with need. Why I grew wetter the longer he remained plastered to me. There was no way I'd feel this way toward him under any other circumstance.

Tugging on my hair, he stared down at me, and I grimaced. The male towered over me, and just as I thought he'd sink his fangs into me again, his lips grazed mine. His mouth was cold, but at the same time, it warmed me up, igniting a fire between my thighs, and with it, a memory came out of nowhere of a time I'd found myself in my room at Sussana's mansion, waking up with a moan on my lips as I'd thought about Atlas.

I lay in bed, breathing heavily, my hips rocking as I slid my fingers between my thighs. It was a hungry and beautiful desire, a torment of release that I'd been holding onto, my sleep deciding to bring me what I refused to do while awake.

My fingers slipped between the seam of my lips, and I found myself soaking wet. I moaned quietly, my legs spreading under the blankets, feeling the building arousal clawing through me.

I pushed a finger inside, arching my back as my greedy pussy drew it in deeper. I wasn't one to play with myself this way since too often someone burst into my room or yelled for me to do another chore. But the sun hadn't risen yet. And I'd woken up embraced by desire.

I trembled, balancing on the edge. So close. My fingers worked and I breathed deeper, building...building.

"Gwendolyn!" Sussana suddenly barked from somewhere in the house.

I flinched so hard, I might have yelped, frantically taking my finger out, clamping my legs shut. I jackknifed in bed, terrified she'd burst through my door any second now.

"For fuck's sake, who broke the vase? Get your ass downstairs."

The memory faded, and I stumbled, finding myself back in a monster's company.

He stood there, grinning, seeming to be enjoying himself. "Such a beautiful memory. Maybe it's something we can re-enact."

Wait! My head twirled with the reality that he'd somehow brought that memory to the surface, and then been able to witness it. Shame coated my tongue, as I panicked what Pan could do with that kind of ability. What he could see... My memories with Atlas, even if he was lost to me forever, were too precious for this creature to get to witness.

I beat my fists against his shoulders.

"Release me, asshole. And don't ever go into my mind again."

The curl of Pan's mouth had my heart fluttering in a way that couldn't be good for me. "Don't worry, it doesn't work too well once you know I can do it. Regardless, my little bunny will be fun to break." My heart collided into my ribcage with how deviously his words rolled off his tongue. "Once I'm finished, you won't even know how to put yourself back together again," Pan whispered against my mouth.

I blinked at his threat, dreading whatever he had planned for me.

Suddenly, his mouth pressed to mine, and he kissed me with a dominant flare. His tongue pressed into my mouth, the sharp points of his teeth grazing my lips. He held me aggressively by my hair, his hand creeping higher up under my dress.

Frustration clawed at me, that nothing I did would get him off me.

I pushed against him, writhing this way and that as I tried to escape…but failing miserably.

His growls darkened, and I felt the sharpness of his nails dragging across my lower stomach, the tear of fabric sounding.

My breath caught in my chest, and I whimpered, panic rushing over me.

So I did the only thing I could think of…I bit down hard on his lower lip, making sure I drew blood.

He flinched back, breaking from me with a low growl, and the first trickle of blood bubbled across the corner of his lip.

Lapping his tongue out, he swept it greedily across the bite mark, stealing all the blood. All the while he studied me, arching a brow in a haughty way.

"I am not your little pet," I spit through gritted teeth.

His depraved grin returned, giving me a slow shake of his head. "Harder next time, okay, little bunny? Make it really hurt," he breathed.

Bastard. I was nothing more than an amusement for him.

A beat of silence strangled the air between us, and I couldn't find the words to speak. All the while, his gaze studied me.

A burst of growls suddenly broke out around us, and in a heartbeat, Pan was yanked backward and tossed to the floor.

My breaths grew shallow as I frantically searched for my savior.

It was Pan...but...wait. I did a double take at the second Pan standing in front of me, wearing all black—pants and a long-sleeve Henley top, eyes red as blood, his jaw clenched in dark fury.

"What the fuck do you think you're doing?" he barked at his...twin, who was getting up from the floor with such fluidity that it seemed nothing he did could be perceived as anything but brutally graceful.

"I'm having a little fun. I had no idea you brought us home a snack." The crazy Pan was chuckling, but, by the tightness of his expression, it was all for show because there was a heated anger behind his gaze.

Pan moved at lightning speed at his double, and in a flash, he had him bent back over the railing. "She's not yours to play with. I'm serious, Crocodile. I'll personally skin you alive over this."

Crocodile...that was an interesting name. Their parents must have been a bit...odd.

I watched as his face went deathly white, and I knew I shouldn't make a sound, shouldn't move, but I was shaking so hard that my fight or flight instincts took over. Evidently, for me that meant flight.

I darted back inside, my pulse pounding, and Pan's words rang behind me. But I couldn't stop, wouldn't.

Not thinking about where I ran, I sprinted back inside, going left and right, my bare feet striking the stone floor.

Heavy footfalls hit the floor behind me, and I kept glancing over my shoulder, but there was nobody there.

I passed elaborate candle chandeliers in the hallways, paintings, and doors, and all I could picture was finding another way out of this insane maze house.

It was only when I burst into an enormous hall made of black walls with gold trim that I slowed down. The trunk of the giant tree I'd seen outside was bursting out of the floor here, shooting up through the ceiling, and the sight of such a strange thing had me coming to a screeching halt.

I felt as if I'd stepped into a dream as I stared around at the enchanting room that surrounded me. Besides the awe-inspiring view of the tree, there was a sweeping staircase, walls draped in tapestries, and golden lights shining all around.

Despite the shudders still running along my spine, I was curious enough to approach the tree. It was at that exact moment that part of the ceiling around the tree began to slide open, bringing in a light breeze. Moonlight and stars glittered from the dark sky, catching the light of the torches on the walls, setting off an explosion of reflecting light.

My mouth might have dropped open as I turned on the spot, taking in the beauty of the grand hallway that could easily be a ballroom for the most elaborate of parties…fit for a king.

I placed my palm on the trunk, the bark rough and bumpy. The tree was well preserved without any damage, despite the fact it was growing inside of a building.

The tap of footfalls on the stone floor behind me signaled that I was no longer alone. I sensed the swish of air at my back, and my breath caught in my chest. A heavy presence washed through the room, and that could only be one of two people.

Turning around, I found the real Pan emerging from the shadows.

I swallowed hard at the sight of him, and at the same time, I was relieved it wasn't his evil twin, Crocodile.

Pan moved like a god. Now that I was examining him closer, I could see the difference. There was an intangible air about him, like he owned the world and everything in it. His brother had been more…desperate.

He prowled towards me. Hard edges, broad chest, muscles, and a steely gaze on mine.

Savage was a word that described him perfectly.

I recoiled, caught in his silvery gaze.

"You shouldn't have left your room until I came for you." His brows knitted, drawing shadows across his face.

I shook my head. "Why? What are you going to do with me?"

"Show you around so you understand the dangers in Darkland."

With him closing the distance between us, I pressed my back flush to the tree. "How about you tell me exactly where Darkland is? And what did you do to me when you bit me because I almost killed a poor maid, and why can't I feel my wolf? Why did your psycho twin want to hurt me, and why is there a tree in your house?" The words spit out of me rapidfire, and his gaze danced with mirth.

"That's a lot of questions. Would you rather I answer them one by one as you try to become one with that tree...or shall we do it while we walk?"

Ugh, his charm was annoying.

"Just answer the questions." I crossed my arms in front of me, the rough fabric of my dress grating against my skin, and frustration tugging on the edge of my mind.

He nodded and began to walk around the enormous trunk of the tree so that I had no choice but to twist around to watch him. "Alright. For your sanity, steer clear of my twin brother, as it seems you've already piqued his interest. And location-wise, we're in the Rocky Mountains in an isolated location that no one can reach easily. A place that's been charmed to fit my...needs."

Well, that was just great. What did he mean by "needs?"

Pan's perfect silvery eyes were fixed on me, and he licked his lips, stepping around the tree, and I turned completely to face him.

"Long ago, I was running for my life and found myself in an uncharted land," he explained. "That was when I stumbled upon this sector of woods and this tree." He tapped the trunk. "I learned that this was a pinus longaeva species of pine tree. They live up to 5,000 years and are some of the oldest trees in the world, but you know what I found fascinating?" He glanced at me, and I hadn't realized how captivated I'd been by his voice until he paused, and with it came my strange need, echoing through me.

"What's that?" I forced myself to ask, steeling myself for whatever he was going to say.

"These trees aren't native to this area, and yet this one grew despite the different terrain and weather. It made itself fit in an alien location. It reminded me of myself–forced to live where I didn't belong. And I took the tree as a sign of where I would set up my kingdom. With a little spell to make it always night...it was home..."

I blinked at him, taken aback, as I hadn't expected him to share so much. "How long have you been living here?"

"Long enough." There was a dangerous edge to his voice once more.

His hand slid forward, his fingers brushing mine softly, giving me the false sensation of comfort. And from the moment our fingers touched, electricity danced up my arms, a warm sensation coiling around me with invisible hands, seeming to almost draw me closer to him.

But I fought the urge, my mind clamping down on my body's instinct to blindly go to him. Even if I couldn't stop studying how absolutely perfect he was, or how the temptation to give this beautiful vampire anything he wanted lingered just below the surface.

"You keep fighting me," he murmured, dark curiosity ghosting behind his gaze. "What makes you so special, Gwendolyn?" he asked. "No one's ever resisted my call before. Or denied me once I bit them."

"Is that why I'm here? For you to study me? Because you'll be disappointed. I'm just an omega, and not a wanted one. There's nothing more for you to find."

"I think you're wrong about that, little Darling," he murmured, his tone mocking as he made fun of my last name...something I hadn't given him. His thumb stroked the back of my hand in small circles, sending warmth curling in my stomach.

A flicker of worry flared over me that he actually believed I was something else, something interesting...he was going to be so disappointed if he looked too deeply.

And I didn't know why that shamed me to think about.

With a grin, he drew me into a walk, away from the tree.

We crossed the great ballroom, making our way to an arched doorway when all of a sudden, snarls and voices filled the room behind us.

I glanced over my shoulder just as Pan guided me through the doorway.

Shadows from the corners seemed to come to life. Figures stepped out of the shadows, like they were coming from the walls. More vampires by the look of the red glow in their stares...like they might very well enjoy making me their meal.

They filled the room in seconds, at least a hundred of them, and Pan whisked me away from them, but I couldn't shake away the dread. I'd been in a room being watched by vampires, and I'd had no idea.

"The castle revolves around this ballroom. It's the center of our home. The hallways follow a circular path. Should you get lost, you keep going around until you find a stairway."

I stumbled after Pan, still shocked at what we'd just left behind, barely noting that his hand was locked around mine.

"There aren't many rules in Darkland, but the few I have can't be broken."

"Like what?" I asked urgently, trying my best to remember the corridors he was taking to avoid getting lost again.

"In Darkland, you are free to be and do anything you want. There are no restrictions here. It's why we live here. If you want to dance around in the nude, go for it." He eyed me darkly, almost as though he pictured me in that exact scenario and enjoyed what he saw. "But be aware that not everything will play nice with you. And one rule is that the basement is completely out of bounds."

I glanced up at him, studying the way his forehead furrowed.

"Why? What's down there?"

Red flashed in his eyes. "Nothing for you," he said darkly. "It's off limits. Make sure you remember that one well because there'll be severe consequences if you break the rules."

My pulse throbbed, fear filling me from his words. "Fine, don't worry. I won't go anywhere near it."

"There's also the rule of no draining anyone else in the castle. Outsiders are fair game, as are animals, but not each other."

I glanced up at him, trying to work out if he was trying to scare me. "Wait, I'm not a member of whatever fucked up kingdom you have here, and it's not like I'll be *wanting* to drain anyone. I'm not like you; I'm a wolf. And I'm never going to drink your blood to let you change me into a full vampire, anyway."

Pan was facing me, moving so quickly that it left me dizzy. He had a hand on the back of my neck, holding me gently, yet firmly, a small, cruel smile on his perfect lips. "Where did you learn your vampire lore from? Movies and books?"

I shrugged, my breaths speeding up. "It's not like there's a plethora of vampires running around where I grew up."

He laughed, the sound akin to the most beautiful song I'd heard. "Draga mea, Gwendolyn, one bite from a vampire king like me, and you've transformed into a full vampire already."

I blinked at him.

My mind was shifting to the realization of what he'd just said. "Wait. I actually died and..." I might have just screamed. I couldn't tell because my knees hit the red rug. "I'm dead." I rocked back and forth, hugging myself, desperation and madness battering at my mind as I tried to figure out how this could be my reality. "And wait, so I can now go around and just bite anyone and they become vampires?" I was just rambling, but I had no control over my mind at that point.

"For someone to be turned, you must drain them completely until they die, your fangs still penetrating them. I recommend you stick to quick feeds, though. I'm big on population control for the most part. I like to think of us as an exclusive club."

I was pretty sure he was trying to be funny, but my earlier panic I tried desperately to fight was taking over me. I clasped my hand to my neck where his bite mark remained. Was this really happening?

Reaching down within me, I called to my wolf, but she didn't answer. No groaning or her fur brushing against my insides. Just a hollowness that terrified me.

I made a whining sound. "You…you took my wolf from me," I gasped, my throat thickening. "She was all I've known, all I've been."

"When you die and are reborn, the vampire you awaken takes over your wolf." He stared at me in a cavalier manner that irritated me. This was nothing to him, the fact that he'd changed my entire existence was nothing…

Pan's shadow cast over me, and he picked me up, setting me on my feet. "Gwendolyn, this is your home from now on. You aren't going anywhere so you don't need to worry about no longer being a wolf. Like everyone else, you belong to me now."

With his cold hands around mine, he drew me back down the hallway, but I pulled my hand from his.

"You just took my wolf from me." I batted the tears away. "My whole life, I've had everything ripped from me. And…" I hated that I felt so emotionally unstable and so out of control.

It was all becoming too much, too quickly, and with it came a heavy growl from my stomach. I groaned, wrapping my hand around my middle as I almost doubled over from the sharpening pain.

"I-I think I'm dying all over again," I murmured.

Maybe it was disbelief or that I was still dealing with shock, but I sure as hell didn't feel dead. Was there a book somewhere that explained how you were supposed to feel when you became one of the undead? I still was breathing, and my heart seemed to still beat, or was that just the strange sensation of a phantom heart confusing me? Just like people who lost limbs and spoke of still feeling them.

"You're just hungry, and I can fix that." Pan collected my hand again insistently, and I idly noticed how his hand swallowed my own.

I still hadn't come even close to terms with being ripped from my old life. My thoughts panned over my last day amid the living, and Atlas came to mine. Would I even see him again? I sighed at the painful memories of him imprisoned, my chest tightening because it seemed my existence had now become one sad memory after another.

Not exactly keeping track of where Pan was taking me, we finally came to a pause outside a black, metal door that looked more like a dungeon door.

I frowned at him, but he wasn't looking at me; instead, he pushed open the door. Standing in the doorway, Pan turned toward me, and I couldn't help myself as I tried to peer past him into the room that showed nothing--it was pitch black inside.

"Your room is farther down this hallway," Pan explained, pointing to the long hallway. "And this room here is where you'll find the kitchen to sate your hunger."

I swallowed hard, the deep ache in my gut groaning as if on cue. "You're a vampire now, Gwendolyn. And your hunger is your deadliest adversary. If you don't feed enough, the creature you've become will come out, and trust me when I say, the carnage you'll leave in your wake will break you."

We stared at each other for a few long seconds. "If you're trying to make me feel comfortable about what you've made me into, you're failing terribly."

Running a finger under my chin softly, he traced the length of my neck, and my insides fluttered. "You'll feed here until you're strong enough to hunt down your own meal." His features stilled as he waited patiently for a response.

My chest squeezed and I raised a brow. "Okay." What else was I going to say? In the span of one day, I'd lost my life, became a vampire, and now I was told I'd be feeding on blood.

I wasn't exactly dealing well with all the sudden changes

in my life at the moment. I was still hoping any second now, I'd wake up, to find this was all some terrible nightmare.

"Good girl," he purred. There was a seductive darkness behind his voice. Heat rushed through me, blending with fear and the warmth of desire he brought out in me.

I was beginning to think he was the kind of man with two faces. The charming one he tried to carry for when he wanted something from someone, and then the creature I'd seen snippets of up to now that left me paralyzed in fear.

Even knowing that I needed to be on my guard at all times around him…it was hard not to fall prey to his charm.

He left me breathless, and even when he wasn't touching me, it felt like his fingers were gliding up my inner thighs, burning me.

Leaving me to my troubled contemplation, he walked into the room, the fluorescent lights automatically flicking on. Refrigerators with glass doors lined two walls, and my gaze fell to the shelves filled with blood bags.

I stood there, unable to move, staring at all the blood, too frightened to ask where it all came from. A tremble skated over my skin. Was this what my life had come down to? Sucking on blood like a parasite?

"Don't overthink it," Pan soothed, studying me as I tried to hold myself together.

He crossed the room in a few steps and threw open a fridge door before grabbing a bag. Over at the island that sat in the middle of the room, he collected a metal straw, then proceeded to stab it into the bag like he'd just made me a freaking milkshake.

"I suggest sticking to the AB+ initially. It has all protein groups for your body since you are still getting used to your transformation. You'll see more changes over the next couple of weeks."

I laughed at how crazy this was while wanting to cry hysterically at the same time. But when he pushed the bag into my hands, and the metallic smell hit my nostrils, something in me changed.

Something primal and raw came over me, the inky void of my hunger roaring to life. It scared me, but I couldn't control the ache in my stomach or how much the scent of blood had me salivating.

I pitched forward, curling over the bag, unable to get the straw to my mouth fast enough, my heart hammering.

Sucking on the straw, blood filled my mouth, spreading over my tongue. The metallic taste was almost sweet, but it left a slightly salty flavor on the back of my throat too. I was too hungry to make sense of it, and with each gulp rushing down my throat, the pain in my stomach eased. Yet the emptiness never went away. I muffled a cry, unable to get enough blood into me. I clawed at the bag, squeezing it to get more out.

I gulped it down savagely, ignoring the panicked voice in my head screaming that I was drinking blood.

I wanted only one thing…and right now, the bag was empty. Dropping it to the floor, I flew toward the fridge when a powerful arm looped around my middle. Suddenly, Pan had me off my feet, and I growled. "Put me down. More. I need more."

His voice sang in my ear, "That's enough. Too much on your first feed will make you sick."

I heard him, but I writhed against him regardless, a wildness thrashing inside me as I stared at the blood sitting only a few feet away.

"It still hurts. I can't do this; I can't be starving all the time," I pleaded, my whimpers growing louder. "I don't want to do this."

Pan stepped out of the room and into the hallway, setting me on my feet, and pinning me between the wall and his strong, masculine body. His eyes glowed red. He felt the hunger too, didn't he?

Our touch was electric, and every inch of me buzzed. With it came a gush of wetness between my legs, every brief touch sending me into a shuddering aroused state. I arched against him, my breasts brushing against his chest, and the thickness in his pants nestled against my stomach.

He groaned, the slip of his fangs showing.

He brushed his hand across my cheek, staring at my mouth, our bodies seemingly moving together in a strange dance where I craved his touch as much as I did blood. "You're certainly going to liven up this place, aren't you little omega." It wasn't a question, so much as a statement of fact.

My hands trembled, fingers splayed against his biceps as I grasped onto him, hungrily licking the last drops of blood from my lips.

His eyes widened, staring at my mouth possessively, like he was upset I'd taken the drop of blood he'd had his eyes on.

"Pan, I'm afraid you're going to be incredibly disappointed when you realize I'm nothing special," I whispered with bated breath. I'd lost my body, lost everything, and now my control was going out the window.

"Gwendolyn, you have no idea." Towering over me, he studied me, his erection twitching with a growing need, and he ran his hands down my arms.

I moaned in response, pushing myself up on tiptoes to reach his face. Pan's cruel grin should have deterred me, but whatever was happening to me was all-consuming.

Pan leaned in close to me, his mouth hovering inches above mine. He didn't breathe, just stared me in the eyes. "This isn't what you want. You're drunk on blood, and I won't mess up your head more than it already is. Not yet anyway."

Everywhere he touched me sent shivers through my body. I couldn't explain it, but it felt like I'd been waiting for his touch forever.

I didn't respond, as I couldn't understand what was going on with me, and in response, he broke away from me. With my hand in his, he pulled me down the corridor, around the corner, and then another, moving faster, and before long, we were standing outside a door.

"You need to rest now," was all he said as he swung it open to reveal the room I'd woken up in what seemed like a lifetime ago. "You'll feel better later."

I was lost for words, confused, starved, and horny. How could one person be so many things at once?

With a gentle nudge at my back, he pressed me into the

bedroom with the enormous, over-the-top bed. My head was dizzy, and the room was spinning as I stared at the bed.

"I'm not tired," I slurred. I turned just as he shut the door, the click of the lock resonating with a finality that told me I'd indeed become the vampire king's prisoner.

CHAPTER 6

PAN

I lingered outside Gwendolyn's room, listening to her pacing inside, mumbling to herself.

The sight of her greedily sucking on the blood pulsed through my brain, my cock growing painfully hard. I couldn't remember the last time I'd seen anything so beautiful that it awakened the creature inside me. My teeth clenched as I held back the desperation to burst into her room, rip her dress off, and fuck her up against the wall.

Over the years, I'd grown used to hunger, but this was new…my starvation strangled my balls, and I ached for release. Obsession kept me pacing outside her room, all while trying to figure out how she had such an impact on me.

It started with that first bite…but why wasn't it fading?

Every vampire was unique. Some of us carried mind abilities like my brother, Crocodile, able to draw out random snippets of anyone's painful or sexual memories to make them experience it again. It weakened him when he used his gift, but the bastard still did it to anyone he could. To bring them pain. He was a fucking sadist.

But with Gwendolyn, she awakened a primal arousal in me.

I wasn't sure that was her "ability" per se, but the longer I stayed by her door, the harder my cock got.

I'd never experienced anyone not reacting to my bite instantaneously.

The little wolf had fought me in the town center. So, of course, I'd brought her back to Darkland to learn more about what made her so different, and why in the world my thrall had such a weak impact on her.

I might regret that decision, I could see that now. I should have just handed her over to the Lost Boys to have their fun. To finish her off as they'd done to so many others.

Crocodile slipped into my thoughts. He'd tracked her down so quickly, the asshole wasting no time trying to pin her down. And why wouldn't he? We'd always played with the wolves we'd destroyed in the past.

But this time, a sliver of irritation cut through me.

Her sweet smell lingered in my nostrils, the taste of her blood like honey on my tongue. She had glared at me when I carried her out of the kitchen, but new vampires hadn't worked out how to temper their hunger. It took discipline because getting into a feeding frenzy would make them lose control, much like sharks mid-feed. They'd become hysterical and attack anything in their way. When a new vampire ate

too much, they also risked putting themselves into a permanent coma.

Gwendolyn screamed once more from within her room,
snapping me out of my muse. A buzz pulsed across my cock
with how much I'd enjoy bringing such sounds from her
sweet mouth.

Her body...fuck, she was going to bury me with that body
if I didn't find control. Gwendolyn had the type of beauty
you fought wars over, did everything to keep. Where you
stared at her, wondering how someone could be so perfect
looking...

A flare of awareness raced down my back as her angry
shouts turned into moans inside her room. She was getting
herself off, the blood craze too much for her to take. The
temptation to show her what being fucked by a vampire king
could do to her grew by the second.

Instead, I left her behind before I jerked off all over her
door. I guessed it was time to get back to work and deal with
the clusterfuck shadowing Darkland. It pissed me off, in
truth, that after all this time, I still hadn't found a way to
best *Him*.

He wouldn't give up until he'd destroyed every last one
of us, that much was clear.

Revenge flooded my veins just thinking of all he'd done
to me.

I warned him I'd be back for him, and next time, I'd wipe
him from existence. And when I finished with him, I'd make
sure no one ever heard the fucking name, Hook Silver, again.

Gwendolyn

I couldn't remember how long I'd been pacing in my room, screaming, ripping the sheets off my bed, throwing all the new clothes out of the wardrobe I'd found in the room. In my madness, I had discovered another door in my room that led to a small bathroom, so that was a relief.

It was childish of me, but I didn't care. Frustration pulsed in my temples, and the hunger consuming me was destroying me.

During my madness, and after I'd...taken the edge off...I must have fallen asleep because I blinked open my eyes and found myself surrounded by a nest of clothes of varying colors and fabrics. My head still spun, but on the bright side, the hunger pains had subsided.

Climbing to my feet, I took stock of the messy room, stepped out of my nest, and wandered over to the window. I threw open the heavy black curtains to find it was still dark outside, just as Pan had said.

Turning back around to the mess on the floor, I randomly picked up a ruby colored dress with a round neckline and long sleeves.

Moving over to the drawers inside the wardrobe, I found all kinds of underwear. They looked new, and I hoped these hadn't been worn by previous victims. Taking a simple black thong, I went into the bathroom, figuring I might be stuck in my room, but that didn't mean I had to keep wearing this horrible, itchy dress from the Rapture ceremony. I wanted to hold my own kind of sacrificial burning ceremony for it, considering it represented all the ugly Sussana had ever done to me.

In the bathroom, the towels were strewn on the floor, and I made quick work of picking them up and returning them to the white shelves built into the walls.

Unlike most of the bedroom, the walls in here were spectacularly white, the windows frosty, concealing the outside world. There was nothing extraordinary about the room, especially seeing the extravagance of the rest of the castle.

I stripped before entering the shower. Hot water sprayed on my back, and I groaned under my breath at how much I missed taking hot showers. I guess that was one potential... big plus for my new home.

This was heaven, and I stood under the spray, letting it wash away all the pain. It brought back memories of the last days I'd spent with Atlas.

I saw him in my mind, the hurt in his gaze after discovering his parents' secret. Closing my eyes, I didn't want to remember seeing him in so much agony, and instead, I remembered the glorious day when the two of us found ourselves alone in the mountains.

Butterflies fluttered in my stomach at the memory, leaving me tingling everywhere. What he made me feel that day would remain with me for life, and no one could take it away. But with it, a burning sharpness remained in my chest, and heartache crept over me that I wouldn't see him again.

He was my first love, and I'd imprinted every second of our time on my mind. But it was so much more than the physical act of him making love to me. He'd paid attention to me...he'd seen me. He remembered my written project for school, that I snuck out to help the less fortunate. His words floated over my head, and my throat thickened over the fact that he'd cared for me for so long.

"I see you, little Darling. I've always seen you. And I think... you might be the only person in this world that actually sees me."

Tears rolled down my cheeks, my breaths hiccupping as I softly sobbed. I cried for the chance at happiness I'd lost. For the man who saw me as I was, who paid attention to what everyone else ignored.

At having something so good just ripped away.

I let myself cry a bit longer, to release the emotions that choked me. A lungful of air rushed out on my sob. Water cascaded over me, taking with it all my tears. Part of me wished it could just as easily remove the sorrow, while another part cherished those painful memories because they were all I had left of Atlas.

Pain.

Heartache.

A desperate hunger to find my way back to him.

A sudden, unexpected movement caught my attention from the window. And I realized it was a tree branch lightly tapping the glass, the whistle of the wind accompanying it. My gut squeezed at the reminder of where I was, so I turned off the water and toweled myself, deciding I'd get out of my room one way or another.

I threw on the clothes, then dried my hair with the towel before combing it off my face with the wide tooth comb on the sink. There were no mirrors anywhere, and I suspected if I could see myself, I'd be pale and ghostly.

I had died, after all.

I found a pair of brand-new, black tennis shoes in the drawers, along with glittery heels and a number of other shoes. Escaping a room and a vampire's lair required comfortable shoes, no matter how much I kept staring at the kind of heels I'd never been permitted to wear back home.

Surprisingly, the shoes fit perfectly, as did the dress, which cinched in at my waist with elastic and tumbled down to my knees. I had no idea how Pan knew my size, but I also didn't want to think too much about it either. Or the fact that these could all be clothes from his previous victims. Maybe he had a thing for my body type.

Back in the bedroom, I headed to the door and pushed down on the handle. Locked, of course. I knew from exploring earlier that getting off my balcony wasn't going to be possible, unless I wanted to test out my newfound immortality by dropping 100 feet. So I would have to get creative.

Glancing around, I paused on the lamp by the bed and made my way to it. Then I ripped off the shade, finding metal pins poking up around the lightbulb. Wrestling with the lamp, I snapped off two of the pins and rushed back to the door where I fell to my knees.

I wasn't 100% sure what I was doing, but I once watched Cook break into the pantry after it had accidentally locked with the keys inside. Sussana insisted on keeping it locked when not in use, as she was afraid someone would take the food…someone like me…

Sticking one rod into the keyhole, I jiggled it until I felt a small click. I jammed in the second rod, remembering Cook saying it was all about detaching the locking mechanism... and playing with the springs. I wasn't too sure what that meant, but I'd seen Cook unlock the door in seconds. So it couldn't be that hard.

Minutes later and I was sweating, my fingers cramping up. "Come on, get open."

With a deep breath, I persistently kept at it when finally I heard the best sound in the world–a metallic click.

I jumped to my feet and rapidly opened the door while doing a silent cheer. Rushing back to the set of drawers, I stashed the metal rods there so no one could find them, then I set the partially broken lamp back with the shade, and I hurried out of the room.

Without thinking, my feet carried me directly to the kitchen, and my stomach growled in anticipation. I pushed at the handle and found it locked. My shoulders sank, and I glanced at the three locks on the door, wondering how long it would take me to break in before someone spotted me.

Just when I made the decision to retrieve the metal rods and break into the kitchen, the thumping sound of footfalls came from the same direction as my room.

My chest constricted, and I pivoted on my heels, running in the opposite direction, convinced Pan was returning for me.

I had no idea what turns I'd taken, but I came across an elaborate descending staircase with shiny black railings and a red rug that tumbled down the middle of the marble steps. It curved around and I followed it downward, ending up in a small foyer with a set of open doors ahead of me.

Tree vines snaked along the walls.

I inhaled in relief that I was alone and crossed the foyer quickly. At the door, I peered out into the night. Lights flickered from my right, with voices coming and shouting. To my left, darkness swallowed everything.

A shiver danced down my spine as I recalled what Pan's brother, Crocodile, had said.

I can throw you out into the woods and you can discover for yourself that there are other dangerous things out there that want to skin you alive and suck the marrow from your bones.

Covered in goosebumps, I found myself creeping forward to see who was out there.

My eyes flew open, and I silenced the shock startling me the moment I saw them.

In the flickering blaze breaking through the darkness, I stared into chaos. It took me a little while to work out exactly what I was seeing.

Flashes of blood. Pale flesh torn. Gurgled screams from the women the vampires were feeding on. Pinned to the ground laid out across the wooden table, caged against a tree.

I stared in horror as the poor women tried to escape; they fought, but none of them stood a chance. Not when they were dealing with monsters.

Monsters like me…

The fire flickered wildly, the light pulsing across the bloody slaughter and all the ravaged flesh. My stomach rumbled at the sweet scent dancing on the breeze, my chest clenching.

I battled the hunger in me, staring in disbelief that this is what I'd become. One of them.

A woman sobbed as a vampire snatched her into his arms. With instinct, I stepped forward, but that had been a mistake because I'd caught another vamp's attention.

A shadow of a creature stood against the side of the house watching the brutal feeding frenzy until he found something more entertaining… Me.

My heart jacked up to my throat.

How long had he been standing there without me knowing?

The vampire stepped out of the shadows. He was lofty and brawny. He wore only low-hanging jeans, and blood splashed across his chest. More of it dripped from his chin from a recent feed, it seemed.

Sickness slithered through my gut, and despite my nervousness over the way he stared at me, the screams of the women carving through the night, and the heavy stench of death around me, a part of me still craved a taste of the blood.

I swallowed past my dry throat, still remembering the sweetness of the blood from the bag. How it sated me, how it awakened something in me that made me feel invincible.

His hostile glare morphed into a wicked grin, the promise of danger playing in his darkening eyes that held a red glow.

He was at my side in a flash, his long, bony fingers snapped around my wrist.

"What a delicious thing you are." A thick tongue slipped

out of his mouth, dragging across his bottom lip, covering me in shivers.

"Let go of me," I hissed, my voice nothing against the screaming that enveloped the air all around me. I shoved my hand against his chest, managing to coax a laugh out of the asshole as he leaned in closer, his tongue dragging across my ear.

Driving my fist against him, an icy shiver ran through me, but he wasn't releasing me. And now I regretted coming out here at all.

"I heard we had a new vampire in Darkland, but you're different, aren't you?" he whispered in my ear. "I can't recall the last time Pan brought us new blood to play with."

Before I had the chance to expand my lungs and take in a breath to respond–since the instinct of breathing as though I still lived lingered evidently–he threw me over his shoulder. We rushed across the open yard, the breeze ripping at my hair.

Panic dug into me, and I joined the screams surrounding us, but just as quickly, I was set back on my feet. The monster loomed over me.

It all happened too fast, and as I wracked my brain for information on how to deal with this guy...monster to monster, I came up blank.

In Darkland, you are also free to be and do anything you want.

Those had been Pan's words, so did that extend to these vamps doing as they pleased to me? I thought there were rules about that...

I shoved a hand against the vamp once more. "Don't

touch me." That was when I noticed we stood in the heart of the monstrous feeding frenzy. Other vamps paused their eating and looked over at us. Blood stained their faces and their clothes, and the grass beneath our feet felt squishy and wet with the crimson blood.

Fear. I hated that feeling and how it made my head race. Hated that it made me appear weak.

I recoiled, bumping right into the vamp who carried me here. Iron hands grabbed my hips, and in seconds, I was sitting on his lap on a log seat while he made a disgusting sucking sound in my ear. I clawed at his hand looped round my middle, keeping me prisoner.

Eyes were on me. So many ravenous vamps.

I swallowed down the shiver as the beast behind me groped my breast, licking my neck.

"Let me go," I shouted, thrashing against him. I fought harder, ripping the flesh on his arm with my fingernails. I looked around for help, but all my gaze found...was Crocodile.

He stood near the flames, blood dripping down his chin just as the girl in his arms slumped to the ground in front of him, dead.

A scream rose to the back of my throat from the way he was greedily staring at me—a monster readying to attack his next victim.

My fingers continued to frantically dig into the vamp's arm around my middle, the cruel desperation to escape stretching through me. I took back what I said about being stronger. I was nothing against this guy.

"If all you're going to do is toy with your food," Crocodile started, stepping over the girl, sauntering towards us. "Then I'll take her off your hands."

The vampire at my back stiffened and hissed over my shoulder. I pictured these two brawling, with me in the middle of them. So much for Pan's rules. Maybe he should talk to his "Lost Boys" about obedience, and not me.

I tried my best not to look at the bodies around me, or I'd really go insane. Darkland was hell. I was convinced of that now.

This wasn't a place for me. It couldn't be.

Around us, the sickening slurping sound of drinking blood echoed, with the victims mostly dead now.

Death. That was what Darkland stood for.

"I'm very much in the mood for a hare," Crocodile growled. He ran the jagged edge of his fingernail along the sharp edge of his jawline, but paused suddenly.

His nostrils flared as he drew a scent in. His fingers extended into claws, his shoulders rising like hackles. Somehow, despite being pale already, he managed to become paler.

Then it happened so fast my head spun. He retreated in the same heartbeat that a flurry of air rushed against me.

The guy behind me was ripped away.

Several vampires nearby snapped to attention, staring our way once more, mouths gaping open with fangs on show.

In the commotion, I was shoved over onto the ground as a savage explosive fight broke out. My mind flew to Crocodile attacking the vamp who'd grabbed me. But as I quickly pushed myself to my feet, I caught sight of him back by the fire.

Hastily, I twisted around toward the commotion and shuddered.

Pan fisted the vamp by the hair, slamming him up against a tree, growling in his face, "You dare touch what's mine? You don't fucking look at her, do you understand? Don't be in the same room as her." Pan paused, his head tilting to the side, studying the squirming vampire who was whimpering apologies in his grasp. "Fuck it, you *won't* ever see her again."

He lashed out, snatching the vamp by the throat, clawed fingers digging into flesh.

The male's scream died the moment Pan ripped out his throat.

Blood and sinew splattered everywhere.

A small scream spilled past my lips, and I stumbled backward, telling myself to not make a sound. But the moment Pan dropped the vamp from his arms, he fell to his knees by his side and stared at me.

There was something strange behind his gaze…a spark of rage like somehow I'd forced his hand to kill one of his own. But, this craziness was all on him. This was his kingdom…his rules.

He raised his hand, holding what appeared to be a broken branch, thick enough that the sharp end caught my attention.

Without pausing, Pan drove the stake right into the vamp's chest. The vampire's gargled cries flatlined instantly, and I watched like a deer caught in headlights, curious about what would happen to the creature. Was he dead?

But nothing happened.

Pan carried no remorse in his gaze, no guilt for killing one of his own. Shadows danced against his face. Even with the dead vampire's blood on him, he was a beautiful creature... too beautiful to be such a terrifying monster of the night. His skin pale and perfect, his eyes brooding, staring into mine.

Getting to his feet, he dusted his blood-splattered shirt, stepping away from the vamp. His mouth fell at the edges as he kept his attention on me.

He stared at me like I had become his prey.

Terror boomed in my head.

I couldn't stay there. I couldn't remain in Darkland.

Darkness descended on my mind, and I turned, pushing into a frantic run across the yard.

I had to find a way out of here.

I sprinted away, taking one last glance back to see all the vampires rushing towards their dead comrade. They tore into him, ripping him to shreds, sucking down on his blood.

My throat trembled and I gagged at the sight.

If I had a heart, it would be banging against my ribcage right now. Instead, I ran for my life, having lost all hope that I was in any way safe with Pan.

The darkness blurred the landscape around me into shapes and shadows that seemed to sharpen.

And all I could smell was the stench of death in the air, following me.

CHAPTER 7
GWENDOLYN

My breath was an illusion, but it still felt like it came out in gasps, puffing into the cold air around me as I ran. I'd thought that life with Sussana was terrible, but this... this place was a living nightmare.

Or maybe living wasn't the right word.

My new vampire speed didn't come with grace evidently, because my toe hit a tree root on the forest floor and I was launched to the ground, hitting the damp earth with a hard thump that seemed to rattle through the undergrowth around me.

I resisted the urge to sob…or at least scream, as I jumped to my feet and continued to stalk through the night. I had no idea where I was going; all I knew was I had to get out of here.

It would be nice if Pan could just decide to cut his losses

and let me go. Especially if he was going to kill his men because of me.

Fuck. Crimson blood splashed through my mind, a nauseating hunger pain flashing through me at the thought. How could something be disgusting, and yet tantalizing…all at the same time?

"Stupid vamps," I muttered, well aware I was cursing myself at the same time. I stumbled again and slowed, feeling like my speed wasn't doing very much for me. I could see much better than usual at night, but in the forest, everything looked the same, and I could have been going in a circle for all I knew.

Something glinted in the moonlight off to my left and I froze, a little impressed with how fast I could stop now. I leaned forward, realizing it was some kind of giant structure that had been camouflaged to melt into the woods. I listened for a long moment for anyone in the near vicinity…aka Pan, but all I could hear was the chirping of crickets and the soft hoot of a nearby owl. I crept forward, stopping every few feet to listen again, until finally, I was just outside the large structure. There were two huge barn doors in front of it, the planks vertical and consisting of trunks complete with tree branches still attached. It was a clever disguise; I doubted I would have even noticed it if it weren't for the fact some of the wood had come undone on a small portion of the roof, revealing the tin underneath that had flashed under the moonlight.

I walked along the side of the building, trying to find a window to see inside. I'd made it all the way to the back when I noticed a canvas cover attached to the wall.

Cautiously, I slowly pulled on it and revealed a solitary window. It was dark inside, but as I lifted the cover higher, allowing more of the moonlight to stream in, I could see outlines of what looked like…motorcycles? Was this the garage where Pan and his men kept their bikes?

Hope flared through me as I dropped the window cover and crept back around to where the huge doors were. Evidently, Pan was really sure no one was going to bother him around here, because I was easily able to get the door cracked and slide inside.

I did an awkward little dance when I saw I'd been right, and there was, in fact, a garage full of gorgeous bikes laid out like a feast in front of me. It was easy to spot Pan's. It was the largest and flashiest, with skulls and replicas of the tree all over it. For a second, I was tempted to grab it and drive away, but I figured that might give him more incentive to come after me, and that wasn't something I was interested in.

I chose a smaller bike, closer to the size I had back home, and I carefully wheeled it out of the garage, stopping again to listen at the entryway just in case this was some kind of trap and I'd been stupidly lured in like a mouse with a cube of cheese.

There was nothing there. Nothing but the sound of the darkness and my breathing.

I slid on the bike and gave it a kickstart. It purred as the engine started, the sound music to my ears.

And then I rode.

There was a trail leading out from the garage, or really, it was just a tire track through the dirt, barely visible in the darkness. I drove down it slowly as the moon slipped behind a cloud and the headlight on the bike barely illuminated the path. The bike wasn't loud, but in the stillness of the night, it sounded like a roar, and there was no way for me to relax even as I made it out of the woods and onto an actual road.

I'd been driving for about ten minutes when I heard it. The whirring rumble of another bike not far behind me. A cold sweat broke out on my forehead as I pushed my bike to go faster. The wind battered at my skin. It usually felt like a caress, but with the way dread spiked through my veins, it was just an impediment, keeping me from going as fast as I needed to get away.

I knew it was him. I knew it without a doubt. Like his bite had transferred some of his essence into my being and now I could sense whenever he was near.

Maybe it had.

And maybe his bike had powers just like he did because no matter how fast I went, and I was flying down the road at over a hundred miles per hour at this point, his bike went faster. Finally, he appeared around a bend, a dark specter in the night, a cruel smile on his face as he leaned forward and urged his bike faster.

Tingles traced up my spine. I'd never felt more like prey than I did at that moment.

Some part of it was exhilarating, though. Like standing on the edge of a cliff, knowing what will happen if you take a step off. We were neck and neck, and somehow there was a grin on my face. The terror was obviously turning me batty.

Pun intended.

Although I hadn't yet seen any sign that that particular rumor about vampires was real. Or at least, I hadn't yet felt the urge to turn into a bat.

Pan let out a war cry that echoed through the night, the sound its own kind of magic because instead of screaming, I felt the urge to answer his call.

The road was a straightway and we both careened down it. Immortality felt amazing in that moment. I wasn't sure what exactly could kill me now that I was turned, besides Pan ripping my throat out and stabbing me with a stake, but I was sure it wasn't a motorcycle crash.

The panic was fading away as we raced down the roadway.

I had a thing for bikes. And apparently bikers.

Because the way he was handling that thing was down-right sinful. It was like it was a part of him. I'd never seen anyone that in control on a bike.

"Fuck off," I screamed over the wind.

He threw his head back laughing, and even through the wind, the sexy sound reverberated through my bones.

Stupid.

"Pull over," he ordered. I groaned as the command reverberated in my head. Fuck. It felt stronger than an alpha bark.

Asshole.

I leaned forward and pushed on.

I could feel his sigh of annoyance as if it was a living, breathing thing.

"Pull. Over." This time, his bike dipped towards mine, nudging it and almost sending me careening into the bushes and trees that lined the highway. It was nice to know that I wouldn't die from a crash. But it would still hurt.

Before I could have another thought, Pan sprung from his bike and landed on the seat behind me, his arms coming around me to grab the handlebars. I glanced back, shocked that he would crash his perfect, beautiful bike, but I swerved when I saw that his bike had come to a magical stop and was just balancing upright where he had jumped off, not showing any sign it was going to tip over.

Pan clenched the brake and our bike came to a screeching stop, his boot dropping to the ground to keep us upright.

My teeth ground in frustration as he grabbed the key. I sat there for a long second, my mind whirring as I debated trying to run away.

I was sure that would just excite him more since he seemed to love the whole cat-and-mouse game.

I really wanted to scream, but I held it in.

Just as I was about to ask him what the hell he was waiting for, since he was still sitting behind me on the bike, his hand trailed down the side of my arm.

I froze. What the fuck was he doing? Chills followed his touch down my skin, and I couldn't hold in my tremble or the way my breath had begun to come out in gasps.

Ugh. Hormones. I might have been one of the undead, but there was definitely slick gushing between my legs as his tongue trailed down my neck, circling my pulse point.

Hmm. That was interesting.

"Stop fucking touching me," I growled, but of course, the growl came out as a whine...

I used the handlebars to pull myself forward, but his arm wrapped around me and halted my progress.

"You know I'm thinking my little omega needs to be punished," he murmured as his tongue flicked out again to brush against my skin.

I couldn't stop the whimper or the scent of my slick that was thick in the air from yet another gush.

"I will stab you in your sleep if you keep touching me like this," I warned. He just laughed, and I huffed, annoyed at how he even made *that* sexy.

"Mmmh. I'm thinking that we both might enjoy your punishment," he answered, and without warning, he struck, his sharp incisor teeth digging into my skin. Pleasure burst through my body, so intense that my vision blurred, the dark night around me fading into a pinprick as my screams filled the air.

I orgasmed instantly. And it wasn't just any climax—it was the orgasm to end all orgasms.

He was sucking in deep gulps of my blood, and it was like every pull from his lips had a direct line to my fucking vagina.

Pan pulled out and licked at the wound. "That's my girl," he purred, and I was frozen in place, the venom from his bite immobilizing me. I would have fallen off the bike if not for his arm still holding me firmly in place.

It was hard to put into words what I was feeling as his hand slid between my legs. I hated him.

But I was desperate for more. I was desperate for him to make me feel like that again.

Was his bite like a drug? Besides the venom's effect, could someone get addicted to it? Because this was how I imagined an addict felt. Desperate, willing to throw away all common sense for more. My neck was tingling where the skin was healing, and I could feel his hard length digging into my back.

He licked again at my neck, where there must have still been some blood staining my skin, and his moan right after was so erotic, I bet the trees around us would have blushed if it were possible.

His hand slipped beneath my dress, and his fingers pushed past the edge of my panties, sliding through my folds lazily.

I was dripping wet. There wasn't any hiding it. He chuckled darkly, laughing in stupid male satisfaction at how turned on he'd made me.

"That means nothing," I choked out, the words difficult to form since I was fucking paralyzed.

"This is how it starts, you know," he mused as his fingers continued their slow, decadent glide, occasionally dipping inside for the fun of torturing me. He didn't wait for me to try and squeak out a reply. "This is how you're going to fall in love with me."

I scoffed. A huge scoff, but it didn't seem to affect him at all.

"There's no one in this world who can make you feel like this…"

My mind flashed to Atlas and how he'd made me feel.

The orgasm might not have been as intense...but the feelings involved...

Those were unforgettable.

As if he could read my mind–and maybe he could; I hadn't quite figured that out yet–his thick fingers sunk into me, another pressing against my clit expertly.

"Are you going to be my good girl and cum again?" he growled as white-hot heat licked up my spine. He was hitting that perfect spot.

God, why did it have to feel so good?

I welcomed the sting of his teeth as he bit down again, blood trickling down the front of my chest as his fingers played. I came.

Again.

This one was just as ridiculously good as before.

Abruptly, he pulled his fingers and his teeth out mid-orgasm and pushed me forward so my back was arched and I was leaning against the handlebars.

"Fuck," he groaned in a rough, gravel-filled voice. He hadn't licked my wound so my blood was still flowing. My sensitive hearing heard the drip, drip, drip of it falling onto the bike's metal.

After pulling my dress up all the way, Pan trailed a finger down the front of me, gathering the blood on his fingers... before he rubbed his wet fingers around my asshole.

I squeaked from the sensation, and he laughed before grabbing up more of the blood. I could feel his hand between us, working his dick—was he really rubbing my blood all over his dick right now?

And why was that so hot?

Another gush of slick and I swore I was coating the seat of the bike. They would need to burn it after this...or give it to me. Because there was no way that anyone would ever be able to remove the scent, and the last thing I wanted was one of Pan's so-called "Lost Boys" to be riding around with a hard-on constantly because my smell was stuck to their bike.

Before I could think of a bunch of pervy vampires getting off on my fragrance, he flipped me around on the bike like I weighed nothing and set me on his lap, moving my hips so I was pressed against his length.

"Fuck," he hissed as he buried his face in my chest and began to lick and suck at the blood still dripping down my chest. I glanced down and saw that he had indeed lathered his dick with my blood. The sight was...

Arousing...

I was disgusted with myself, but I was blaming the vampire venom for addling my brain.

"Pan," I weakly protested as my bare ass rubbed against his leather-covered thighs.

"You're so fucking wet, but I want more. Can you give me that, little omega? Drown me in your slick. I want to feel it," he murmured in my ear before pulling my face back by my hair and taking me in a fierce kiss.

My lips were barely able to move against his, but it didn't really matter. Pan would have controlled the kiss no matter what, licking, sucking, and biting at my mouth savagely as he rubbed his blood-slick dick through my folds.

It felt so filthy.

But yet freeing at the same time. I'd had years of being a servant in the house that was supposed to be my home. And before that, it had been made clear behind Caleb's back how unwelcome I really was.

Years of having to say yes ma'am, no ma'am. To make sure everything was perfect. To ensure I was perfect.

This messy, out-of-control bonding felt like it was ripping the cages down around me that had been erected.

The moon was slicing across his face, making him look every bit the dark prince from hell, or wherever it was that vampires like him came from.

My lips were regaining even more movement, and I was suddenly desperate to take back a little control. I wiggled my fingers, almost shouting in celebration when I could move almost my whole hand.

"Show me why they call you a king," I whispered, enjoying the surprise in his eyes at my words, followed by a rush of heat.

He groaned, and like we were tethered, the sound reverberated through my skin as his hands moved to my ass and he squeezed and massaged my cheeks.

"With pleasure, little Darling," he purred as he surged into my tight core, right as he bit down on my breast, an inch away from my nipple.

My scream reverberated around us. I swore there were colors I'd never seen before that appeared in my vision as he lifted me up and down on his cock, fucking me from underneath. His gulps were long and hard, and I was getting lightheaded as the tip of his dick hit the spot inside me perfectly.

It wasn't so much that another orgasm was building, as it was that it never really stopped.

"You are not leaving me," he grunted through gritted teeth. "You are never leaving me," he swore as he continued to pound into me.

In the back of my mind, I was faintly aware of what he was saying, but I was swept up in the sparks he'd created in my body. His movements somehow quickened, and he let out a rough groan that reverberated through the night as his warmth filled me.

Fuck.

My breaths came out in gasps as I floated down from my high, moaning when he slipped out of me and hating how empty I felt.

Pan tucked himself back in his pants and reached behind me towards the handlebars...and then we were moving. My eyes sprung open as my soaked core rubbed and vibrated against the seat, almost setting me off once more. I struggled to get my boobs back under my dress and bra. Pan's face was completely blank, like what had just happened...meant nothing.

He made no move to slow down as I attempted to right my clothes, not feeling excited about my chest flapping in the breeze.

As the wind whistled past my face, the melancholy seeped in.

I had failed in my escape plan.

And not only had I failed, I'd also allowed my captor to fuck me.

This was not cause for celebration no matter how good the fucking actually was.

I moved my head and winced, realizing he still hadn't closed my wound.

Did all vampires bleed like this? Or was I just special like that? And why did I still have some of my omega qualities?

We were back at the castle before I could think more closely about my multitude of questions. I could see the ever-present bonfire in the distance, and the sound of the raucous partying of his Lost Boys. I shivered, thinking of the scene that had caused me to run in the first place.

Pan pulled up to one of the side entrances and stopped. He slid off the bike and began to stride towards the door, making no move to check if I was following.

It was only when he got to the door that he turned back to look at me.

"There's no place you can run that I won't find you, Gwendolyn," he purred, the nonchalance on his face clashing with the power and tension in his voice. He glanced lazily down my body as I slid off the bike, trying to adjust myself. A cruel smirk appeared on his lips. "But it will be fun every time you try."

With those parting words, he walked into the castle, leaving me alone in the cold breeze, his cum still sliding down my leg and blood from my wound still dripping along my skin.

CHAPTER 8
GWENDOLYN

I woke up the next morning to a drenched pillow and feeling like I was going to pass out at any moment from all the blood loss. I fingered the tiny holes in my neck, wondering what to do. I'd tried to use my own saliva to close them last night, but it hadn't done anything. Pan must have some kind of super venom that could only be stopped by him or something.

I had no interest in trying to hunt down Pan to help me, especially when I could still feel the ache inside of me where his cock had been, but I needed some kind of help.

After sluggishly throwing on some clothes, I wandered into the hallway, the steady drip of blood sliding along my neck. I leaned against the wall as I went along, trying to concentrate on one step and then another.

I was starving. The need for blood was...almost overpowering.

The world was starting to fade as I turned onto another hall when, all of a sudden, a figure appeared out of a doorway in the distance. He stutter-stepped backward in surprise when he saw me, and before I could comprehend who it was, my legs failed me...and the world went back.

————

It was the whistling that woke me up. Cheerful fucking whistling that my brain felt at odds with in the dark place I'd found myself. I tried to open my eyes, but they felt as if they'd been glued shut.

"Easy there, sweetheart. Drink this and you'll be good to go in a jiff," a happy-sounding—familiar—voice soothed from next to me. A second later, a straw was between my lips and I was greedily gulping what I knew to be blood, but what might as well have been chocolate cake from my former life with how freaking incredible it tasted.

"Mmmh," I groaned, only somewhat aware of the fingers softly stroking my face as I gulped desperately at the straw. It only took a minute for me to get to the end of the blood bag, and I whined as the straw was removed from my lips. Half a second later, it was back and I was once again getting access to the blood. I worked to open my eyes and inwardly cheered as they finally popped open, and I was staring into an unfamiliar pair of sea green eyes.

"Hi there, sweetheart," the male murmured, a playful glint in his gaze as he stared back at me unblinkingly.

I wrinkled my nose at him, and that was the best I could give him as I continued to desperately suck at the blood.

He let out a surprised laugh that caused a weird feeling to twitch in my stomach at the sound. "You're cute," he murmured as we continued to stare at one another.

The stranger was dressed casually, in jeans and a faded T-shirt that stretched across his broad shoulders, emphasizing very capable-looking biceps—if that was a thing. And he was tall and lean, taller than even Pan had been, towering over me. I would have thought I'd be intimidated by how utterly large he was, but as I watched him run a hand absent-mindedly through his golden brown colored hair, I found myself relaxing. His hair was short on the sides but longer on the top, and spiked upward, which added even more inches to his height. His bicep flexed and moved as he continued to run his hand through his hair, and I found myself a bit entranced.

There must have been something in the air in this place that was turning me into some kind of demented ball of lust...because I was finding myself way too attracted to the creatures here.

"I'm Luke," he finally greeted in a pleasant, smooth voice that was as warm and friendly sounding as his appearance. "And you're our beautiful Gwendolyn." He bopped me softly on the tip of my nose when I scrunched it up again, my sips finally growing slower as my haze of hunger began to lift.

I still finished the entire bag he was holding up to my lips. My tongue peeked out to get a drop that was sliding down my mouth, and his eyes tracked the movement, the pupils widening in arousal as he did so.

I cleared my throat and pulled away from the straw.

"Thank you," I whispered in a gravelly voice, and he clucked his tongue and shook his head at the sound.

"Let me get something for that," he murmured, almost to himself, before turning and rummaging through some cabinets.

For the first time, I glanced around at my surroundings and realized I was in what appeared to be some kind of medical room. There was medical equipment on the long metal cabinet across from me, and I was on a cot with handrails, just like the ones in the hospital. I also belatedly realized that there was a line in my arm connected to some kind of machine, and clear liquid was being pumped from the machine into my arm. An I.V.

"Where am I?" I asked, settling against the fluffy pillows I'd realized were behind me and hoping somehow I was out of Darkland—even while I ignored the faint pang in my heart at the idea of not seeing Pan again.

Stupid heart.

"Still Darkland, sweets. This is just the infirmary. I had to take you here after you passed out in the hallway."

Well, fuck.

"I passed out in the hallway?" I asked, trying to think back a second before remembering stumbling down the hallway after Pan...

Fucking Pan.

"That filthy fucking bloodsucker," I screeched, still hoarsely, as he turned towards me with a small shot glass of milky blue liquid.

He threw his head back at the sound, giving the room another one of those happy, full laughs I was strangely attracted to.

I'd never met someone who came across so…sunny. Even Atlas, my beautiful golden boy had come across as moody and brooding most of the time. This guy—Luke—embodied sunshine. From his laugh to the golden red tinted color of his hair.

"Pan got a little exuberant last night, did he?" he asked with a wink, not appearing outraged in the least bit. Or shocked, for that matter. A flash of what was suspiciously close to jealousy sparked through me at the idea of Pan doing last night's events with others.

Not that I'd enjoyed it. At all.

"Hey," Luke murmured with a frown, a rough finger coming to tip my chin towards him. "There's nothing to be ashamed about. Pan can be quite…persuasive."

My eyebrows rose. "First-hand experience?"

He laughed again, the sound wrapping me up in its warmth like a lover's hug. "Mmmh. I'm afraid I only have eyes for the fairer sex." His eyebrows went up and down like a comic book villain's. "But in a pinch, blood from Pan does the trick."

Now my insides were clenching just thinking of watching them feed from each other. I shook my head free of his finger that was still touching my skin, trying to clear my head as my hand reached toward my neck.

"I sealed the wound. Only Pan or one of the inner circle can do it."

"The Lost Boys, you mean?" I asked, cocking my head, unable to stop myself from admiring his pretty face.

Now he was the one scrunching up his nose. "I hate that term. As you can see," he said, gesturing to his gorgeous, built body, "I'm anything but a boy."

"A bit full of ourselves, aren't we?" My voice came out far more flirty than I would have liked, but I couldn't help it--his personality was contagious.

"I just know who I am," he responded easily, and for some reason, his words hit me hard, burrowing deep. When had I ever known who I was? I was a daughter, and then an orphan. An unwanted foster kid, then a servant. A weak omega.

Now I was a sacrifice. A vampire.

I really wanted to be more.

"Are you the MC's doctor?" I asked, moving on from the uncomfortableness I was feeling.

"Yes, I guess you could call me that. I was in med school when I was turned. Two years there, and then I've figured things out from there over the years."

"You were turned in medical school?" I asked tentatively as he adjusted the I.V. bag, knowing that was probably something you weren't supposed to ask but deciding to go for it anyway. I knew absolutely nothing of what I'd become…and I was thinking Luke could help me with that.

It was the first time a shadow passed over his features, but he quickly shook it off.

"I'd worked late in the lab that night. It was probably one a.m. or so. And some rabid vamp jumped me and pulled me into the alley. Next thing I knew, I was waking up in some homeless person's piss...changed."

He fell silent for a moment as I pictured him, left for dead somewhere. I might have been turned without my consent, but at least it hadn't been like that.

"A rabid vamp?" I finally asked, picturing how out of my mind I'd been with hunger when I'd first woken up, and wondering if it was like that.

His thumb was absentmindedly stroking across my bare knee as he stood in front of me, and I shivered from the sensations.

"A vampire who's become lost to the bloodlust. For some reason, there are some vampires who never calm down, no matter how much blood they get ahold of. They're usually put down, but that one, for whatever reason, hadn't been discovered yet."

"What did you do when you woke up?" I whispered, lost in the story.

"Well, as I'm sure you can imagine, I was a bit rabid myself. I believe I fastened onto the first creature I came across, and was just a menace to society in general for a bit." He bit his lip as he stared at the wall above my head, clearly lost in his memories.

"I was a bit bitter about losing my dream of becoming a doctor—"

"There wasn't any way you could go back?"

He laughed, the sound of it far from the sunny ones before that. It was harsh and caustic.

Pained.

"Well, I tried. But then I almost killed my lab partner…who happened to be my fiancée. So I figured that wasn't a good idea."

My hand flew up to my mouth, my heart clenching for him. His whole body shuddered for a moment, and then he pasted on a fake smile.

I found myself missing his real one. He was the first seemingly nice person I'd encountered in this hell hole.

"Hey," he said gently, his voice rough as he tried to control his emotions. "It happened a long time ago. I've—I've gotten past it."

I bit my lip, wondering why I felt like I was going to cry all of a sudden, for a stranger. Not only a stranger, but someone complicit in my current fate.

"How did you end up with Pan?" I asked, when I'd gotten ahold of myself.

He snorted and rolled his eyes, as if the story was ludicrous, and I leaned forward, a little too eager for the tale.

"I'd gotten in the habit of trolling nightclubs for my meals," he began. I raised an eyebrow, picturing him seducing his victim amidst the music. I'd never been to one, of course; there weren't any "clubs" in the packs I'd grown up in, but I'd heard about them in the cities. He just grinned at me unrepentantly as his thumb continued its maddening sweep across my skin. "I'd see Pan from time to time at one of them. But the rumors about him were enough to keep me far away. Then one night, a fight broke out; someone pulled a knife and literally slit the throat of one of the MC. Of course, somehow, I ended up right in the midst of it, trying to sew the guy's throat together since his body wasn't healing rapidly enough to save him. I guess Pan liked the idea of having his own guy around to help with injuries. So here I am."

"You're understating the story just a bit there, Luke," came Pan's cool voice from the side of us.

My gaze widened and shot over to the doorway where Pan was leaning against the stone, looking like a dark prince in a fairy tale come to life.

"Mmh, yes, I left out the part that makes you look like a hero," Luke mused, mischief thick in his voice. My gaze bounced between the both of them, wondering how I was feeling equally attracted to them at the moment.

Except I hated Pan.

Couldn't forget that.

Since he was the reason I was in here to begin with.

"Please tell me how Pan could look like a hero," I drawled sarcastically, garnering another heady laugh from Luke and a darkly amused grin from Pan. A tendril of hair had fallen in Pan's face, and I could have sworn his eyes were daring me to jump off the med bed and move it.

Or maybe that was just my imagination…

"Luke was trying unsuccessfully to kill himself by poisoning his body with whatever drug he could get his hands on, so he was lucky he was able to help at all," tossed out Pan.

"Well, he seemed to have performed well enough to impress you," I shot back.

Pan's smirk widened. "My, Luke, you move quickly. You've already got our Darling defending you."

My cheeks flamed at his insinuation, and I shot Luke a glance, only to see that his smile had widened. He was delighted at what Pan had just said.

"Come talk to me later, Luke," Pan commanded, before leaving without a word to me.

"You can apologize any time now," I called out after him, very unwilling to let anything go.

His laughter bounced into the room, but he didn't come back.

"Pan always keeps things lively," Luke commented as he took my arm and carefully removed the I.V. He was good. I barely felt a pinch. "Alright, sweetheart. Now that I've got you up and running again, and you've managed to get me to bare my soul to you, let's see if I can get your other parts running."

"Pardon me?" I asked, my insides clenching at the insinuation, especially after what Pan had said.

"Your stomach, of course, sweetheart," he murmured knowingly, like he could see in my head what I'd been thinking. "But I'd be up for other things as well."

"I'm good, thanks," I squeaked, ignoring the slick coating my panties suddenly.

"Pan's good at sharing." The comment had my mind going down dangerous paths. My body burning up between theirs as they moved in and out—

Luke cleared his throat, a blush staining his cheeks as he

took deep inhales. Fuck. I realized I was perfuming, my scent thick throughout the room.

"How is that possible? Aren't I technically...dead?" I gasped, a gush of slick drowning my panties even more.

"Fuck," he growled, as he pinched his nose closed, a pained furrow on his brows. "You smell like fucking heaven."

I snapped my legs tightly closed, like that could seal in the smell somehow.

"Well, doctor?" I cried out, thoroughly embarrassed. "Any ideas?"

"I'll have to look into it. I've never heard of an omega being turned. You're my first," he tried to joke, even though it still appeared as if he was suffering. "I also wasn't clear on the fact an omega would have such an intense—" he gestured to the huge bulge in his tight black pants. And when I say huge...I was more than intrigued by what I was seeing. There was no way it could fit in someone.

I mean, not that I was thinking about that.

He lunged towards one of the cabinets and pulled out a bottle of vodka, unstopping the cork and taking deep inhales of it as he walked towards the wall and turned on a fan so my scent was cycling out of the room. We were both quiet as we tried to calm down, nothing but the whir of the fan and the sound of our deep, desperate breaths filling the room.

When my perfume had faded, Luke let out a long sigh and walked over to put the vodka back in the cabinet.

"You're going to make things interesting around here, aren't you?" he asked, amused.

"I don't know what you're talking about," I answered haughtily.

Just then, fire licked through my insides and my stomach and esophagus...they burned.

"Okay then, back to what I'd intended to do before you decided to make me hornier than a three-peckered toad."

"A three-peckered toad?"

"Believe me, they're horny," he nodded sagely.

I giggled, and his eyes turned warm, like he was pleased he'd made me laugh.

Clearing his throat, he continued. "I think today is a good day to see what you like."

I cocked my head, confused.

"To see what blood type you like," he clarified.

"They taste different?"

"Oh yes. And different species taste different. So you might think you love an A type nymph, but the B+ version might blow you out of the water. The B+ version of a troll would most likely make you throw up, however."

My face must have shown my disdain at the idea of trying a nymph...or a troll. My stomach, however, was quite intrigued.

He snorted again, turning around and walking towards a fridge tucked in the back corner. Opening the door, he reached in and pulled out a multitude of blood packs.

A groan escaped my lips, and he smirked at me before closing the fridge and walking toward the counter with the bags. I could see labels on them. Dragon. Fey. Nymph. Wolf...

Blah.

"Alright," he mused, staring at the blood packets. "What to try first." Luke grabbed the dragon blood bag and a straw and then handed it to me. "Try this."

I bit my lip, as usual, disgusted with the idea of drinking blood even if it tasted incredible.

"Come on, sweetheart. Might as well play along."

My stomach's growl finally convinced me to grab the drink and take a good long slurp.

Wow.

"That's...incredible," I moaned as I drank faster.

Suddenly, he yanked it out of my hand.

"What!"

"This is a taste test. You'll get to pick your favorite and drink to your heart's content at the end," he chided teasingly.

I definitely pouted. I was sure there wasn't going to be something better than dragon blood. That had been...

The fey blood was brought to my lips next, and my taste-buds exploded as the blood rolled across my tongue.

Luke chuckled, watching me avidly like I was the most interesting thing he'd ever seen. It was heady to have his attention like that. Or maybe it was just how freaking amazing the blood was that had me feeling like preening in front of him.

My good feelings rapidly disappeared when he yanked the blood from my mouth. "Alright, let's see," he shot me a glance. "I really think you'll like this wolf one." I quickly shook my head, inanely feeling that it was a little too close to cannibalism for comfort.

He grabbed the nymph one and I...spit it all out. "Ugh," I

hissed. "I thought you said I was going to like the nymph one!" It tasted like I'd just tried to drink dirt. Even my greedy stomach wanted no part in that.

His laughter reverberated around me, and I glared at him, realizing he'd set me up. "I mean, that makes it clear that blood does taste different."

I scoffed. "I'd already figured that out with the fey blood tasting better than the dragon blood, asshole."

He laughed even harder, and I couldn't help but admire how freaking gorgeous his smile was. Like Pan, everything about him was designed to drag you in. Even though you knew he would kill you, you still couldn't help but want to be closer.

"Okay," he drawled, leaning closer so I could see the specks of gold in his seafoam eyes.

"Okay, what?"

"I know what species of blood you should try next," he answered calmly.

I cocked my head, wondering if he was going to pull out witch blood or something like that.

"As long as it's not wolf, I'm game."

His grin widened, the pupils of his eyes expanding as I watched.

"How about vampire?" he purred.

It took me a second to realize what he was insinuating. But when I figured out that he wanted me to feed off him, my hunger flared.

Both kinds of hunger flared.

My perfume came out again, so thick and cloying, it felt like syrup in the air. I was sure there was a puddle under me from how much slick was gushing from my core. My gums ached as my incisors, which had stayed in the entire time I'd been drinking the blood today, came shooting out.

"You like the idea of that, don't you, sweetheart?" he growled, leaning forward.

"I'm up for it if you are." My voice was a rasp, almost unrecognizable.

"Let's just say that I'm up for a taste test whenever you want." Luke took a step towards me, until he was standing just an inch away. My hands were trembling as they landed on his chest. A purr slid out of me as I felt the strength beneath my fingertips and admired the long lines of his neck.

"Come on, baby. Have a taste," he cajoled.

At this point, it was becoming really clear that I had little to no willpower, because his words were dripping with sexual connotations and I didn't even try to fight it. Instead, I leaned over and slowly slid my teeth into his neck, taking a long draw of his blood.

His erotic moan filled the room.

He was delicious. By far the best thing I'd ever tasted in my entire life.

"Fuck, you're perfect," he growled.

I wasn't exactly sure what he meant by that. Could you be perfect at feeding on someone? But what I did know was that I didn't really care because he tasted too freaking good to really care about anything at the moment.

Or at least I thought I didn't care about anything, until his front started rubbing against my core, my drenched underwear and his thin pants doing very little to detract from how good it felt to have his enormous dick rubbing against my most sensitive areas.

Honestly, I had to admit to myself, I wasn't sure I was ever going to be able to eat without it being tied to something sexual again after this experience with him...and with Pan.

I also wasn't sure if I was ever going to be able to feed on anything but Luke again, because I was 99% positive that nothing would ever taste better than this.

His thrusts quickened, and then his groan was long and loud, and I could feel his heat through my panties as he came in his pants.

I wanted to keep going, but unlike that first day, when I felt unable to stop myself from draining anyone dry, I finally was able to withdraw my fangs, licking my lips to make sure that I got every last delicious drop.

His eyelids were heavy and there was a soft, content smile on his lips as he stared at me.

Luke pushed a hand through his hair, before his thumb went to his lower lip, and he softly caressed it as he eyed me hungrily. I felt like I had drained at least half of his blood supply, but he looked perfectly strong standing there...with a large wet spot across his crotch, which was strangely a turn-on.

Hell, at this point, let's just admit that everything about him was a turn-on to me.

"Need any help?" he said huskily, taking a step back towards me so I could feel his still hard dick.

I did want help. I wanted all the help. But I was also afraid that I was turning into a nymphomaniac, and while last night's venture with Pan was a stupid mistake, a romp with Luke would probably be an even bigger one.

Because it was much easier to keep feelings out of the picture when someone was a giant asshole. Like Pan.

Luke was far too perfect for me not to have problems with that.

"I'm good. Nothing I can't take care of myself." My voice didn't come out as strong as I would've liked; there was too much lust in it. But his eyes still widened, the black almost completely overtaking the sea foam green as he got my meaning.

"Well, sweetheart," he purred after a pause. "Let me just make sure it's on the record that you're welcome to have me whenever you want." He leaned forward until his lips were just a breath away. "In whatever *way* you want me."

"What about Pan?" I asked, because the offer sounded too good to be true, and I wanted to accept it, badly. Unless it led to Pan killing Luke in a jealous rage.

"Little secret about Pan, sweetheart." He paused for dramatic effect. "He likes to share."

His lips were against mine then, kissing me relentlessly, pressing against my center in tune with his tongue as it swirled with mine. I groaned as his lips moved away, his teeth nipping gently on my lower lip as he did so.

"Breakfast, lunch, and dinner, sweetheart," he whispered.

And like a coward, all I could do was nod and then slide off the cot and run away, feeling his hot gaze licking at my skin until I disappeared around the corner.

I was screwed.

But his offer of breakfast, lunch, and dinner...

I didn't think it was something I could refuse.

CHAPTER 9

GWENDOLYN

They say that when you died, your life would flash before your eyes, but I didn't remember any of that when Pan took mine. Only panic and fear, followed by a strange excitement that confused me. Then darkness swallowing everything.

I wanted to believe that becoming a vampire wasn't a true death, since I'd been reanimated. To me, true death was ascending from this different plane of existence, so perhaps this was more like a temporary death.

I scoffed at how crazy I sounded and pushed up from the floor of the main ballroom.

For the past two days, I'd found myself gravitating to this room. Most of the vampires were giving me a wide berth for the moment…maybe Pan's actions after the bonfire incident had been enough of a warning to keep them away…either way I spent time in this room studying the grandiose tree growing in the middle of the castle. The roots that had broken out of the walls and spread across the room like they gradually planned to take over the place.

Aside from feeding in the kitchen most days, I hadn't given up on my potential plan to escape either. I was waiting though, because I knew the vampires watched me. They might be leaving me alone, but I still felt them, saw them at the corners of my eyes, sneaking about.

There was one particular vampire who wasn't leaving me alone though, and he was prowling down the steps and into the ballroom, his eyes immediately finding me. The corners of Pan's mouth lifted, as if just the sight of me amused him.

I blinked at him, quickly realizing my mistake. It wasn't Pan, but Crocodile, and I cringed on the inside at his appearance.

The differences were noticeable when I really studied their facial expressions. Whereas Crocodile always looked ready to pounce on me and make me wish I was really dead, Pan stared at me with pure, unadulterated obsession and lust. The vampire king made me crave him while Crocodile made me want to scream and run.

What did he want now?

"Hello, Bunny. Are you ready to come out and play?" Crocodile asked, closing the distance between us and taking my arm by force.

I immediately pushed away from him, my hackles raising at how easily he manhandled me. "I'm not going anywhere with you," I snapped.

He laughed maniacally, then the sound ended abruptly as he stared at me.

Lifting my chin, I held his gaze, even as a shiver wormed along my spine. I knew he could easily make my life terrible– or at least more terrible than it already was. But I was practicing my new mindset that consisted of reminding myself I wasn't a mere omega shifter anymore.

I was a vampire.

Saying those words in my head still felt odd, but it was a mindset I really needed to master before I became someone's meal when they realized how weak I really was.

He cocked an eyebrow. "Here I was under the impression that you liked me."

I rolled my eyes while he most likely contemplated how to torture me next.

"Have it your way, Bunny, but I'll see you out there. You'll be lost in the darkness with the rest of us soon enough," he growled with a threatening promise behind his words.

He licked his lips, and I recoiled, watching him stalk out of the ballroom and outside.

The odd thumping in my chest only lasted until I remembered that I had no working heart. Talk about being psychosomatic.

When the heavy thud of footfalls came in behind me, I swiveled around toward another vamp I didn't recognize entering the hall.

Round cheeks, short hair perfectly combed off the side, and a softness in his eyes I didn't expect. The vamp was more gothic rockstar than vicious monster of the night. He wore tight black jeans, heavy boots, and a white, untucked shirt with frills running down the front, painting the picture of what I'd come to expect from vamps in the movies.

"I'm having some major *Interview with the Vampire* vibes right now," I said teasingly.

The vamp's eyes lit up like I had just given him the best compliment in the world. "You have no idea how much I love hearing that." He suddenly paused at the base of the steps, straightening his posture, and turning his face into a broody guise. With his chin raised, he stalked toward me in a manner that could be incredibly mesmerizing and terrifying. He was tall, on the thin side, but with vampires, it didn't come down to muscle, as they were already extraordinarily strong.

Pausing in front of me, he suddenly broke out laughing, falling back into his curled shoulders and relaxed expression. "You're the first person to have recognized what look I was going for. You'd think that living with all these vampires, they would know all the lore and myths out there, all the fiction, but most haven't even seen the movie, as they'd been turned before the invention of television. Anyway, I'm rattling on. I'm Finn."

"Hi, I'm Gwendolyn." I offered him my hand to shake but then paused mid-way, feeling awkward and unsure how one greeted a friendly vampire. Was it normal to shake hands, hug, or…exchange blood?

Finn took my hand regardless, and I noted he'd painted his fingernails black. He shook my hand vigorously.

"I know exactly who you are," he murmured. "The whole den's chatting about the new girl Pan keeps protected. And I can see why." He eyed me up and down, and I felt slightly uncomfortable. He ran a thumb across his chin, tilting his head, studying me. "You have a very unique and hypnotic kind of beauty, don't you?"

I shrugged. "I've never really thought about it." I wasn't the kind of girl who grew up wishing she was different from everyone else, to stand out, be independent. I just craved to be like everyone else and fit in. To be loved.

"Well, the Silver family has never been known to possess natural beauty. But you are gorgeous."

I glanced down at myself. At my deep blue mini shorts, black combat boots I found in my cupboard, and a loose tee. Nothing extraordinary here. "What do you know of the Silver family?"

"That they're hugely in debt to Pan and the rest of us, and as far as Pan is concerned, he'd slay the whole bloodline before letting them pay off their debt." He offered me his bent arm, and I don't know what came over me, but I placed my hand on his.

"What did they do?"

He walked us outside the castle as he muttered, "Such things are not for me to tell. What you need to know is that everyone in this place fears Pan. It may not appear so, but he's a lot more dangerous than he might appear. So, one rule most of us follow is to never speak about his business."

I almost choked on my breath. "More dangerous. He already scares me half to death."

"I saw you out here a couple of nights ago, you know,"

Finn admitted, his eyes narrowing on me. "Liam was a bastard, so not much grief was lost for his death."

"Guessing Liam was the vampire who Pan killed?"

He nodded. "Liam had taken boredom to a new level and was making it his mission to start up his own personal fight club. Vampire against vampire, to the death. The asshole enjoyed seeing others suffer, so he got what he deserved." He smirked, looking a bit bloodthirsty at that moment.

He had an easy nature about him, even if his fangs peered out from under his lip when he smiled.

He was also…a talker. Something I wasn't used to, but found myself liking. I liked the idea of having at least one friend until I found a way out of Darkland. Something I'd given a lot of thought over the past two days. How I'd find my way back to collect Atlas, then together we'd run away and find a place to live where no one could take us away from each other.

"This way," Finn directed, his soft voice slicing through my thoughts. "We've got to be quick. Pan hates it when anyone's late."

"Umm, where are we going?" I glanced around us at the empty yard. The bonfire crackled, spitting embers and chasing away the shadows. The sky was a midnight blue…as usual. But no sign of anyone.

"The hunt," Finn stated in a knowing tone, as though I should know what he was talking about. "Every full moon, we do it. Believe it or not, not everyone in Darkland wishes you harm. Some of us are happy for another person to befriend to escape our boredom."

At the mention of others wanting to harm me, my mind went directly to Crocodile, and just as quickly, I shook the thought away. "Hunting what?" I asked, a bit too panicked with a squeaky voice. I blinked up at him, and he gave out a laugh where he threw his head back and sent the ruffles running down the front of his shirt into a small dance.

He was a beautiful vampire...most vampires were like that I'd realized. Perfect bone structure, porcelain skin, and piercing stares. But Finn seemed different. He was missing the hard, psychopath edge the rest of them had. It made me wonder if he was a new vampire.

"Depends on what Pan's found for us. It's always different. Last month, it was a vampire who broke the rules. But everyone participates. It's an unspoken rule. So you need to join us too, because trust me, you don't want to see Pan angry. I learned that lesson when I first arrived in Darkland, and he broke every bone in my body."

"Ouch. That's awful."

He shrugged. "To be fair, I did bring complete strangers into our home without notifying him, then I let them leave. Let's just say, there was a huge hunt that night to capture every single one of those humans to avoid anyone discovering this lair."

I was lost for words at hearing his horrifying story. "Oh, I'm sorry that happened to you. So that means you're new to Darkland too?"

"If you consider five hundred years new, sure." He laughed softly and nudged me to keep moving.

When I composed myself, I reached over and laid my hand on his arm. "Were they your friends?" I asked.

He shook his head and patted my hand. "Just strangers I met at a tavern, and I wanted to surprise Pan, you see, with a free feed, but when the mortals panicked, I panicked and then showed them the way out, which was clearly a huge mistake on my part. They could have led others here who wanted to hurt everyone in Darkland. But it's all in the past now." He paused, and gave me a strange and curious look. "Thanks, though," he said softly. "You're very kind. Maybe too kind for this place."

He paused in front of me, and while he said I was sweet, I could see the sweetness behind *his* eyes too. "I hope Darkland doesn't break you too quickly, Gwendolyn. This place has a way of destroying every one of us." With a long exhale, he seemed to change before my eyes, his mouth curling upward.

"We should hurry." He dragged me quickly across the grounds to the rear of the castle where there were several motorbikes lined up in the yard, just waiting to be taken.

A roar echoed in the distance, along with hoots and shouts flooding the woods. Birds burst out of nearby trees from the sounds, blotting the darkened sky with their beating wings.

"We're hunting on bikes?" I asked, slightly excited about getting to ride freely, which also gave me ample opportunity to slip away should the chance present itself.

"Have you never ridden a bike?" he asked with slight concern on his face, and I realized then that I really liked him.

He was the first person in Darkland to show such compassion. I could just imagine Crocodile telling me to suck it up and ride the bike even if I couldn't. Pan, he'd lift me onto his bike, and just the thought of that brought back images of him ravaging me against it. And how much I'd loved every moment of it. A buzz of tingles from what he'd done to me raced like fire between my legs.

I glanced at Finn, heat dotting my cheeks. He studied me, amused, waiting for a response. I cleared my throat. "I grew up riding bikes. So, should we join them?"

If Pan and his Lost Boys wanted to play games, then I'd play...and hopefully learn something I could use alone the way. As my father once told me while trying to teach me to hunt, even the scariest beast has a weakness—it's just a matter of watching them until you discover their Achilles heel.

I chose the closest bike, mostly because it was the smallest compared to the others, and it meant I could easily touch the ground with my feet once I straddled the seat to hold my balance. These were dirt bikes with thinner wheels and narrower, flat seats. Mine was inky black, which meant it was less likely to be seen in the dark. I was also dressed in dark colors, which helped...well, except for my violet hair.

Finn had his bike grunting to life in a heartbeat, and he shoved his head back, unleashing a half-howl, half-whistle. Seconds later, others responded to him from within the woods, making a similar cry.

Adrenaline surged through me. "A hunting we will go," I yelled, a smile sliding along my lips.

Not wasting another second, I turned the throttle, my foot

pushing down on the kickstarter several times, the bike starting almost immediately. It purred beneath me, vibrating between my legs. I kicked up the stand and took off right behind Finn, throwing dust in my wake.

My bike roared through the forest, the sensation of wind whipping through my hair and tugging on my clothes reminding me of being back home and driving towards the lookout. I ducked under a low-hanging branch and tried my best to keep up with Finn who glided through the woodland like he was flying. Luckily, the trees were sparsely spaced, and darting between them proved no problem for me.

There was something primal and exciting about racing in the woods. I found myself smiling, embracing the freedom as I swerved around a dead branch.

Finn cut sharply to his right, and I tracked him, catching up quickly. He kept glancing over his shoulder at me, yelling, "You're fast for a little girl."

My chest rose with adrenaline, the competitive nature in me soaring.

Shadows fell around me suddenly, and the shapes of vamps on bikes racing all around me came into view. They moved madly through the woods like they saw something ahead of me I didn't. Whatever we were chasing, they had to be fast, and part of me contemplated staying back. Did I want to see them hunting down an innocent animal?

I cringed on the inside. Great vampire I made. Pan had said I would soon start fending for myself at mealtime, yet the image of feasting on humans out in the yard has me sick to my stomach.

Did I have it in me?

The hunger that snarled in my stomach each morning said a different story.

We raced faster, night seeming to chase us.

In seconds, we all burst out of the woods, finding ourselves in a huge open field with a jagged rock face in the distance, and the landscape on my left jarring upward. Darkness stretched over the sky, which held a heavily pregnant moon so bright and so big that I could easily make out the craters on its surface.

But my attention refocused dead ahead where all the bikes were funneling toward one thing...

I narrowed my eyes, leaning forward and speeding wildly after them. From behind, it was close to impossible to tell who was who on the bike ride, but by the sheer number, we'd easily be close to forty bikes. I couldn't help myself; I kept scanning for Pan or Luke, unable to see them.

Regardless, I sped with the rest of the gang, torn about how much I enjoyed the ride beneath the bright moon's gaze. No lights on the bikes were needed. The silvery hue lit up the landscape like it had received a fresh coat of snow.

I swerved around a boulder in my way, the bike jostling beneath me across the uneven earth. I clasped the handlebars tightly, but just then I caught a glance of what we were chasing, and I frowned in confusion.

A pig!

What the fuck?

So all of these vampires were getting revved up on chasing a pig?

That didn't add up.

Not the way the bikers were howling in their chase, or the fact that we were all moving so damn fast, that we should have already caught the animal by now. No pig ran that fast...none. I kept swerving across the land to get a view of the creature we chased, to understand what was really going on here.

But just as I swerved around another large rock, the pig tumbled over his own feet and fell forward, head over heels, rolling before coming to a dead stop. That was all the vampires needed because suddenly, there were a dozen bikes circling the animal, calling out taunts as they circled their prey.

I soon came to a pause outside the circle, blinking at the animal that I soon discovered was no longer a pig, but was mid-transformation, turning into a quivering male. My mouth gaped open in surprise at discovering the existence of a pig-shifter. I grew up associating mostly with wolf shifters only. Sure, I'd heard rumors that other kinds of supernaturals existed, but never before had I encountered one of them until that fateful day in the town square.

Darkland was opening my eyes in more ways than one.

Unlike the others, I remained on my bike in case I needed to make a quick getaway, feeling like an intruder in that moment. Even if Pan and Luke had been at the forefront of my mind.

I stared, entranced at the shifter who finished shifting into a younger-looking man. The vamp bikers circled him, kicking up dust, while the man pulled himself off the ground, completely naked.

His terror floated on the air. It smelled vinegary and like perspiration, and instead of pity, a strange sensation came over me. One of hunger and craving to see him on his knees. I surprised myself, and not in a good way either, by having such thoughts over a stranger.

Was this how vamps felt all the time? No remorse or pity for those they killed to feed?

I wasn't sure I was cut out for this. Disgust rose to the back of my throat, the taste of bile making me sick.

I started to roll my bike backward, an urgency to get out of there hammering in my chest. But evidently, it'd been too late because the vampires were already off their bikes and launching themselves at the man.

His screams left me shuddering. Tears pricked my eyes at the panicked sound I'd never get out of my head. Convinced I was going to throw up, I hastily pulled back, and with my bike's engine still grunting, I twisted the throttle and took off. One glance back told me no one paid me any attention, but I also watched that poor shifter being torn physically apart, and the vampires feeding on him savagely.

I can't do this. I can't kill mercilessly.

The wind wiped my cheeks free of tears, and I sped away, merging into the woods. I wasn't sure where I was going, but for now, I just needed to be as far from them as possible. That was how they saw me, wasn't it? A shifter who was nothing more than something to hunt, to have fun with.

I don't remember how far I traveled, but when I emerged from the woods in a rock field where the landscape ascended up a hill ahead of me, I came to a stop on the bike and parked. I climbed off and took a few steps forward to where the cool breeze swished through my hair, and I could breathe easily.

I had no idea where I was, but I didn't care as I fought to get the image of that shifter out of my head.

But whatever tranquil peace I thought I'd found, it didn't last long when the crunch of branches came from behind me.

Of course, someone had followed me, and when I twisted around, it was Pan who emerged out of the wood's shadows and into the moon's glow.

His unflinching stare stayed on me, while the hormones in my body had a mind of their own, leaving me turned on almost instantly in his presence. I fought the urge to squeeze my thighs together and make it obvious, though seeing my underwear was already slick with my arousal, I had doubts I could hide anything from him.

For a second I imagined him kissing me roughly, forcefully driving me up against a tree...his mouth dragging over every inch of my body.

I swallowed hard, well aware of how quickly I'd lost control, and I fought the desire in any attempt to rein myself back in.

The primal, raw lust he awakened in me owned me, and I hated him for it. For most of my life, someone else had always controlled every aspect of my life, and now this monster influenced me with simply the way he looked at me.

"I'm disappointed in you," he murmured, stepping closer

and coming to a pause barely a foot from me. The guy held no concept of personal space. "Are you going to keep running from me?"

Defiantly, I squared my shoulders. "Of course. Would you expect anything less?"

His hand was on my arm before I saw him moving, his long fingers playing to an invisible tune on my skin. As a vampire myself, I knew his touch was cool, even if I was just as cold as him. And yet, I'd also come to enjoy the soothing sensation in some kind of macabre way. My head was still twisted with fully accepting that I was a creature of the night.

Telling myself the words was one thing, but to have it sink into my thoughts was a very different thing.

"You are going to bring me trouble, aren't you? Last time we were together, I promised you punishment, which isn't going to work, is it?"

He was gripping my chin now, forcing my head back so I glared into his eyes. "I'm beginning to suspect that we may have more similarities than I first thought."

"I'm nothing like you." I pulled back from his grasp, my thoughts swishing like the wind billowing against me. "Or like those monsters back there in the hunt. I will never be like that," I snapped, anger pouring through my words.

Disgust came over me. "He was a shifter. Is that how you all see me too? Disposable? Only good for your entertainment?"

His head tilted to the side, like he saw a different side to me and wasn't sure what to make of it.

"Did you think that *pig* out there was innocent? And that

us *horrible* vampires were simply torturing him?" he asked nonchalantly.

"It's what your kind does, isn't it? On my first day, you said soon I will hunt down my own food, so what's the difference?"

Adrenaline and fiery frustration rushed over me the longer I stared at Pan. Even I had to admit that it was a strange sensation to find myself turned on and furious at someone at the same time.

"Come on, let's go for a walk; you have a lot to learn, my dove."

"Dove?"

"You fly away on assumptions without all the information."

"So, you're not a killer?" I asked, so quickly that I wanted to retract the words the moment they left my lips.

"As a vampire, you need to kill to survive. I have no guilt in what I do, and you will understand very soon." Despite his remark, he spoke softly, yet I didn't miss the chill beneath his silky voice. All the while, his gaze roamed over my body, which left me both mesmerized and unsettled.

Half the time, I couldn't tell if he used his thrall on me or if everything I felt around him was real.

His hand slid down my arm, leaving a tingling trail over my skin. Fingers interlaced with mine, and before I knew it, we were strolling in the night. Normally, I'd be wary of walking alone in the middle of the night, especially in the woods....our world was filled with men who like to prey on omegas like me.

But now, there was nothing to fear, for I held the company of the most dangerous creature out there. The vampire king.

It was comforting…

"Okay, I'm listening," I encouraged, but he didn't respond right away. Rather, his thumb stroked the back of my hand, filling me with the raw desire he ignited between us.

This was a cruel joke that the creature who killed me, ended up keeping me as his own.

"This way," he directed as we followed a worn track on the ascending hill.

"One thing you'll learn quickly in Darkland is that nothing is as it seems. The shifter we hunted has been our enemy for a long time."

I glanced over at him, slightly surprised. "I would have never guessed that someone like you had a pig shifter for an enemy. Everyone fears you."

"It may seem that way," he responded, meeting my gaze, and there was something surprising I hadn't seen before behind those silvery eyes that watched my every move. They held a sense of vulnerability.

Hair the color of midnight draped over half his brow, and underneath the moon's hue, I found myself studying his chiseled cheekbones, a bone structure that could easily make angels envious. In his leather jacket, he looked suave, the image of this tall, perfect vampire striking and hypnotic.

The longer I studied him and let my thoughts carry me away, the more my panties drenched.

Oh, hell. "Stop. Please just stop using your thrall on me."

He grinned, the corners of his mouth coming up a bit too

much, like he enjoyed knowing that his power influenced me so easily. "I honestly wasn't influencing you. That beautiful, sweet fragrance, your desire, is all you, little omega."

I eyed him, not sure I believed him. But when he laughed, my muscles trembled.

He drew me against him so fast that I both bristled and gasped at the same time. It seemed my body was a complete contradiction. My breasts pressed to his chest, and I drew in a fake breath, purely out of instinct.

Soft, cold fingers traced along my jawline. "You are beautiful to watch, reacting so easily to me. We're in tune, you and I, our bodies calling to one another."

"I thought only wolves were linked with such a bond. Not vampires." My words came out breathy, and I tried my best to not let him see how much he'd already influenced me. How wet my panties were.

"Why wouldn't it be so with vampires?"

Heat filled me, and I was too distracted since I was acutely aware of everywhere we touched. "B-Because you don't have a beating heart or a soul."

"Well, that's where you're wrong. You see, vampires do indeed retain part of their soul... Otherwise, we'd be nothing more than the undead." His fingers swept through my hair, and my body pressed in closer to him, completely betraying me. "I'm going to teach you everything you need to know about vampires. You'll discover how unimaginably beautiful the world can be. How you've become a god among mortals. The things we can see and experience together will be unlike anything you've ever seen. I just need you to...give me a chance. Give yourself completely to me."

I blinked at him. "I was taken against my will. So, I'm not thinking that's a possibility."

He grinned, like he'd expected me to say that. "I'm going to change your mind, little Darling. One bite at a time."

Heat built in my core, pushing away all my thoughts while fire licked between my thighs, sending a desperate surge of desire through me. It came too intensely, again and again, leaving me whimpering for more.

Leaning closer, he whispered, "I could take you right here and you'd lose the fight. You'd beg me for more, spreading your creamy thighs for me to sink into your perfect little cunt. Would you like that?"

The storm of arousal came at me once more, stronger this time, ripping through me with an orgasm.

I cried out, my legs wobbling beneath me, and I held onto him, my hands fisting his jacket while it felt like I floated in the air.

"I love watching you cum." Pan held me, staring at me with hungry eyes, his top lip curling up and over unsheathed fangs.

Convinced he'd bite me, I did my best to wriggle out of his arm, while my body still thrummed from the incredible climax.

I finally ripped out of his arms, stumbling away from him, gasping and completely flushed. "I guess no matter how beautiful you are, you're still a monster. Taking what you want with your mind games."

"On the contrary. I was giving you a small gift."

"Well, don't do me any favors." We stood there in the dark, me trying to accept the fact that Pan wasn't the kind of creature who'd let me walk away. Obsession glinted in his eyes, his predatory instincts in full force.

"Well, that time, I did use my power on you so you'd see that, if I wanted to, I could easily take what I need from you. But I far more enjoy when you come to me willingly."

I clenched my jaw, knowing he'd used his power on me so much at this point, that I wasn't sure I could tell the difference when he didn't.

Still buzzing, I changed the topic because I worried if I didn't, I might be the one who'd ask him for more. And I'd hate myself even more if I did that.

"How about you get back to telling me what was going on in the hunt, instead of using your thrall to seduce me."

"Alright, I did promise you an explanation."

We moved once more up the side of the hill, and only the distant yells of the other vampires sang on the night air. Around us were mountains and woodlands, offering no easy escape. I still hated this place, but I had to keep reminding myself that staying in Darkland was only temporary until I found a way out.

I wasn't dealing with wolf shifters anymore who were tied to societal expectations, I was dealing with an undead who didn't have any rules. All I could hope was that he tired of me sometime and then allowed me to leave...without a stake in my chest.

"The shifter we hunted tonight is a fucking pirate," Pan

began to explain. "We aren't alone living in this part of the country. Our enemy wants us dead and has been doing everything in their power to eliminate us. Including sending these asshole shifters onto our land to gain intelligence on us. Last night, one of my vampires was found strung up by his throat from a tree in the woods, his heart carved out of his chest. And the culprit was the fucking pig. So yes, I hold no mercy when it comes to paying back the pain they bring us."

I gasped, listening carefully, completely shocked at the news. "I had no idea."

"Of course, I made sure you were kept out of the drama. But the Lost Boys deserved retribution for a lost friend."

"And that was the hunt tonight," I finished for him, thinking of them tearing the pig shifter apart. "Why do these shifters hate you, though? Are you taking sacrifices from them as well?" I asked, thinking of my own situation.

"The shifters work for a vampire—Hook Silver," he said darkly, loathing thick in his voice. We continued to walk, the sudden silence burrowing under my skin, leaving me tense. His last name–Silver. Was he related to Alpha Silver or was that a pure coincidence?

"It seems safe to assume there's no love lost between the two of you…"

"Hook and I were once as close as family," Pan murmured. "I shared everything with him, and then…he stabbed me in the back and he killed my fated mate."

I gasped, but Pan just continued on. "When I was a mortal, I'd found her and the kind of happiness I'd only dreamed of. Lillian lived in my village, and I knew right away that one day I would marry her..." He paused and kicked at a rock in front of him, scattering it over the edge of the cliff we were walking by. "I asked for her hand on her birthday, one summer night. I'd worked to make the perfect ring with the village metalsmith...I knew she'd love it." His voice cracked, and that vulnerability I'd seen earlier surfaced beneath his words.

"I'm so sorry," I murmured, feeling his ache suddenly as if it was my own.

It was terrible, but hearing about someone he once loved–maybe still loved–had my chest squeezing. I shouldn't have felt anything, I had every intention of leaving Pan the second I got a chance. But that ache in his voice when he said her name...I hated it.

"Why did he do it?"

He tensed, his jaw clenched in frustration. "That's the thing. I have no idea. For some reason, I can't remember anything else from that night except seeing him attacking Lillian...then everything's blank."

That was...horrible.

Pan didn't say anything more while we reached the top of the hill we'd begun climbing, where the stars overhead twinkled brightly like tinsel on a Christmas tree. He paused at the edge of another cliff. From our location, we overlooked an ocean reflecting the enormous moon across its surface.

It still was incredible to me that this realm had been created like this. Obviously there were no oceans in the Rocky Mountains, where we supposedly were located...but in Darkland there certainly were.

It was only once I stepped forward that I realized how close I was to falling off the rocky edge.

A guttural growl rolled over Pan's throat, and he spat over the edge, fury darkening the shadows across his face. "He lives out there on his ship, reminding me constantly that he's coming to finish me just as he did to Lillian."

"He turned you, didn't he?" I didn't know why I guessed that, but it made sense that he would have gone after this Hook guy after he killed Lillian… and perhaps in the process had gotten himself changed. I raised my chin to the cluster of lights in the distance from the ship, bobbing on the water, convinced I could see a skull and crossbones flag in the moon's glow.

My mind swam with questions, but Pan wasn't done.

"He took everything from me. These blank spaces in my memories…I know he's responsible somehow. Parts of my past are fogged, and I'm going to make him bring them back."

Only the wind shrilling filled the silence between us. I might have had a million reasons to hate Pan, but in that moment, I was torn at seeing the pain on his face as he stared out into the water toward the boat.

"If he took so much from *you*, why is he still trying to kill you?"

His gaze turned to me after my question, a small smirk spreading across his full lips. "Ahh, yes. That's the only *fun* part of the story. My brother, Crocodile, has always been an asshole, and he's responsible for Hook's present vendetta."

"What did he do?" I was hanging off every word he said,

completely invested. It seemed it wasn't just my life that felt chaotic.

"Let's just say that when we first moved in, Hook and Crocodile had an...encounter, and the bastard barely survived meeting a real crocodile because of it. My brother shoved Hook into the Arcadian River, where he got attacked by one. And now Hook is thirsty for vengeance...he also...is missing a few parts now."

Pan shook his head, his mirth quickly fading as he stared out at the stars. "But I'm finished talking about him," he growled. "He ruins enough of my nights already."

A red glint sparked in his eyes, and I steeled myself for whatever mischief he had planned, a shiver racing down my spine. My mind wavered over what he'd told me. I wondered if that incident with Hook and the crocodile was how Pan's brother got his name...I still hadn't found out his real one.

I had a million more questions about Hook, but with the tension still laced through the vampire king, I decided I didn't want to push him anymore.

Distraction seemed to be my best friend at the moment.

CHAPTER 10
GWENDOLYN

"You don't happen to have a boat lying around?" I asked, peering out at the pirate ship in the distance, my voice light with a hint of mirth.

He chuckled, and I liked that he thought I was funny. "Now why would I need that when I have such a better option for transportation."

His words seemed to hold a hidden meaning, and I cocked my head, trying to ignore how stunning he was standing there with the stars as a background.

"I'm not swimming, if that's what you're suggesting. There are definitely sharks out there."

"Scared of sharks, are you?" He grinned. "Did you forget you were immortal?"

I shivered, just thinking of something waiting in the dark water. "Sharks are evil. They'd find a way to kill me. I know

He laughed again, but this time he did it with his whole body, throwing back his head in delight. He was relaxing, the tension of our earlier conversation leaking out of him.

There was a freedom about him in that moment, I didn't know how to explain it. It wasn't like he was usually reserved. He never failed to take whatever he wanted, consequences be damned. But right then, he just seemed lighter.

"Little omega, I'm not going to make you swim with the sharks tonight. Although skinny dipping is definitely on my list of favorite activities," he taunted with a charming wink that had butterflies swooping around my stomach. "We're going to fly there."

My mouth dropped. "Fly?" I asked, sure I hadn't heard him right.

He looked pleased with the shock written across my face. Before I could say anything else, I realized he'd risen in the air. Glancing down, I saw his feet were at least two feet in the air. And it wasn't like he sprouted wings or anything like that. He was just hovering there, effortlessly, it seemed.

He reached out a hand towards me. "Come take a ride, Darling," he murmured.

One thing about me, I was incredibly afraid of heights. Even just standing on this cliff was giving me heart palpitations. So the idea of willingly soaring through the air...

Even as fear shot around my chest, my mind was racing with the idea of floating through the stars. As a little girl, before everything had gone so off-track, I used to lay in the meadow by our house and stare up at the clouds as they passed by. I'd had no idea that you couldn't walk on clouds, and I'd imagined all the grand adventures I'd go on if only I could get up there.

"Come on," he cajoled, extending his arm out even further. "Don't you trust me?"

"No, of course not," I responded back quickly, and he grinned before lunging forward and grabbing my hand tightly in his.

And then suddenly, he was pulling me off the ground. I couldn't hold in my terrified scream as I got farther and farther away from the safety of the dirt. "Don't let go," I begged, holding onto his one hand with both of mine before lunging forward and wrapping my arms around his neck as he soared up into the sky.

"Little Darling," he murmured, his voice a caress against my skin. "Haven't you realized by now, I have no intention of letting you go?"

Maybe I should've been worried about the hidden meaning in his words, but I found them comforting in that moment. We flew so high that I forgot to be afraid, because there was nothing but stars and clouds around us, illuminated by the moon which appeared twice as large as usual.

As a shifter, I'd been taught the moon held power. Up here, it was even easier to believe in the stories I'd heard all my life.

The stars twinkled around me, a dream come to life.

"How do you ever come down?" I whispered as the sky sparkled around me.

"I haven't minded it as much recently," he answered. I happened to glance at him at that moment, and I saw the intent in his gaze as he stared at my face…almost with…longing.

"When you say things like that, I'd almost believe you care," I told him quietly.

He continued to stare at me intently. "The problem, little omega, is that I do, far too much." His hand went up to my cheek and he softly stroked it. His eyes gleamed back at me.

I tore my gaze away, and I heard his soft sigh of disappointment, like there were words he wanted me to say. I wasn't sure I could ever admit to the darkness growing in my heart for him. And that's what I characterized it as–darkness. What I'd felt for Atlas was bright and shiny, like a spark of light that warmed me. But the feelings that Pan brought out in me were nothing like that. And I didn't quite understand how the heart could feel something for both the light and the dark.

It's just Stockholm Syndrome setting in. That's what I kept telling myself, but when he peeled back the arrogant façade, what I saw under there was undoubtedly…attractive.

Suddenly, we were flying through the air. He firmly unwrapped my arms from around his neck until I was only holding on to him by his hand.

"Spread out," he called as he unfurled his arms like he was a bird flying through the sky. There was a delighted grin on his face, and he looked more boyish than a dark king then.

Deciding to be a little brave, I tentatively spread out my arms, sending a silent prayer into the universe that I wasn't going to fall to my death.

After a minute, the panic started to recede and I could just enjoy the wind whipping through my hair. He dipped us lower, and I could make out little bits of light in the landscape where creatures were living.

We turned towards the east. Pan was holding my hand very loosely at this point, his tense shoulders curling forward, he appeared more relaxed than I'd ever seen him. "Where are we going?" I called, the wind doing its best to muffle my voice.

"You'll see," he answered with a sexy wink. I wrinkled my nose at him but didn't press for more, eager to see whatever Pan wanted to show me tonight. We'd gone for about fifteen minutes before he pulled us higher. A minute later, we were above the cloud line, and I gasped in surprise when I saw pink and purple and green lights dancing across the sky as if set to a melody. Pan brought us to a stop, and we just hovered there, staring at the colors.

"What is that?" My mouth was hanging open, I probably resembled an idiot, but I'd never seen anything so beautiful in my life. My gaze shot to Pan's profile, and I amended my statement in my head. I guess it was the second prettiest thing I'd ever seen.

"It's fairies," Pan stated lowly, not taking his eyes off the scene.

"Fairies? Like the fey?" I asked, thinking of the blood I'd drank and feeling a small spark of inane hunger as I remembered how good it had tasted.

"They're a bit different. They come from the same place, but the fairies are far slighter in stature. The fey look like you and me, but the fairies are small, almost like fireflies. Every month, under the full moon, they come up here and dance. Their magic is what creates those colors."

I squinted, trying to see the little creatures, but however they flew, they sparked like electric shocks of light.

"There are very few individuals, love, who've seen the fairy dance," he commented, shooting me a mischievous grin. "You're going to owe me, I think."

I scoffed at him, resisting the urge to punch him since I was still holding onto him in the air, and he was the only thing preventing me from plummeting to my death. "I'm not sure I should need to remind you of this, but you did kill me and make me one of the undead."

He shrugged. "Semantics." His thumb stroked my hand. "Besides, there's a lot of perks to the whole undead thing. Don't you think?" he purred, gesturing to the incredible light show in front of us.

I forgot to answer as the colors changed before my eyes, teal and fuchsia joining the mix.

"Bet you weren't able to do that before," he said. I glanced over at him, wondering what he was talking about because we'd already covered that very few people ever saw the fairies.

And then I realized that his hands were crossed in front of him. Which meant that…

I shrieked as I began to plummet down, through the clouds, popping out and seeing the ground in the distance below me.

"Just relax," Pan called out, appearing in front of me and

matching my speed as I fell. I reached for him, holding out my hands desperately, but he stayed just out of my grasp.

"You can do this. Just relax, think of the air as solid around you."

"You fucking asshole," I screamed, unable to relax in the least bit. Pan rolled his eyes, amusement dancing in his eyes even as I fell towards my death.

"Think of your best memory!" he called. Finally realizing he had no intention of grabbing me, I put my focus into doing what he said, even though I had no idea how it was going to help. Unless a memory was all of a sudden going to act as a giant pillow, sheltering me from the ground.

I still tried anyway.

It was a funny thing. The longer I was just there in the air, the more a sense of calm did rush over me. A feeling of weight-lessness and a sense of freedom, if you will. Finally, it came to me. There was one day when my father, before he'd lost his job and everything had fallen apart, had taken me out to teach me about the stars. The memory evoked the same feeling I'd had watching the fairy dance. I remembered the peace I'd felt just laying in the grass next to him, fireflies flickering in the tall reeds, and the forest beyond us. We stared up at the sky as he pointed out the different constellations, telling me stories about the lore of the wolf hunter and the fated mates who'd begged to spend eternity together on their deathbeds and were given the gift of living together in the sky as a result.

I'd wanted that moment to last forever, and even now, all these years later, I longed for the peace I'd felt. I ached for the feeling that all was right in the world, and if it wasn't, my father could make it so.

"Look at you go," Pan said, bringing me out of my reverie. I hadn't even realized I'd closed my eyes.

Wait...my gaze shot down, and I saw I was hovering about two stories in the air, the ocean laid out like a dark jewel beneath me. I was...flying!

No sooner did I have that thought, than I started to fall again.

But this time, Pan caught me.

We stared at each other, and I couldn't help but grin wildly. I'd been flying. Even if I ended up falling at the end. I'd still been flying. I couldn't believe it. Only in my wildest dreams had I imagined something like that happening.

Pan appeared fascinated as he stared at my wide grin, and eventually, I became a little self-conscious.

"Well, thanks for catching me this time," I commented. "I wasn't really feeling like testing out the whole immortality thing."

He flew us down until our toes were just inches from the water. Under the dark night sky, I was suddenly imagining a great white shark breaching out of the water and swallowing me whole. Hopefully things like that didn't happen in Dark-land. There was only so much room for apex predators, and Pan had the title covered.

"What were you thinking about?" he asked, cocking his head and looking almost...impressed.

"Just a moment with my father," I explained, my wide

grin fading into a bittersweet one. "Just something that happened a long time ago."

We were still just hovering above the water.

"Tell me," he insisted.

I went ahead and told him, not knowing why it was such a big deal.

"You must've loved your father a great deal," he finally said.

I frowned and then nodded, not understanding the significance.

"I've never had anyone who was able to fly on their first try like that," he admitted softly, staring intensely at me.

One thing about Pan, when you had his attention, you *really* had his attention. Everything about him was focused on me. It was a heady sensation to feel like this vampire king was eating out of the palm of my hand at that point. Or thought I was the most interesting person around. No wonder he had so many followers. If he gave them all that kind of attention, I'm sure it was easy to garner loyalty. No one really gave attention like that anymore. They were too busy thinking about whatever they were going to say about themselves, that they lost the significance of whatever you had just told them. I had a feeling that Pan was listening to everything I said. So intensely it was like he was carving it across his soul.

"No one's flown before? But you just dropped me."

He shrugged, a bit sheepishly actually. "I was going to catch you before you hit the water," he objected nonchalantly.

"Right."

"Does everyone have to think of a memory that makes them happy?" I asked.

His face went blank then. "Yes, everyone but me."

I hesitated but went ahead and asked. "What do you have to think about?"

I could feel the air chill around me at my question. "That's a story for another time, little omega," he chided stiffly before beginning to fly towards the shore.

It left me wondering if his memory involved Lillian, his fated mate. Again, the fiery streak of jealousy crossed my chest, but I told myself I didn't care. I shouldn't care.

We flew the rest of the way in silence, pirate ships and fairy dances left long behind us. We flew until we were back at the castle and we were landing on the stone balcony outside my room.

He continued to hold my hand as he led me through the french doors inside. He touched my cheek softly, an air of melancholy about him before dropping his hand and striding towards the door.

"Pan!" I called out. He stopped but didn't turn around to face me.

"I'm sorry for whatever I said," I whispered. I could've sworn that a tremor ran through his body at my apology. There was another long pause, so long I was about to speak again. But then he suddenly turned around and strode towards me determinedly. He stopped when he was just an inch away, his silver eyes staring down at me, heat and lingering anger in their depths. The rest of his face was impassive, but I could feel the energy below the surface. I couldn't tell what kind of energy it was, only that there was a strong emotion there.

He leaned in, so slowly it was almost as if he was waiting for me to stop him, and then his lips just barely grazed mine. Once, twice, before they finally melted against mine in a deep kiss. It took a moment for his tongue to slide between my lips, senselessly molding with mine, like he was just enjoying the taste of me. Suddenly, his kiss turned aggressive, and all the softness went away. He attacked my mouth with his tongue, the deep, long licks spiraling through my body. Everything about him in that moment was the dominating king, and I could feel my body preparing itself for him. Slick was gushing from my core, my insides were softening, and my breasts were achy and desperate for him to touch me.

We kissed like that until I felt like I was about to cum, and then he abruptly ripped himself away, gripping the back of my hair and angling his head until his lips were inches away from my ear. "I want to feel your delicious heat soaking my cock," he growled.

Just when I was about to tell him to go for it, a knock sounded on the door. He froze, not asking who was there. I opened my mouth and he just laid a kiss across it, silencing me. The knock sounded again.

"Pan, I know you're in there," came Luke's voice through the door.

"Mother Fucker," Pan snarled under his breath. "This better be important."

I heard a soft snicker, even through the thick door. "You know I wouldn't bother you otherwise," Luke murmured, and Pan groaned loudly before his lips were suddenly back on mine, his thick tongue aggressively taking my mouth.

"Pan," Luke interrupted again.

Pan ripped himself from my lips and swore before striding towards the door and throwing it open without a word to me. I saw Luke staring at me knowingly before he gave me a hot wink and followed his king.

I sat back on the bed behind me, my legs trembling and unable to support me.

Just when I thought things couldn't get crazier, a night like tonight happened. I fell to my back, and then I squealed. I'd flown. I still couldn't believe it

And a part of me, for the first time, had the thought that maybe this new life of mine wasn't so bad.

————

It seemed like I'd just fallen asleep when there was a single knock on the door, and then it was pushed open. I scrambled to sit up before relaxing when I saw it was just Pan standing there, a determined pull on his features.

"I didn't think you'd be coming back tonight. Was everything with Luke alright?" I asked.

"Everything was fine. Just a little thing I had to attend to," he murmured before closing the door behind him.

He prowled towards me, and when I say prowled, I meant I felt like the rabbit the wolf was coming after just then.

"Now where were we?" he growled before he fisted my hair and began to devour me. His sharp incisor teeth were out, and he pricked my bottom lip as we kissed, the salty metallic taste touching my tongue and making me groan.

I would examine that particular thought later, that I was getting turned on by the taste of my own blood.

He pushed me back on the bed so I was lying down, and thrust his thigh between my legs, rubbing against my aching core as low moans dripped out of my mouth.

"Come for me. Come just like this," he ordered, and it was only a second later that my insides tightened and pleasure shot up and down my body. I sucked on his tongue in my mouth desperately. I didn't quite know how we'd gotten to this point, but I was here for it. The front of my shirt was ripped open, and a second later, he was tearing his lips from mine, and then…

His teeth were cutting through the skin on my upper breast savagely, pleasure pulsating from the bite, and I was cumming again, my core pulsing, and my body shattering as he drank. I could feel blood trickling down my breast and pooling between them. His hand went up and smeared it against my skin. His other hand went between my legs, and his fingers trailed through my dripping folds. My perfume was all over the room. And I was screaming because there was so much pleasure pulsating through my body. He ripped his lips from my breast and growled lowly.

"What a good girl," he purred as his lips trailed along my skin, licking and biting. Even with just the tips of his teeth, whatever venom he was injecting was driving me absolutely wild. There was the familiar numbness around the bite area, but the pleasure was still soaring through my veins.

"Be a good girl for your king. Again," he ordered as he pinched my other nipple at the same time his teeth pricked against my neck. Another scream rang through the room as I came.

I didn't know if we were doing some kind of role-play, but the idea of him acting like my Alpha...it was really doing it for me. The hand that had just pinched my nipples went back between my folds, and he ripped the underwear off that his fingers had been slipping under. His fingers slid back until he found my puckered flesh. I gasped, a strange mix of shame and desire flashing through me as he rubbed across it gently.

"Has no one taken you here yet, little omega?" he purred, and I shivered as he applied more pressure, spiking me towards another orgasm. Suddenly, his finger popped through the ring, and I yelped as he began to move it in and out at the same time as another finger slipped into my sopping wet core.

My hips were moving desperately against his fingers, wanting a certain rhythm, and he quickly matched it. The parts of my brain that should've been telling me...really anything, had completely switched off. In that moment, I was pretty sure I would've let him do whatever he wanted to me. And then there it was—his head lowered and his teeth struck in the opposite breast from before. My fists were in his hair, pulling and holding him to me as I moved my hips frantically against his fingers, scream after scream rushing out of my mouth.

"You're fucking beautiful," he murmured as he continued to fill me up in both holes with his fingers. I moaned as another orgasm tore through me. I was faintly aware that there was blood dripping down my whole body, and I probably needed to make sure he actually closed the bites this time, but besides that, I felt incredible. I whimpered, suddenly needing something more substantial than just his fingers.

I wanted him. Pan.

"Do you want my dick, little Darling?" he asked with a grin, blood smeared across his lips. It should have been macabre, but instead, it was incredibly sexy.

I moaned in response and he clicked his tongue, chiding me. "I want your words, little Darling. Can you give them to me?"

The glide of his fingers had slowed until they were barely moving, threatening to drive me into madness.

"Yes," I panted.

"Yes, what?"

The words came instantly to the tip of my tongue. "Yes, Alpha," I rasped desperately.

With a gleam of satisfaction in his gaze, he tore his hands from my body and replaced the fingers that had been in my core with his enormous dick I hadn't even noticed him getting out of his pants.

I was immediately lost in him, completely fuck drunk as he thrusted into me. We moved against each other like we'd been doing this forever, and for a second there, I saw something in his gaze. Something stronger than affection, but more akin to madness than love. He closed his eyes, like he didn't want me to see it, and then his lips were against mine once again and his hips were pounding into me.

Suddenly, a throat cleared, happening to coincide with yet another orgasm. I froze in place, feeling the mixture of annoyance and embarrassment that someone had caught us in this position.

But when I looked over...

Pan was standing there, leaning against the wall with an amused smirk on his lips and a fevered glint in his gaze.

Stunned, fear crept into my insides. I glanced back and forth between the Pan against the wall and the Pan currently balls deep inside of me. They wore identical grins, and I just knew...it had happened again.

I let out a shriek, this time it wasn't one of ecstasy, even though his dick still felt incredible inside of me, and my body was ready to continue.

"Get off me," I screamed, pushing against his broad shoulders.

Crocodile's broad shoulders.

Lust and disgust were at war in my body. I needed a knife so I could scar Crocodile's pretty face to differentiate it from his brother's. When had he developed that skill, of being able to mimic his twin brother perfectly, and why had he needed it?

"Don't stop on my account," murmured Pan, still at the same spot on the wall. A dark fantasy slipped in, of my body held between Crocodile and Pan's. I quickly shook it away.

Since Crocodile was taking his sweet time, I reared back my fist and then punched it right at his nose. Pain reverberated through my hand, but I inwardly cheered as I felt the crack of his nose breaking.

"Fuck," Crocodile moaned with a laugh as he finally slipped out of me, his slick-covered dick hanging out for us all to see.

"Is this just some kind of kink for you?" I hissed as I struggled to cover my body. There was a dirty shirt on the ground that I hadn't picked up, and I tossed off the ruined shirt Crocodile had ripped and threw on the other so I was at least slightly covered before their gazes.

Crocodile grinned as he nonchalantly tucked himself back into his pants, blood trickling down from his nose where I'd broken it. I watched in numb disbelief as he squeezed the bridge of it between two fingers and cracked it back into place until it was once again perfectly aligned. I was trembling from blood loss and exhaustion, but adrenaline was now running through me over the realization I'd just been conned...

And I lost it.

In a blur, I flashed out of the room, the speed I had seen in the other vampires finally coming out in full force. I didn't hear any footsteps following behind me, and I had no purpose in mind; I just had to put as much distance between myself and those assholes.

I went down one hallway and another, only faintly aware that I was rapidly descending floors. I'd never explored this part of the castle before. There was a chill in the air with how deep I'd gone, and I wondered just how many underground floors this place had and why. I finally came to my senses when I got to yet another set of stairs. Although the walls of the dark hallway in front of me were made of the same stone as most of the rest of the castle, every breath I inhaled was full of the dark, earthy scent, just hinting at the dirt that surrounded us. A shiver ran down my spine as I peered around me, finally noticing a large wooden door just a few feet away. Of my many fallacies, being too curious for my own good was definitely one of them. And of course, I found myself walking towards the door.

Maybe it was an empty room, long forgotten, that I could turn into my own when I needed to hide from everyone and have some space to myself. The scent was almost comforting, and the quiet, although most would probably find it unnerving, after the chaos of what had just happened…it felt nice.

I knocked on the door, just making sure someone wasn't going to bark something at me from inside, and after a minute passed and no one had answered, I slowly opened the door.

It was dark, but it was like my vampire senses were getting better and better, because I could still see everything clearly. I frowned when I saw the unmade bed on the far wall, swathed in black sheets. This was someone's bedroom.

It only took a second to realize just who it belonged to. This was Pan's room. I knew it was his room and not Crocodile's, because his scent was everywhere. Looking back now, Crocodile had started everything so quickly that the one thing that would've set them apart–their scent–I'd totally missed because I was lost in lust. Scents were a big deal for an omega, but so were orgasms, and he'd known just the right buttons to push to keep me occupied.

I didn't feel bad at all about walking into his room and looking around; whether he'd be furious or not, his sins against me were rapidly ratcheting up.

The first thing I noted was that the room appeared lived in, which perhaps sounded inane, but I almost would've expected Pan to have an austere bedroom with no personality, because his actual personality was so big. There were carelessly tossed clothes all over the floor and the furniture. The room was enormous, large enough to fit a bed area, a sunken living room area filled with sumptuous, comfy-looking black leather couches, and a kitchenette. I could see through one of the open doors where a black tiled bathroom lay.

It was the artwork on the walls that caught my attention next. All of them were various depictions of Hell. Kind of a strange thing for a vampire, I thought. The devil was sitting on a pile of skulls in one of them, the mouth sockets on the skulls in various states of panic. In another picture, there was a man screaming in a pile of flames as various creatures with horns and long tails laughed and pointed. Every picture was terrifying. How did Pan sleep with these things staring down at him?

There was a dagger in a glass case that caught my attention next, lying on a dark paneled dresser. The handle of the dagger was black, with red leather wrapped around it. Just staring at the dagger gave me shivers, like I could tell it held an enormous amount of power, and not the good kind.

"What are you doing in here?" came Pan's furious voice.

I turned around in shock, feeling like the child who got caught with her hand in the cookie jar.

"Did anyone say you could be in here?"

I thought I'd seen him angry, but this was on an entirely new level. He was furious–past the point of furious, if that was possible. Like he was seconds away from ripping my throat out.

I didn't really have a defense, I'd known it was his room and still chose to sneak around.

"Get out of here," he snarled coldly. "And don't ever come in here again. I'll kill you, Gwendolyn."

There was firm conviction in his words, and terror sliced through my veins.

I raced towards the door, feeling his dark gaze tracking me the entire time. I could sense the violence in his body, like he was holding back from tearing me to shreds.

"I'm sorry," I choked out once I reached the hallway. But he didn't answer me. The door slammed behind me, and then I could hear the loud clack of the lock as it engaged.

I threw myself up the stairs, my body trembling with how close I'd come to actual destruction. What I'd just seen had been far stronger than territorial; he had almost been...panicked.

As I finally reached my thankfully Crocodile-free room, the fairy dance and our night under the stars seemed a lifetime away.

Pan's cold and deadly stare followed me into a fitful sleep where demons and devils chased me through my dreams.

CHAPTER 11

GWENDOLYN

The next week was a lesson in the coldness of being ignored.

It was like I didn't exist. I didn't see him, or Luke, or even Crocodile. I did run across one of the Lost Boys in the hallway, but anytime I did, their attention would be focused on the floor, or the ceiling, or beyond me. They would flat-out ignore my whispered hello.

I'd been alone for much of my life, so the experience was almost debilitating. Being ignored, being unseen. I'd forgotten how much it could burn.

This continued on.

I was tempted to find Pan and try apologizing again, because I liked the version of him giving me flying lessons much better than the other sides I'd seen of him. But when he never appeared in the walks I took around the castle, it felt like a hopeless endeavor because I certainly wasn't going to risk going back to his room to see if he was in there.

I would've thought they'd all left on a trip with how silent the castle had become, if not for the times I could hear their revelry in the forest, just out of sight. It was clear everything was intentional.

It was the seventh night of my silent treatment, when I woke up to the sound of loud laughter outside. Not just laughter, a chorus of excitement and cheers. I walked outdoors to my balcony and looked down, shocked to see that at least fifty of the MC were gathered below on the ground. Pan was at their head, and I greedily devoured the sight of him.

A part of me wondered if this was some kind of psychological way to try and get me to be more dependent on him, because after a week of speaking to no one, the sight of him was like water to a dying man.

"I have a special treat for you for the hunt this week!" Pan crowed, and the masses roared and cheered once more, until Pan held up a hand to quiet them.

"We have a special guest who's wandered onto our lands, just asking to play. It's been a while since we had an alpha to play with boys. Let's make this a night to remember!"

An alpha...what on earth? I hadn't heard anything about them keeping wolf shifters hostage, and a bad feeling developed in my chest.

With a loud war cry, as if they were all connected, I heard the click of their fangs extending, all at the same time.

"Bring out the prisoner!" Pan bellowed. I noted Luke

standing nearby, a feverish glint in his gaze. He was clearly excited about what was to come.

It took a few minutes, and then the bad feeling I'd developed turned into sickening dread. Because the prisoner...

It was Atlas.

"No!" I gasped, and as if Pan could hear me, his gaze met mine. And he grinned, like he knew exactly who Atlas was, and it was giving him great pleasure in taking him away from me.

I shot him a glare of fury and raced to throw on some clothes before striding to the door. To my shock and fear, it was locked. And however it had been locked must've been magical, because not even my enhanced strength or my metal pins could get it open.

Outside, there was another loud cheer.

"Let the games begin," I heard Pan yell, then their footsteps started to spread out into the night.

Fuck, fuck, fuck. What was I going to do? My gaze flicked between the door and the balcony, a rather stupid idea forming in my head. The only way out of here...was to fly.

Okay. Channel happy thoughts, I told myself. I could do that. The only problem was that anxiety was spiking through my veins, making it rather difficult to think of anything good, let alone something good enough to keep me in the air long enough that I didn't spiral to my death on the ground. I tried to think of the field again, but I couldn't evoke the same childhood nostalgia as before. *Think*, I chided myself. The problem was, there weren't a lot of great memories to grab onto. So I stood there on the balcony, trying to think happy thoughts. I didn't raise even a centimeter in the air, the situation made worse because I could hear the sound of the Lost Boys hunting in the woods. My dread was thickening, and then...

Atlas. I could think of my first time with Atlas. I hadn't really thought of it before; after all, I'd tried my best to get him out of my head because I'd thought he was lost to me forever. But now, somehow... somehow he was still in my realm of possibilities. If only I could figure this out.

I closed my eyes and took a deep breath, spreading my arms out wide as the breeze trickled through my fingers. I thought of that afternoon, of the sun on my skin, the smell of the wilderness around me, the sunset in the distance, and him. My golden boy who was actually here.

I remembered his hungry lips against mine, the way his rough hands had stroked my skin. I remember his growled words of praise, I remembered it all happening right then. That feeling of weightlessness from before enveloped me, and when I opened my eyes, I was floating in the air.

Yes!

As soon as I let myself celebrate, I crashed back down on my ass on the stone.

Fuck, that hurt.

Okay, so momentary lapses in concentration were not allowed, evidently. I struggled to my feet and worked again to channel the feeling that Atlas had given me, the sense of pure happiness, pure hope.

It worked quicker this time, and before I could distract myself with another thought, I leaped over the balcony and soared through the air. There were two of Pan's men discussing something in the courtyard, and their eyes shot up as I passed above them, almost identical expressions of shock and awe visible on their faces. I gave them a wide grin and a salute before I determinedly pushed forward.

I was going to find a way to save him; there wasn't another option.

I soared toward the woods, falling a bit in the air when I realized the quickest way to do the task was to fly in and out of the tree line. Which would take a lot of finesse. I wasn't really wanting to impale myself on a tree branch if I could help it.

I could see some of the Lost Boys running around below me, their muffled shouts floating up. At least they hadn't caught him yet, although I had a feeling Pan liked to play with his food before he ate. He wouldn't want the hunt to be over quickly.

Ugh, I cried out as I clumsily hit a tree branch while I was trying to dip a bit closer to the ground. The branch tore into me, and it was a testament to my burgeoning ability as a flyer that I didn't fall to the ground and break my neck.

Taking a deep breath, I pushed off from a nearby branch and went into the air, staying just ahead of where I saw a large group of Lost Boys hunting.

But where was Pan? And Crocodile? I had a feeling their hunting abilities blew far past those of the rest of the MC.

Deciding I was heading in the wrong direction, I began to travel left and then right, at least a mile past where I'd been, to see if I could spot anything.

I was feeling hopeless when, all of a sudden, a flash of gold caught my eye. Being more careful this time, I allowed myself to float below the tree line, inwardly congratulating myself when I did it without bodily injury.

There it was, another spark of gold. I surged forward, going as fast as I could while winding through the trees, and I caught a whiff of a warm, cinnamon apple scent.

It was him.

I got a better look at him and realized he was in wolf form, his enormous creature having the same golden hair color as he did in his other form. I'd always loved his hair, but I was cursing it right now. Black or brown would've been much better for blending in than gold. I pushed myself to go faster and tried to whisper call for him.

"Atlas!" I softly cried, hoping his wolf hearing could pick me up and that somehow my voice would evade Pan's hearing.

His steps didn't falter.

Alright, I just needed to get a little bit closer. This time, unfortunately, I wasn't able to control myself, and I hit another tree...with the side of my head. All the thoughts I'd been using to keep me afloat were knocked out of me, and I fell, my flight down hindered in speed by all of the leaves and branches I was passing through on the way down. I landed with a solid thunk, feeling my shoulder snap as I did so...and also my leg.

The world was spinning around me, the forest above going in and out of focus. Until suddenly, a golden wolf appeared above me with glowing jewel-green eyes.

Suddenly, the form melted in front of my gaze, and a familiar-looking male was staring down at me. I'd obviously gotten a head injury, because it took me a few moments to realize that it was Atlas, staring down at me in terror. His lips were moving like he was talking to me, but the words got confused entering my head.

Finally, my body started to stitch back together. I could hear the bones snapping into place, and the tendons and ligaments sealing together.

But it wasn't enough, I needed more. I needed...

My incisors popped out, and I eyed Atlas hungrily. I could finally make out the words he was saying now. He was asking if I was alright. His head snapped back in surprise when he saw my teeth pop out, and then determination glinted in his gaze. He lifted me into his arms gently, and I shivered at the feeling of his touch. Pulling me up, he extended his neck to the side so I could see his pulse beating softly in his throat.

"Get something to drink, baby. Help yourself heal."

My vampiric nature didn't need him to say more. I snapped my head forward, my teeth slicing into his neck as the delicious flavor bubbled over my tongue. He tasted just as good, if not better than Luke had. I was faintly aware of Atlas's soft moan and could feel him start to harden underneath me. At least it felt good to him and he didn't find me disgusting in this form. He held me tightly against him, his whole body shaking as I drank.

"That's it, baby. Take whatever you need," he purred. As his blood flowed through me, and my strength returned, the situation came back into focus in my brain. With a gasp, I forced my teeth from his throat and met his gaze before erupting into tears.

"I'm here, little omega. And I'm never going to be away from you again. No matter what," he whispered, his promise sounding worshipful.

"Is that so?" Pan's voice floated from behind me. Atlas's body froze at the sound of his voice.

Determination flew through me. Whatever happened, I was going to save Atlas. He'd come for me. No one had ever done something like that for me before. No one had cared enough. No matter what, I wasn't going to let him go. I slowly turned in Atlas's lap, ready to fight.

But I was taken aback by what I saw in Pan's features, and right next to him, in Luke's. Jealousy. That was what I was seeing. In both of them.

"What the fuck is this?" Luke growled before Pan could say anything. Pan seemed momentarily confused by the ferocity in Luke's voice, but he shook it off and centered his attention back on my shaking body.

"Yes, little omega, what the fuck is this?" Pan drawled.

"You can't have him," I growled as fiercely as I could, realizing that the look I'd seen from Pan earlier hadn't had anything to do with him thinking I knew Atlas. He was just gloating at me because he had been punishing me all week. Asshole.

"And why exactly do you think I can't have him?" Pan asked lightly.

"Because he's mine." The words settled into my chest,

clicking into place like they'd become a part of me. Maybe I hadn't hit my head as hard as I'd thought before. Maybe I'd held a part of me back because something in me could sense that I couldn't have him forever.

But now, everything in me had claimed Atlas as mine.

"And you're mine," commented Pan. "So what to do about the situation?" He took a step towards me and a growl ripped from Atlas's throat, only adding to the jealousy and fury on Pan's face.

"She's mine. She'll always be mine. I've done everything to come and find her," rasped Atlas hoarsely. It came to me then, that I'd just fed on him, weakening him when he needed all of his strength for a fight.

Fuck.

I couldn't match Pan's strength in any way, I knew that. Even at my fiercest, I was nothing compared to him.

"Please, I'll do anything. Don't take him from me," I pleaded. Pan's face was impassive now, unreadable. Atlas growled again, obviously unhappy at my supplication. He was the big bad alpha. I knew it was in his nature to think that he was supposed to protect me. But there was a reason that everyone was scared of Pan.

"Are you hurt?" Luke's voice cut through the thick tension in the air. My attention went to him, shocked to see his entire focus on me, his own body trembling as he stared at my injuries. I realized I was quite the sight; even though my body was still in the midst of repairing itself, it didn't change the fact that I was covered in blood and scratches. The leggings I'd been wearing were torn all over, and you could see blood and bruising through the holes. That tree and subsequent fall had certainly done a number on me.

"Yes, she is," Atlas answered before I could respond. "She fell from the fucking sky and bounced through the trees. She just fed on me, but she needs more."

A whimper burst from my lips. What was he doing?

Luke suddenly lunged forward, and with supersonic speed, pulled me from Atlas's lap, cradling me gently but firmly.

"We need to get you back to the castle and get you looked at," he said worriedly, his hands feeling all over my body. I cried out as his hand passed along my broken leg which was still in the process of sealing itself back together.

"I'm fine," I objected stubbornly, my gaze flicking back and forth between Pan and Atlas, who were staring at each other in mutual distrust and fury.

Atlas sighed exasperatedly. "Just kill me if you're going to, but make sure she's okay."

"If you kill him, I'll never forgive you. There won't be a day, a moment, where I don't hate you with every fiber of my being," I swore softly, glaring into Pan's still impassive stare.

The silence was deafening around us as I waited for Pan's answer.

"Pan can inform you of his decision later, sweetheart. We're going back to the castle," Luke snarled, continuing to hold me close to him.

"No!" I screamed, struggling to get out of his grasp and back to Atlas. Atlas had leaped to his feet, his hands in fists as he stared at me, tortured.

"This is so freaking dramatic," purred Pan, not sounding nearly as exasperated as his words would assume.

"Take her to the castle," he ordered. "Make sure that she gets better. And you," he gestured to the crowd of males I hadn't noticed gathering nearby. "Take him back to the castle and throw him in a cell."

I opened my mouth to object, but he held up a hand to silence me. "Don't test my patience, Gwendolyn. I believe I am being far more generous than I should be with your lover." He turned his attention back to his men. "Make sure you only have a little bit of fun with him on the way over. I don't want him harmed."

At his words, Atlas sprung into action, fighting back as Pan's Lost Boys swarmed him.

Pan sighed and shook his head before glancing at Luke. "Get her out of here."

With a nod, Luke was suddenly springing into the air and we were soaring above the trees.

"Atlas!" I screamed, feeling lightheaded. The last thing I saw was Pan pushing up his sleeves and strolling towards Atlas as if he didn't have a care in the world, and then everything faded around me.

———

Luke

I stared down at her beautiful face. She seemed so fragile passed out in my arms. I hated how helpless she looked. Since the moment I had seen her, I felt like there was a thread connecting my heart to hers. Everything about me was attracted to her.

It was her beauty that caught my attention first. I'd never seen anything so extraordinary in my entire existence.

But the glimpses of her personality, that I'd seen far more than she knew—since I spent all of my free time watching her —had been what had really done it. Those hours I'd gotten to spend with her in the medical bay, I went over them constantly, every detail highlighted in my mind.

I got to the castle as quickly as possible, striding through the hallways until I reached my office where I could lay her gently on the medical bed. It took everything in me not to keep her in my arms. I knew that would make it a bit difficult to check her out though. At least I was trying to be rational.

She looked like she'd been through hell. When I first stepped into the clearing and saw her, I'd almost lost my mind. There was blood all over her, something that certainly could be sexy in specific situations, but not when combined with the bruising, cuts, and scrapes that were marring her perfect skin. I could tell her bone had snapped in her leg. The skin was a shiny pink color as it healed, signaling the grave injury that once had been there.

Thank God Pan had turned her. Not that she would've been up in the air in general if she hadn't been turned, but I couldn't imagine her walking around unprotected. The wolves thought they were so strong, but they were nothing compared to us.

I grabbed a clean cloth, wet it, and then gently rubbed it over her skin, removing the blood so I could get a closer inspecting her injuries. She was strangely giving off tiny bursts of perfume, and I frowned, hating how lost I was when it came to what she'd become. She was a vampire, most certainly, but she was also still an omega, which didn't make any sense. There weren't many females that we'd turned, but the ones that some of the others had turned had definitely been full vampires, no matter what species they were before. It was like her turn had only partially happened. And no matter how many hours I spent in the giant library Pan had collected over the last thousands of years, I couldn't find anything that explained the phenomenon that was her.

But hell, her perfume was potent. Even with how concerned I was over her injuries, I was hard, unable to beat down my erection. My gums were aching from the need to bite into her skin. I hadn't partaken of her blood yet, but it was number one on my bucket list. That and having her feed on me over and over again.

When I was satisfied I'd removed enough of the blood to look at her injuries, I examined every part of her body.

I was pleased to see beyond a couple of particularly bad cuts, her body was doing its job. Just as a precaution, I set up an I.V. with a fey blood bag to help her heal. Their blood had more healing properties than others, so it should help her to recover faster.

I pulled up a chair next to her, knowing I wouldn't be able to leave her side until she woke up. I had plenty to think about, after all, even if it took a couple of hours. The most pressing thing was how to get this girl to fall for me like I was falling for her.

I didn't really think of it as competing with Pan. He wasn't like that with me. Although he was more territorial of her than I'd seen him with any other being over the long amount of time I'd been around him, he had enough confidence to not feel threatened. Pan knew that even if she had fallen for someone else, it didn't take away the feelings she had for him, which were obvious even though she was doing her best to fight them.

My problem was having her see me. Pan had a certain magnetism about him. When he was in the room, he was what the focus was on, and since it wasn't like I was getting a lot of time with just me and her, it seemed an impossible task to make her see me when he and I were in the same room with her. What I needed was more alone time with her, but most of my alone time with her seemed to be when she was comatose, which may have helped strengthen my feelings for her, but was certainly doing nothing to strengthen hers toward me.

I knew she'd felt something with that kiss though, and I knew she really enjoyed the taste of my blood. So at least I had that going for me. But now I had to worry about the alpha. He was a pretty boy, just like Pan, and I guess Crocodile, too, since Crocodile was Pan's mirror image, just with a lot more screws loose. I'd seen the devotion in her gaze, how her body gravitated towards his even when she was held in my arms.

I sighed, brushing some of my hair out of my face. I needed a fucking haircut.

I was so caught up in my pity party that I almost missed

that she was beginning to stir. Glancing at the clock, I realized she'd been under for only about an hour and a half. Unfortunately, that hour and a half had probably done nothing to soften the fury she'd been feeling as I swept her away from her boy toy.

Her eyes snapped open then, and as usual, I got lost staring at the amber color, a shade I'd never seen before in someone. Amber had become my favorite color since she'd been around.

It took a minute, but she soon remembered exactly why she was lying there. And when she did, she tried to spring from her bed, the I.V. still attached.

"Fuck," she growled as the needle bent awkwardly in her arm. I jumped up, moving to help her.

"Don't come near me," she hissed, and it broke my fucking heart to see the tears in her gaze. She was glaring at me like I'd betrayed her.

I held up my hands in front of her. "Please let me help you. You're still healing from some pretty serious injuries. I promise he's okay." I took a deep breath, hating the next words I was going to say. "And I promise that I'll take you to see him as soon as you're strong enough."

She eyed me for a moment, before reluctantly nodding her head. I carefully removed the needle, cleaning the wound out of habit even though her vampiric nature would take care of any bacteria.

"How are you feeling?" I asked.

"Far better than I should after falling a few stories and almost getting impaled by a bunch of trees." She bit her lip, examining me, and I patiently waited for her verdict. "How long has he been here for?" she finally asked.

I bit back the jealousy churning in my gut. "Two days. Pan had some business to attend to, so he delayed the hunt. Normally, it would have occurred that first night. Nothing the Lost Boys like more than a hunt."

"Was he captured? Did they...feed off him?"

I shook my head. "One of the men found him milling about in the woods. He refused to tell them why he was here, and as far as I know, he was taken to a cell and left there. Pan hadn't spoken with him until that rendezvous just a bit ago."

Her shoulders relaxed a bit at that. I was leaving out a little bit, like how the wolf had almost fatally killed two of our men. Pan hadn't been happy when he heard that, but he had been distracted by Hook's latest antics, and so he decided to wait to deal with it until the hunt.

"I want to go see him," she said stubbornly, lifting her chin.

Her skin was taking on a more rosy glow, and where her bone had popped out was completely smooth. She was well on her way to recovery. I nodded, wishing I could have more time with her where she wasn't wanting someone else. "I'll take you there, as long as I can carry you there as a precaution." I didn't really need to carry her as a precaution, but certainly, it was another chance to feel her body against mine. Maybe make her think of me a bit. I did have a pretty good body if I did say so myself. Maybe she'd even get hungry and want a snack from my throat as we walked.

Wishful thinking, but a guy could dream.

She scoffed and then sighed. "Fine, whatever." I managed to hold in my grin as I lifted her into my arms. We strolled out of the med room and back into the hallway, turning this way and that until we got to the lower level where the prisoners were kept. Two of our guys were stationed right outside the cells, and they both nodded when they saw me and said nothing as we passed. Unfortunately for me, she didn't ask for a snack, but she did seem to be cuddling against me. I didn't think I was imagining that.

Finally, we were there, and I lost all of her attention. It was focused on the male slumped over on a threadbare cot in the corner of a dusty cell.

"Atlas," she sighed with relief, and his head snapped up as he immediately got to his feet and rushed towards the bars that separated him from us, looking none the worse for the wear, I noted.

"Is she alright?" he asked me, and I nodded but didn't say anything. I set her down and she moved towards him without a look back.

"Are *you* all right?" she pressed, reaching through the bar to touch his chest.

Fuck, I was already missing her being in my arms.

"I'm totally fine. They just brought me here," he lied through the skin of his teeth. I knew Pan wouldn't have "just let him come here", but whatever bruises he'd left on his body, he'd managed to make sure they were hidden under his clothes, I'm sure foreseeing that Gwendolyn would want to see him before he could heal all the way.

Atlas's nose started twitching.

"You smell…different," he said softly.

She shrugged, biting her lip anxiously. "Obviously I've changed." She cleared her throat.

"Am I…disgusting to you now?"

I tensed, ready to rip his head off if he said yes, but of course, golden boy just shook his head with a soft smile. "You still smell good enough to eat," he teased. "Even if you're the one doing the eating." He winked at her, and I watched as she swooned. I'd noted she really liked winking, I needed to put that more in my arsenal.

"How did you find me?" she asked, a blush spreading across her cheeks at his flirting. "I didn't think anyone could find this place without Pan leading them here."

Now it was his turn to blush. Interesting. He side-eyed me and then turned his attention back to her. "This," he finally answered, pulling up his sleeve to reveal an infinity sign that seemed to be glowing on his wrist. I'd never seen anything like it before.

"After you left, it appeared on my wrist. I'd been in severe pain before that, and then…it was there and it was like there was a map inside my head, telling me how to find you."

Before I could ponder anymore on what he'd said, Gwendolyn swayed on her feet, and then I was holding her in my arms as Atlas reached out for her.

"Vampires are fast motherfuckers," he noted, and I just grinned at him smugly.

"You can come visit him in the morning, sweetheart," I cajoled her. "For right now, you need some more rest."

She opened her mouth to object, but then Atlas pitched in.

"Go get some sleep, little omega. I'll be here in the morning, and everything will be fine."

She scrunched up her nose in that cute way she did, obviously thinking hard about it. "All right," she finally agreed, more exhausted than she was letting on. Atlas and I exchanged a glance, and his gaze promised retribution if anything happened to her. I just glared back at him. Like I would ever let anything happen to her. Over my dead body.

Literally.

"I love you," she called after him as I strode out the door with her wrapped tightly in my arms. I flinched at her words, wishing desperately that they were for me, but I forced my feet forward.

"I love you too," he called after us.

She was asleep before I even got out of the first hallway, and I promised, as I stared down at her beautiful face, I was going to make her feel something, no matter how long it took.

CHAPTER 12
GWENDOLYN

I woke up feeling strange.

Not the kind of strange where I forgot where I was, but like something inside me had twisted and left me feeling empty. I couldn't explain it even to myself, but the jarring sensation lingered in my gut. Even two bags of blood didn't sate the desire growing deep inside me.

Was this another stage of becoming a vampire? Another change that Pan forgot to tell me about?

My thoughts funneled in on the demonic artwork in Pan's room above his bed, wondering if they had any significance with his story.

Maybe I was still burning on the inside that Atlas had followed me into Darkland and got himself imprisoned by Pan? The vampire king wasn't someone who often showed mercy, and considering his obsession over me, I was terrified for Atlas' fate.

I was also…overjoyed he'd come for me, like an integral piece of me had been returned. I'd thought I'd lost him forever.

I paused in front of my bed, not realizing I'd been pacing, and decided that my strange feeling had everything to do with my emotions around Atlas' return.

My stomach buzzed with butterflies at the thought of seeing him again, and I made up my mind that I'd find a way to save him, even if it would infuriate Pan.

I left my room behind and wandered the corridors, attempting to remember where I'd found the door to his cell. Some days it felt like the halls and doors moved in this castle because how could it be that I got lost nearly every day I left my room?

As normal nowadays, I didn't pass any of the Lost Boys, but up ahead, I did spot one of the maids. They were illusive things…Rarely seen and yet my room was always immaculate once I returned to it.

"Hello," I called out, figuring she might hear me from such a distance.

The woman in her maid outfit twisted her head to glance at me over her shoulder, and I recognized her instantly from my first day…when I'd attempted to eat her. Oops.

Her eyes widened with panic at seeing me, and evidently, she recognized me too. Hastily, she turned away and ran down the hallway and vanished around the corner.

Well, that went badly. I wanted to make it up to her though, so I picked up my speed and raced after her because it was always better to have more allies than enemies.

Back in the mansion with Sussana, the only way I survived was by having Cook and the other staff who worked for her as my friends. They shared things with me, snuck me food, and kept me company.

Rounding the corner, I ran right into someone so hard that I rebounded, thrown off by a hard chest.

Pan's hands clasped me hastily around my middle, catching me before I landed on my ass.

Almost instantly, fire licked between my legs, and slick drenched me. It came so fast, it left me dizzy with arousal. An inferno flared through me, burning across my skin, my cheeks flushing. Every place he touched left me covered in goosebumps, sending jolts of delicious sparks across sensitized nerve endings. With my nipples hardening, I quivered against him, my hips thrusting forward like they had a mind of their own.

What in the world was wrong with me?

"Pan..." his name turned into a moan on my tongue, and my body was completely wired. Which meant one thing only: he was using his damn thrall on me again.

I lifted my chin to Pan, meeting his gaze, glaring at the powerful, huge monster peering down at me with a questioning expression—a raised eyebrow and parting lips, as though he might finally tell me what the hell was going on.

"Do you have something to say?" he finally asked, sounding half amused.

Was he kidding? Couldn't he see that I was losing my mind and control of my body?

"Stop it," I shouted. "Stop using your stupid thrall on me."

His brow furrowed, putting on the best fake, confused look. "This isn't me."

Being this close to Pan, I was drowning in his dark, masculine scent, and I craved rolling around in it. But I shook my head, and I shoved my hands into his chest to escape his grip. I stumbled a few feet from him, panic clawing at my mind. What was happening to me?

That was when a blaze of the earlier empty sensation rippled across my body, tightening my stomach, and causing another gush of my slick. It called to me, and like an invisible cord wound around my body, it tugged me closer to him once more. My body tingled with desperate anticipation for his touch.

A whine pulsed over my throat at how much I wanted to ask him to touch me.

His silvery eyes narrowed on me, his nostrils flaring. "You smell like sex and slick. What did you do, little Darling?" He studied me, his face as beautiful as always...hard lines, strong cheekbones, and the darkness in his expression that I was growing obsessed with. He was a walking sex god, and I wanted to demand that he touch me.

I shook my head, recoiling once more, trying to see clearly through the heady sensation coming over me in waves. "I don't know. I woke up with something wrong with me, like nothing was enough...with a hunger I couldn't satisfy with blood."

He dragged his tongue over his lower lip like he wasn't

sure if he wanted to lick me all over or grill me about what was happening to me.

I took a step backward, heaviness pressing down on me.

"Come to me," he ordered, staring with such lust in his gaze, such possessiveness, that I worried what he'd do if I gave myself over to him.

"You smell so good," I whined. "Please stop what you're doing to me."

He stepped forward, and my skin tightened the closer he got. I lifted my chin, attempting to show my defiance and that I had control. But the moment his knuckles ran down my cheek, I was moaning, my knees close to giving out beneath me.

"My little Darling, I know what's going on with you. It's the onset of your cycle."

"What does that mean?" I breathed, desire stretching across my stomach. I pressed myself closer, realizing then that no matter how much I tried, I wasn't going to be able to draw myself away from him.

Every inch of me strained, slick soaking my underwear, my scent so strong now that it left me dizzy.

Pan's expression turned almost feral, and the moment he moved closer, pinning me to the wall, I lost any kind of control I jokingly assumed I had.

"You've gone into heat, my little Darling. Your pheromones have gone wild, and there's only one thing to ease the ache."

"I-I...how?" I made a crying sound.

Fear twisted within me, but each time another wave of

arousal undulated through me, I moaned, my body arching against Pan's. The sensation came faster, ebbed and flowed, the emptiness I hadn't been able to fill, billowing inside me. Soon, I'd be nothing but a lustful thing in so much pain, that I'd lose myself.

"This is your first heat," he murmured, almost to himself.

I writhed against him, a sharp ache of yearning cutting across my stomach, and it dug deeper, doubling me over. Pan lifted me into his arms, holding me upright.

I grabbed his shirt, fisting it, and dragged him impossibly close where I saw the flecks of red forming in his silvery eyes.

"Please, Pan, it hurts so much. I need you to fuck me. I need it. I can't stand this any longer." My libido was starved, my head spinning with the overwhelming endorphins running wild in my body.

"I've got you, little Darling. I'll make the pain go away." Then our mouths clashed with such fervor that my body shuddered. Fresh arousal dripped from my core, and I pushed myself against Pan, ripping at his shirt desperately. Buttons popped and flew in every direction.

I should have been mortified that I was begging the vampire king to fuck me out in the hallway where anyone could walk in on us. But I didn't care as Pan bunched my dress, tucking the hem into the thin belt I wore, or that he tore off my panties with a single rip.

The sensation alone had me moaning louder, and I didn't even want to glance down to see how wet I'd actually become.

Pan kissed me aggressively, and a long-drawn out purr

came from the depths of my lungs. A deep sound I didn't recall ever making before.

Heat tugged between my legs, the intensity so severe that I frantically yanked at Pan's pants. With our mouths never breaking apart, he managed to push them down his legs before he kicked them off.

I frantically pushed his shirt off his shoulders, needing skin-to-skin. Pan wrenched at the neckline of my dress and tugged it down, the fabric tearing, freeing my breasts.

The cool air across my nipples sent me into a flurry of whines. I desperately reached for my nipples, flicking and pulling at them, eager for release. Craving it like my life depended on it.

Pan pushed my hands away. "I didn't give you permission to touch yourself. Every inch of you is mine. Your perky tits, your dripping wet, tight pussy, your ass, your mouth... All of it. You don't touch unless I say so."

"Then do something about it," I groaned.

My stomach turned on itself once more, and I curled a leg around Pan's, needing him closer. He lowered his hand between us, his fingers finding the slick that dripped down my inner thighs.

I cried out at the cold sensation of his fingers sliding across my slit. That's all it took, and I pulsed, my hips rocking back and forth against his hand. Every nerve ending seemed to burst at the same time. I had never felt so high from such a touch. Whatever he was doing, I was about to cum. I gasped for air I didn't need.

He tore his mouth from mine. "Is this what you want, my little omega?"

"Please, yes. Rut me, please, I need you inside me." I heard myself and how desperate I sounded, and yet nothing I did soothed the ache that was showing no signs of easing.

"Fuck. Your smell. I want it all over me. You're drenched, I want your slick on my cock."

He growled, his lips widening into a grin. But there was something more than just satisfaction at finding me so ready. He looked purely feral.

If I had a working heart, it'd be hammering in my chest right now with anticipation. Was it wrong that I longed to have him hurt me, knowing that the pain would make the pleasure that much better?

I arched under him as he slid his large hands to the back of my thighs and pulled me off my feet.

His mouth lowered to my neck, his tongue running from my collarbone to my ear as his cock pressed into my core. A low purr grazed my throat over every inch he pressed into me, stretching me. Even with being so wet, Pan was huge, but the stretch felt incredible.

And something inside me told me that things would never be the same after today.

————

Pan

Gwendolyn cried out, her fingers digging into my shoulders. My name formed on her lips as she wrapped those gorgeous legs around my waist. She tasted and smelled like the sweetest candy, and I was thrusting into her so hard her entire body shuddered.

She had her eyes closed, sucking on her lower lip as she continued to make those delicious sounds.

"Open your eyes." My voice echoed around us, my command coming with enough power to make her listen. Omegas in heat were lost in the desires that consumed them. It swallowed them whole and if not helped, their pain would escalate until they passed out. "I want you to look at me as I fuck you. And I want you to remember that you're mine."

Her eyes slid open, and they were hazy from how aroused she'd gotten herself. She moved on my cock, her tits bouncing, grabbing my attention, the purrs in her throat insanely beautiful.

I drove in and out of her, my need bursting forward, spreading her sweet pussy with each thrust. She held on, moving her hips too, her heels digging into my rear.

"Don't ever stop." Her mewls filled the hallway as she arched her back, offering me her bare neck.

She was spectacular and all mine.

A growl rumbled in my chest.

"Make it hurt more," she panted.

And I was more than happy to oblige, because I'd been holding back on my speed, and so I went faster, harder to where she cried out, her body sinking back against the wall as I slammed her against it.

Her pussy clamping down on my cock drove me wild, but I never relented, even when her legs twitched, trembling around me from how exhausted she was getting. But this felt like Nirvana, and I couldn't stop...wouldn't stop. I'd been waiting for her heat, knowing I would be the one to get her through it.

With her arching back, I leaned down and tongued a nipple, taking as much of her sexy breast into my mouth as I could. I starved to taste her once more and lengthened my fangs, biting down into the soft, creamy flesh of her breast.

Blood seeped over my tongue, and fuck, she tasted incredible.

Her cries grew louder, her body writhing wilder. Instead of stopping me, she rode me harder, begging for more.

When she finally screamed, her body suddenly no longer rocking to meet my thrusts but convulsing, I let go of her breast.

Licking blood from my lips, I stared down between us, where my little omega was dripping all over my cock, squeezing me so hard that she shoved me off the edge. I grunted as the euphoric sensation thundered through me. My muscles coiled as I pumped into her, while her tight core sucked down on my cock, milking me.

"That's it. Fuck. Take it all. Squeeze me." Pulsing into her, I roared, both our cries a ballad to my ears.

We shuddered together, and the grin curved on her lips had primal satisfaction running through me.

Orgasms as a vampire, fucking rocked, the intensity of it a gift. Who needed a heartbeat when you could cum like that?

When we finally settled down, I leaned forward and licked the dripping blood from the bite mark on her breast.

She blinked at me, her cheeks on fire, her chest rising and falling. Even if she didn't need to breathe, she still held onto human actions.

"How was that?"

Her body shuddered against me, her core still fluttering around my dick.

"That was incredible," she gasped.

With me still buried deep inside her, I walked her back to her room. "Let's get you washed up, and then get some food before the next wave hits."

Omegas in heat were hard to predict, their hunger could come at any time, each wave as intense as the next, and they'd beg anyone near them to fuck their brains out. All they sensed was a desire so strong it felt like crippling pain and the need for it to stop. For males, an omega's scent drove them to insanity if they didn't rut her. And vampires were not immune. The Lost Boys were probably out of their minds over her scent floating through the castle air. I shouldn't have taken her in the hallway, but I didn't think she could have made it to her room. Or that I could have for that matter...

"Okay," she sighed, leaning against me.

"Good girl."

Her body was soft and exhausted against my chest. But by the time we reached her shower, she was brushing her lips across my neck, her nipples puckering against my chest.

My hunger for her returned just as quickly. Pulling out of her, I set her down in the shower. I grabbed the skirt of her dress and pulled it up and over her head, leaving her completely naked.

Then I stepped inside with her and turned on the shower, letting the warm water spray over us. Water trickled down her face and body. Blood slid over her breast and stomach, while my seed seeped along the insides of her legs. A beautiful sight.

"How are you feeling?" I asked, as she remained especially quiet, her body trembling. I hoped I hadn't hurt her... more than she'd wanted at least.

"I don't know. I loved that you fucked me that way, but...I still need more."

"It'll get better. I've seen omegas before who would sleep for a day after such an episode, then wake up with no heat. Now, let's get you cleaned up."

I knelt in front of her. "Widen your legs a bit for me."

"You don't need—"

"I do. Now tell me what you did this morning when you woke up. Focus on something other than how you feel." An omega's heat was brought on by a trigger, and as much as I hated to admit it, the only major change in her life in recent days was the fucking furball, Atlas. But I was hoping that I was wrong and her reaction had nothing to do with him.

"Nothing. I fed, then stayed in my room trying to work out why I felt so strange."

"Okay, little omega. It's going to be alright, I promise." My voice came out gentle, as I was starting to see that getting her to come around to doing things my way didn't work if we clashed head-to-head. She had a tendency to be stubborn, and while I usually broke anyone who opposed me...Gwendolyn was different. She was special. I wasn't ready to destroy her...maybe I wouldn't ever be ready. Maybe I wanted to keep my Darling longer than a few weeks.

I trailed my hand between her thighs, my gaze glancing to her face as she watched me, a shy blush crossing her cheeks. I loved seeing this beautiful, gorgeous omega melt under my attention. The temptation to lean in and lick her silky wet pussy played on my mind, to suck on her flesh, to bite her just above her clit and send her to heaven with an orgasm she would never forget.

Water ran down her curvy body. There was so much I wanted to do to her, so many ways I wanted to take her. I couldn't wait to show her all the pleasures I could give her body.

Gwendolyn suddenly shuddered as my fingers ran across her inner lips and hovered around the rim of her entrance. That was when I noticed that her reaction wasn't just being sensitive to my touch, but something completely different. She rocked her hips across my hand, her eyes closed, nipples beaded tight. And with it came that fragrance I was fucking addicted to at this point.

But it also rang alarm bells. Fuck!

Lowering my hand from her beautiful cunt, I got to my feet, much to her protesting moan. Her eyes flipped open and the haze of lust filled them once more.

"So soon, my sweets?" I asked.

She pressed herself to me, hands splayed across my chest, and her body burned up. A harsh purr came out of her.

"It hurts," she whined desperately. My chest constricted,

and I wrapped her in my arms, knowing with certainty now what she needed…even if I hated it.

"Your heat must have been triggered by Atlas' arrival, by your connection to him," I growled, gritting my teeth so hard that pain dug into my jaw. "And as much as I fucking hate to admit it…" My voice trailed off.

"What," she gasped, her hips thrusting against me.

"There's only one reason he'd have an influence like this just with his presence."

She stared at me with huge eyes, and I wasn't sure how much she was able to process what I was implying in her lust-ridden state.

Sharp waves of anger and jealousy carved me up, just knowing he'd gotten to my little Darling first and marked her as his own. The fucker had mated her, bonded himself to her, hadn't he?

Everything in me was objecting to what I knew I had to allow to happen in order to help Gwendolyn.

It went against every fucking thing I stood for. I'd hated shifters for what seemed like forever, and destroyed most who crossed my path.

"Atlas," she moaned as she finally realized who I'd been talking about. "I need him."

I grimaced, hating his name on her lips. But the more Gwendolyn rutted against me, the more I couldn't ignore where this would end.

"I'll fix this," I promised, even as a sharp spear of jealousy pierced my dead, cold heart.

But she barely heard me, and she kept calling for Atlas.

"Please. I need him," she mewled. What was I going to do about the fact the girl I'd claimed as mine...had a mate? He had to be her mate. His arrival had triggered her heat. I'd seen the mark on his wrist.

My chest twinged, and I resisted the urge to drive my fist into the wall. Or into his face.

"Okay, change of plans then," I suggested, turning off the water and guiding her back into her room. Holding her by her arms, she kept purring and rubbing herself against me, peppering me with kisses.

"I need Atlas, please, Pan."

My insides turned colder than they already were, and my brash words came out dark. "Don't fucking move. I'll be back with your loverboy in a few moments." There was no doubt about it in my head. After I helped my little Darling, there was no room for Atlas in this world. Not if I had anything to do with it.

I threw myself out of her room and rushed to grab my discarded pants in the hallway. I dragged them on, then I flew through the castle and down to the dungeons. Snatching the keys from the hook, I unlocked the door and was in the cell half a second later.

He barely had time to react before I had him slammed up against the wall, gasping for air, his eyes huge and bulging. Why did he have to exist?

"Get the fuck off me," he snarled in my face, his strikes to my arms doing nothing but irritating me worse.

I was desperate to let out some of this anger, but for Gwendolyn, I restrained myself from killing him. The fact that a member of the Silver clan had managed to seduce *my* omega still blew me away. But living with those assholes, her offerings would have been limited, she'd probably just felt sorry for him.

"You mated with her, bound her to you, didn't you?" I spit in his face.

He stared at me for a long pause, shock I'd figured it out clear in his features. "Go fuck yourself. She's mine," he finally hissed.

I bristled. His words struck me, and I knew he'd seen how they affected me by the smug glint in his gaze. It wasn't like me to show weakness, but never mind that right now. I might not be able to kill him, to avoid Gwendolyn also dying since their lives were now connected...but I could make his life hell.

"You have no idea who you're dealing with..."

"Yeah?" Fury strained his face. "You have no idea what I'd do to save her and be with her. Now that I've found your little hidey-hole, I can easily share the knowledge." He leaned forward, his teeth shifting and lengthening as he stared daggers at me. "I will get out," he promised. "And I will be taking my mate with me. It will just be icing on the cake that I know I'll be destroying *you* when I do it." He paused, grinning at me as he watched the words sink in.

I just laughed, enjoying the way his eyebrows bunched in confusion. I didn't give a shit about others finding us. I'd slaughter the whole damn world if I needed to. This prick... oh, he was going to be a delight to torture. I pressed my forearm harder against his neck, until he was clawing at my arm for breath.

"It would be so easy to finish you right now," I hissed, wishing with every fiber of my being that I could. Gwendolyn's desperate words, her cries for help, filled my head. If I didn't hurry back, she'd wander outside for help, and knowing my luck...my dick of a brother would find her first and make it his mission to *help* her.

Fuck. I released the wolf who fell to his knees, choking. I snatched him by the back of his shirt, my aching fangs wanting nothing more than to rip him apart. Instead, I hauled him behind me, dragging him like the dog he was out of the prison and back to my Darling's room.

Moving at lightning speed meant Atlas got no chance to get up as I dragged him up every step, until I finally dumped him outside her door.

Grabbing him by the throat, I yanked him to his feet and shoved him into the wall. "Now listen up," I grunted in his face. "Gwendolyn's gone into heat, and she needs you." I hissed the words through clenched teeth. "And you are going to go in there and give her what she needs."

He stared at me dubiously. "Wait. This whole time you've been going all ape-shit with jealousy on my ass, and now you want me to go in there and fuck her?" He stared at me incredulously. "I mean, yes, of course, I would do anything for her. But what's your angle? What do you get out of this?"

"I can't take her being in pain," I admitted truthfully, feeling like the words were being sliced out of me. "She—she means the world to me."

He growled under his breath at my words.

His stare grew cocky as he studied me, and it was a miracle he was still breathing. "You're serious? You actually care for her? I assumed it went against your nature to care about anyone. How are you not bursting into flames right now that you're showing signs of compassion?"

I wished Gwendolyn was there right now, so she could witness the sheer willpower I exercised in deciding to not completely destroy him. The arrogance in his voice had me seething, and refraining wasn't exactly my forte.

"Do it or you'll wish you were dead. Your choice," I grumbled nonchalantly.

"You're an idiot. Of course I'd help Gwendolyn."

"Atlas, is that you?" Her sweet, anxious voice floated from behind the door, and I swallowed my anger, accepting my loss of control for the moment, the taste of it like swallowing barbed wire.

I drew my fangs back and opened the door, finding Gwendolyn on the bed, writhing in agony as she stared at us with tears in her eyes, wearing nothing but a towel wrapped around her body, her wet hair combed off her face.

Atlas sprang into the room, his nostrils flaring from the pure strength of the scent of her slick, so intense it fogged my head and my cock immediately stood at attention.

"Gwen," he murmured, taking her into his arms. "I'm so sorry I wasn't here the moment you went into heat. But I'm here now and I've got you. I'll make it all go away."

Her mouth was instantly on his.

A vampire could only take so much, and I couldn't help

myself; I snatched him by the back of the neck, and yanked him away from her. But she followed him like a cute puppy, calling for him.

"Atlas, I need you."

"Do we have a problem?" he asked, turning to glare at me. "This is what you wanted, right?"

I gritted my jaw, fire burning through me, while his wolf's growl rumbled in his chest. It was at that moment my little Darling slid her hand into mine, our fingers interlacing. I noted then, that she also held his hand.

"I want you both. Please don't fight. Please. I need you."

Atlas stiffened, his face scrunching up like the ugly bastard he was. "Are you sure that's what you want? I'm your mate and I'll take care of you."

I cleared my throat, but no one turned toward me.

"I–I need you both. I *want* you both." Her voice shook, and I saw the ache on her tight face as she fought the pain pummeling into her. She began to twitch too, a moan rolling over her throat, and her scent suddenly intensified. She swayed on her feet.

"Enough of this. She comes first, not your insecurity," I snarled.

I stripped out of my pants, standing there naked and fucking glorious. I had nothing to hide, only a huge cock to parade.

Gwendolyn eyed me, practically swooning on the spot. I reached over, catching her instantly, my arm tucked around her back and leaning in toward her mouth.

She gasped, her scent deepening, and we kissed like our

lives depended on it. I speared my tongue into her mouth, stoking the flames. With one deft movement, I pulled her towel off, needing her naked because she was so much more beautiful that way.

When a shadow fell over us, distracting my Darling, she glanced over to Atlas who quickly scooped her into his arms.

My deadpan expression went amiss. She kissed him too, but went feral to rip his clothes off. In moments, he stood naked, his body pressed to hers.

My instinct had me stepping close, so I stood inches from them. It would be so easy to reach down and take her into my arms, to bend her over and claim her all for myself.

I'd never had any qualms about sharing my toys with one of my inner circle, but with Atlas, he brought out the monster inside, flames of jealousy licking at my insides. How good it would feel to shove him out of the window.

Except I was playing nice, wasn't I?

To my surprise, when they broke apart from their kiss, Atlas lifted his gaze to meet mine. "Are we doing this? And just so it's clear, I'm going to hate every fucking second you're here with us. I'm doing this for her. Whatever she needs."

I might have responded with a clever comeback, or better yet, strangled him, but when Gwendolyn's thin fingers wrapped around my cock, I lost my thoughts. Lowering my gaze, I found her kneeling before both of us, a dick in each hand, and she was moaning.

"I want them both in my mouth, at the same time," she demanded.

I growled. "Fuck no—" Then she licked the tip of my erection, wrapping those delicious lips around my shaft. I shuddered, all the blood going to my cock so I couldn't think straight. But she pulled away too quickly, and just as fast stuck Atlas' member into her mouth, coaxing a longing grunt from the bastard.

I wasn't one to compare sizes, but it brought me endless joy to know that I was so much wider in girth than him.

With her hand shifting down to my balls, she literally had me by my jewels, guiding me as close as she bid. Every nerve and muscle in my body twitched. I was born of death and carnage, a fucking vampire king, and yet she had the power to bring me to my knees.

Atlas didn't protest, and maybe that was *his* kink, but I didn't cross swords.

And just when I was going to object, she slid us both into her mouth, the tips mostly going in, and her tongue going frantically, flicking both our heads. The sensation was completely overwhelming, and I found myself moving closer to the fuckhead, not giving a fuck that our dicks touched because the things she was doing with her tongue were fucking madening, making me forget my dick was rubbing up against another's.

"Little omega, that's so perfect."

The fragrance of her slick intensified, the slurping and purring sounds she made telling me she got off on this.

Atlas had his eyes closed, and I had to refrain from using the moment to knock him out. Another wild flick of her tongue sent my hips into a rocking movement because I needed to be completely inside her.

I withdrew out of her mouth, and she looked up at me, still sucking on Atlas like he was the world's sweetest lollipop, her hand between her legs, rubbing her clit feverishly. Lust rippled in her gaze, and I knew she wouldn't remember much of this after she was out of her heat.

"Let's get you on the bed," I said, taking her hand, helping her up, and Atlas' dick flopped out of her mouth. I swept her into my arms as she clawed at my chest.

"Please. Fuck me. Stop the ache. I'm…empty. So empty. It hurts."

"Good idea," Atlas murmured, already hopping up on the bed, laying on his back. Gwendolyn couldn't writhe out of my arms quick enough as she literally jumped on him, straddling him. Atlas groaned from the impact, but he laughed at her. "Fuck, you're beautiful. Now sit on my cock, baby. And let me take care of you."

I watched as she hungrily rubbed herself on his erection, then pushed down on him. His eyes rolled into the back of his head as he growled, hands fisting the bedsheets. "You're so tight. You're going to kill me."

Fury and jealousy thrashed inside me, flooding me as I watched the asshole fuck her in front of me.

Panting, she bounced up and down on him a few times before twisting around, reaching for me.

"Pan," she moaned. "Please. I need you."

Torn in two about being in this situation and yet wanting

to fuck her brains out, I guessed the latter won out because I accepted her hand and climbed onto the bed behind her.

"I've got you. Now, are you ready for me?" I whispered in her ear, my hands lowering to her curvy ass.

"Yes, oh God, yes."

Atlas might have been giving me a death glare, but I rather enjoyed myself in this position. I squeezed her cheeks, before sliding a finger along her crack. Completely drenched, she wouldn't need any added lubrication, and pushing a finger into her rear confirmed it. I replaced it with the tip of my cock, and she was moaning, fucking herself against me as I pressed into that tight little hole.

I unleashed a moan at how hard her ass gripped me the deeper I pushed into her. She cried out, and purrs danced in her throat. Holding onto her hips, I guided myself deeper, and then back out in slow motion, mostly to help stretch her out a bit before I fucked her how I wanted.

Atlas and I started off slowly in motion, trying to keep the same pace, while Gwendolyn tried to move faster. My poor baby. She just wanted to be fucked like an animal, while we tried not to rip her apart. Literally because she was tiny compared to what we were packing.

But it wasn't long before we picked up speed. With my mouth on her ear, I asked, "I'm the first to fuck you in your ass, aren't I?" The whole time I spoke, I watched Atlas whose lips peeled back, a growl rolling over his throat.

He reached up, cupping her breasts. "And I'll always be your first, isn't that right, my little omega?"

She just moaned in response. Unable to answer as her heat tore at her consciousness.

I smiled. "Let's make you scream, little Darling. Let's make all of Darkland hear you."

We both moved faster, my hips thrusting as we fucked her savagely. Just as she wanted us to. I wrapped an arm around her, snatching a breast in my hand, squeezing it, pulling on it.

I grunted from how she gripped me.

"Scream, angel," Atlas commanded. "Let it all out." He had his hand down between her legs, no doubt teasing her gorgeous little clit.

I pummeled into her brutally, the three of us moving into a rhythm that could set the room on fire with how much heat we generated.

She started quivering, her body convulsing, and a scream tore from her mouth as an orgasm barrelled into her. Thrashing hard against me, I wrapped my arms around her middle, holding her, letting her lean against me so I took her weight.

My own climax slammed into me at her pulsing ass around my cock, and for the second time that day, I thrust deep into her, flooding her with my cum, giving her every-thing I had. White stars danced behind my eyes, and I might have heard furball grunting his own release, but couldn't care at all about him. Only my little Darling.

Her screams turned into mewls and purrs, and then weeping cries and laughter. "Fuck. Yes. The pain's gone," she admitted hoarsely.

She was trembling as we all came down together, barely

able to hold herself up from exhaustion. She shivered in my arms, and I pulled out of her. An arm still locked around her middle, I lifted her off Atlas and brought her up with me as I climbed off the bed.

"Feeling better, baby?" he rasped, his gaze heavy lidded and lazy with pleasure.

"Like I'm normal again. Like I could sleep for a week straight." She wriggled out of my grasp, but then almost fell over.

Atlas and I both reached for her, but he caught her first. Quickly, he carried her towards the bathroom, glancing over his shoulder at me as he walked.

"I suppose I've served my purpose…but you know she'll have more of these heats. Maybe I'm not so bad to keep around."

I studied him for a long moment before I responded, well aware that he'd do anything to remain near Gwendolyn. "I don't like you, but right now, I refuse to deal with you when I've got Gwendolyn in my nostrils, on my cock, and on my mind."

"Understood," he said, disappearing into the bathroom.

A few moments later, they emerged, and she threw herself onto the bed, curling herself in the middle of it.

Atlas reached down to grab something from his pants where he'd discarded them, then he sat next to her on the bed. "I've got something for you," he explained softly. "You forgot this back home and I'm certain you want it back."

She made a cute sound and shuffled to sit up, while I stood there, curious myself to see what he brought her.

He placed a ring on a chain into her hand. "I found it in your room."

She blinked a few times, her eyes glistening with such heartache, I was certain she'd burst out crying.

Throwing herself at him, she embraced him. "That's all I have from my mother," she whispered. "You have no idea how much this means to me."

Their heartfelt moment reminded me of a past I tried to forget because I'd lost so much, and I had nothing of that time, not even all my memories. I held back as they hugged, watching as she finally pulled away, rubbed her eyes and drew Atlas down on the bed with her. She glanced over at me, her gaze exhausted and still watery from unshed tears.

"Are you coming to join us?"

I didn't need to be asked twice and moved to lay alongside her, her back against my chest and her head resting on my outstretched bicep.

Atlas, wiped away a stray tear and lay a hand on her hip, his lips on her ear. "I've never seen anything more spectacular, little omega." She turned her head, kissing him. Then she rolled onto her back and smiled at us both.

"I barely have the energy to talk. But thank you," was all she murmured. Her eyelids slid closed, and she lay unmoving. Atlas cuddled up against her, just like a puppy would do.

I hated this feeling, watching them. I hated how Gwendolyn made me want her so badly it ached in my chest.

I didn't move from her side. I couldn't bring myself to.

A knock came at the door, and before I could respond, it opened.

Luke stuck his head inside, his eyes instantly widening with shock when he saw what he clearly hadn't been expecting.

"Pan?" His brow furrowed with disappointment. "This is a surprise." He studied a curled-up Gwendolyn fallen asleep and pinned between me and my enemy.

Atlas craned his head up too, then flopped it back down on the pillow when he saw who it was.

It must have been a strange image indeed. His eyes roamed all over my little Darling.

"She's asleep," I explained. "Something I can help you with?"

I was a bastard when I saw the answer was scribbled all over his face, and I'd be honest–it shouldn't surprise me, but it did. It seemed Atlas and I weren't the only ones vying for Gwendolyn's attention.

A raw, feral look crossed his eyes. "No, all good," he snapped and left the room, shutting the door a bit too loudly. Not enough to wake up the beauty in my arms, but enough to tell me he was pissed to find that if he wanted her, he'd have to share.

I curled up next to her, my lips dragging on the soft flesh of her shoulder, before I lifted my gaze to find Atlas watching me.

"Don't get too comfortable," I instructed. "Your room is down in the cell."

CHAPTER 13

GWENDOLYN

The world was moving. Was there an earthquake? That was my first thought when I opened my eyes and promptly fell off the bed because the room was rocking so much.

Except it only took a second to realize that it wasn't my bed that I'd fallen off. And glancing around, it was obvious that I was no longer in the castle. What I appeared to be, was on a boat.

What the fuck?

I struggled to my feet, feeling like I was going to be sick. I'd never had the strongest stomach when out on the water. My dad would try and take me on his boat sometimes when I was little, hoping to pass on the family business, but those attempts definitely lessened when I threw up every time he took me with him.

You're fine, you're fine, I murmured to myself, trying to get a hold of my stomach. I breathed in through my nose and out through my mouth, and that helped a little bit. But I still wanted to punch whatever motherfucker had put me on the boat without my permission.

The last thing I remembered was being wrapped up in Pan and Atlas's embrace. Had Luke been there too? I was certain I remembered hearing his voice or something. Had I dreamed that?

I shook my head, like that would help me to clear it. And then I walked over to the wooden plank door, surprised when it opened easily.

That was a good sign, right?

Taking a deep inhale, salty air floating through the small corridor ahead of me confirmed I was indeed out on the sea.

Alright, that was concerning, but I wasn't going to panic yet. I carefully walked down the hallway, hearing the distant hum of people speaking. There were wooden steps at the end of the corridor, and I could see the night sky above. I hesitated on the stairs, not sure what I should do, but eventually, I pressed forward. One thing I hated was the idea of being in the dark. And not in the dark, dark, since I was a vampire now, but not knowing what was going on around me, which had been kind of the state of my life since Pan had taken me that day. I was rather sick and tired of feeling that way.

I slowly walked up the stairs, stopping when my eyes could see my surroundings. My heart sank when I saw the skull and crossbones flag that I'd seen the other night. I was on a pirate ship. And it was most likely Hook's pirate ship unless there were a bunch of pirates in this part of world and Pan had just failed to mention it.

For being the middle of the night, the deck was lively. There were men tying ropes, others sewing what looked like parts of the sails. Others were gathered in a circle, joking and laughing as they drank and ate. And farther away, at what I thought was the front of the ship where the helm was, I saw the outline of a male I could tell even from here was huge.

How had I gotten on this ship?

I threw up then, and I wish I could've blamed the waves bashing against the sides of the boat, something the men were quite calm about, all things considered. But I definitely threw up because of panic.

It was weird to see my vomit completely red and bloody. But I guess everything was rather weird lately.

Wiping my mouth with the back of my hand, I steeled myself and then trudged up the stairs. As soon as I came into view, what felt like a hundred eyes were upon me. Trying to be as brave as possible, I walked forward, the wooden planks echoing beneath my feet, and the wind whipping at my hair as I moved toward where the captain was standing.

The walk seemed to take forever, and of course, he made no move to meet me halfway. My insides were trembling, and the closer I got, the more I could make out his form. The helm was set higher than the rest of the ship, so I had to go up a small set of stairs to get to him.

He was as huge as I'd thought.

Over 6'5 at least, with an aura about him that made you feel insignificant. He had a large hat on, that was triangular in shape, the ends turned up almost like a furrow. There were feathers coming out of the side, jaunty looking if you didn't know who they were attached to. As impressive as the large hat was though, my attention got caught on the captain's bare chest. There was a large metal almost shield-looking piece that covered half of his chest. And it wasn't on top of his chest, it was a part of his chest, like something had gotten torn out of his body and that was all they could use to stop up the hole. My gaze traveled from his chest, down his right arm, to where I realized a long, sharp, silver hook acted as his hand. It was fitted snugly against his arm, with no room for a hand to be under it. Meaning he was missing one. Pan had mentioned chunks being taken out of him...but this was more than I had imagined. That was some crocodile.

I dragged my gaze away from his missing hand, not wanting to offend him by staring longer than normal, and I went about examining the rest of him. He was wearing brown leather breeches with tall white socks. I finally glanced at his face, forcing myself not to take a step back as I took it all in. His eyes were black, soulless depths. Dark eyes could look warm, but his held no semblance of warmth. They were cold, and just staring at them had me envisioning death. His face was severe, his full lips pursed in disapproval as he eyed me. There was a small gold hoop earring in his right ear, and his hair was a dark black color, with streaks of silver at his temple, even though I knew if he was Hook, he shouldn't be aging since he was a vampire.

All of that being said, he was incredibly intimidating, and it was all I could do not to shake as I stood in front of him.

He bowed then, catching me completely off guard. His hand grabbed his hat and he brought it to his chest as he leaned forward. "Hook Silver at your service, my lady," he purred before sweeping himself back up.

I wasn't sure what to do. Was I supposed to curtsy? Was he expecting that? If I didn't curtsy in front of a king, I wasn't inclined to curtsy in front of a pirate, even if everything about him was telling me he was dangerous. Perhaps the most dangerous creature I'd come across yet in this place.

"You seem to know me, but I'm afraid, sir, I don't know you. Or what I'm doing here," I replied stiffly, forcing politeness I didn't feel. I glanced around again, half expecting Pan to jump out of the shadows and tell me this was some kind of test. "Where's Pan?"

No sooner had I said his name than the hook came slicing down beside me, embedding itself in the wooden wall I'd been standing against, chunks of destroyed wood flying through the air.

Note to self, don't mention Pan's name.

He apologetically smiled a second later, and I was getting whiplash from the back and forth.

"Forgive me, Gwendolyn." I noted that the rest of the ship had gone silent, but I didn't dare look away to see the expressions on their faces. It was best not to take your attention away from the scary guy.

And he was scary.

He extended his other arm, the one that didn't have a hook at the end of it. "Would you do me the honor of accompanying me to my lounge to discuss things?" he asked politely.

I didn't really feel like I had an option, even if the last thing I wanted was to go with this creature. I didn't miss the way his stare was gobbling up my features.

I tentatively looped my hand around his enormous bicep and he led me down the stairs and around the corner to a door I hadn't noticed before. Opening it up, he glared over his shoulder to the rest of the ship. "Get to work," and I heard their rapid movements as they listened to their captain.

The door opened up into a sumptuous apartment. Unlike the rest of the ship, which had rough plates on the floor, the floors in here had been polished to a smooth shine. There was a huge walnut desk on one side of the room with a luxurious high-back leather chair behind it and an expertly woven rug underneath it. There were dark wooden bookshelves on either side of the desk loaded down with an assortment of leather-bound books. In the middle of the room was a long table that could seat at least fifteen people, made of a cherry oak color that looked like it was polished daily. Black leather chairs surrounded the table, and on the other side of the room, which I looked away from quickly, was an enormous bed with silk sheets and assortments of black and red pillows.

"Can I offer you a drink?" he asked, and I startled when I saw he was no longer standing beside me and was instead by a small circular table loaded down with an assortment of glass decanters filled with various red liquids.

Blood. The bottles were filled with blood. My stomach gurgled at the thought, but luckily, I still felt sick from the rocking motion of the boat, and my hunger was not full force yet.

"Thank you, but I'm fine," I answered politely.

A hard glint came to his gaze. "It's rude to refuse your host, Gwendolyn. We'll have to help you with that."

Help me with that? What the hell did that mean? But I sighed and suddenly understood that the question of if I wanted to drink had not been a request at all–it had been an order. Had he poisoned it? Drugged it?

With my continued hesitation, he poured himself a glass and then took an exaggerated draw from it. He licked the excess blood on his lips, but unlike when Pan or Luke had done the same thing, instead of feeling lust, I just felt fear. "See, just run-of-the-mill blood."

I finally nodded, feeling like I didn't have a choice but hoping at the same time I wasn't making a huge mistake. He poured me a glass and handed it to me, watching expectantly as I took a sip. It was sour in my mouth; not as bad as the nymph blood had been, but definitely not good either.

"It's an especially tasty vintage, isn't it? It was amazing how much blood your alpha had to give," he remarked casually.

I froze. Alpha?

"Alpha Silver," he clarified, and I immediately set the glass down, unable to hide my distaste. He laughed heartily like I'd made a particularly amusing joke.

"It's hard, isn't it? When you know what you like, but you just can't have it...yet."

"I'm not sure what you mean," I answered slowly, feeling like I was in a game where I didn't know the rules.

"But maybe though, waiting is what makes it particularly good," he mused, acting for all intents and purposes like he hadn't heard me.

I said nothing, because what could I say? He obviously wasn't interested in anything I had to offer.

"Do you know what I want more than almost anything, Gwendolyn?"

The fear inside me deepened, and I slowly shook my head, holding my breath, dreading what he was going to utter next.

"I want you, my dear. I want to trigger your heat, slather your slick all over my face, and fuck you unconscious. And then, after that, I want to drink all of your blood." He offered all of that mildly, like a true psycho would, and I found myself taking a few steps back, something he didn't miss.

"You don't even know me," I stammered. Hook sat on the edge of his desk, calmly sipping at Alpha Silver's blood like we were talking about the weather.

"Oh, but you see, I don't have to know you. I only had to smell you during your heat, when your perfume was so strong that I bet every motherfucking citizen in this kingdom was hard." He ended the sentence with a growl, making sure I understood his frustration.

I was frozen in place now, shame coating my throat. It was one of the most personal things that could happen to an omega, and the fact that this asshole had experienced my perfume was almost more than I could take.

"It wasn't unintentional, I assure you." He laughed, and the sound of it felt like oil against my skin.

"I suggest you drink the rest of that blood, Gwendolyn. You're going to need the energy."

"How did you get me? How did you get me from Pan's castle?" I spit out, not understanding how any of this was happening.

"Your lovers had evidently tired you out. They were letting you rest after your were torturing the rest of us with your heat. It wasn't hard to come in through the balcony and grab you." He smiled, and I inhaled in fear when I saw that his mouth didn't just have sharp incisor teeth like the rest of the vampires I'd met. Instead, his mouth was full of serrated sharp teeth, like a shark.

I'd been right to fear the waters here. I could only imagine what that mouth felt like as he was tearing into your skin with those teeth.

"Please. You don't even know me," I gasped again. "You don't have to do this."

"You see, I have something in common with Pan, as hard as it is to believe," he said silkily. "We both want what we want, and we don't let anyone get in the way of what we want."

My mind was racing as I tried to think of a way out of this, but everything was coming up blank.

Would they come for me? Self-doubt trickled through me, my inner self-loathing questioning whether they cared.

"Drink your blood," said Hook, his voice coming out as a

warning. When I made no move to grab my glass, he set down his own.

"Drink your blood, Gwendolyn," he repeated.

But I was frozen, unable to do anything.

The smile stretched across Hook's lips suggested he wanted me to ignore him. He sauntered towards me until he was standing just a foot away, a predatory gleam in his dark, haunting gaze.

Finally, my senses kicked in and I bolted back towards the door, screaming when he grabbed me around the waist and brought me against his body, his hard length rubbing against my back.

"You're not going anywhere," Hook growled. "I told you everything that I wanted to do with you." He took a big inhale, his face buried in my hair, and I swear he got harder against me. He walked me towards the bed, even as I struggled in his grasp. "And all of that is going to start...right now."

He laughed at my efforts to get away, a dark, cruel laugh that sent sharp daggers down my spine. He threw me on the bed, and I stared at him in horror as he loosened the string holding up his breeches. He wasn't wearing anything underneath, and his red, swollen cock greeted me as his pants slipped down.

I couldn't believe this was happening. After everything I'd been through, after everything I'd survived...I wasn't sure this was something I'd get past.

No. I couldn't let this happen.

Something unfurled inside of me as he grabbed my chin and thrust his dick toward my face.

Something I'd never experienced before.

And as my features began to transform, and a terrifying growl ripped from my chest, I wondered what monster he'd unleashed inside of me, and where had it been hiding all this time.

CHAPTER 14

PAN

Luke growled, gripping and thrashing the metal bars, frothing at the mouth like a rabid dog.

He stared at me like he'd rip me to shreds, and I might have thought he was spelled or something if I hadn't heard him whispering Gwendolyn's name when I first walked down here to check up on him. I recalled the shock on his face when he walked in on us yesterday, and he hadn't been right since. Not after discovering Atlas and me in bed with her.

The doc had it bad for Gwendolyn, to the point where he was losing his mind. I just had to get it into his thick skull that I had no aversion to sharing with him. He was one of mine after all, but he first needed to calm the hell down, because you couldn't reason with a madman.

"What the hell's wrong with him?" Crocodile asked, slouching against the stone wall down in the dungeon, arms folded across his chest. "Found him like this out by the bridge."

"He'll be fine," I confirmed. "He's just got some stuff to sort out and process. I'm certain he'll be right as fucking rain any day now. Until then, let him cool down here."

Luke went back to the corner of the cell, cursing like a sailor to himself. Vampires didn't deal well with feeling like something had been taken away from them.

"Luke, come over here," I commanded, enunciating every syllable, the power behind my voice thick.

He lifted his head almost instantly, eyes glassy like he wasn't fully with me. His feet moved forward, until he was standing right in front of me.

I reached through the bars, my hand clasping the back of his head, holding him still, forcing him to look into my eyes. "There is nothing for you to be worried about when it comes to Gwendolyn. She's mine, but I *will* share her with you. So calm the hell down because I need you back to your less crazy self."

He just stared at me, unblinking, and I released him. The connection broke and he stumbled backward, catching himself, looking suddenly lost.

"Shake it off, and I'll be back for you later," I said on my way out, knowing he'd needed it. The thing with vampires was that we could lose our heads and go berserk over the smallest thing. We were wired differently...death did that to you. It messed with the emotional synapses in our brains, which was part of the reason I founded Darkland for those Lost Boys who went astray with no way of getting back.

In Darkland, they were free to be themselves.

My brother, Crocodile, was a prime example, except something hadn't been right with him from the beginning no matter how much I'd helped him. But he was also the only family I had left, and you couldn't choose your family. No matter how fucked up they were.

I was standing outside Gwendolyn's door before I knew it. It stood ajar, and I entered.

"My little Darling, where are you?"

The moment I stepped into the room, the hairs on my arms raised. Something felt off instantly... The remnants of her perfume carried with it a smell of the ocean. The bed sheets were messy, and one pillow was on the floor. I closed the distance to the bathroom, finding it empty.

The answer did not come immediately, and yet a sense of alarm rang through my head.

Not wanting to panic just yet, I headed into the hallway, about to scour the whole fucking castle. It wasn't like she could have vanished with Atlas, seeing he was down in the cells, and yet something still felt off.

I stepped on something and immediately looked down as I lifted my foot to find a small bolt. Picking it up, it rolled across in my palm, letting off tiny sparks. There was only one person who'd use this to secure the metal plates on his body...

Hook.

Fuck!

He patched up the crocodile bites with good old fashioned fairy magic. Most vampires healed over time from injuries with a good feed, but if our kind didn't take blood for a long time after an injury, well, your body never fully repaired.

Hook had spent too long after the crocodile had bitten him without feeding. So now he wore a metal plate for skin across the side of his body where the croc had taken a chunk out of him, and a hook for his hand, keeping them attached to him using these fairy bolts.

A growl rumbled in my chest, urgency pulsing over my thoughts as I saw red.

I unleashed an ungodly sound, fury shooting through me.

"I'm coming, my little Darling."

Rage ripped across my chest, and a roar burst from my mouth. Curling my hand into a fist over the bolt, I darted out of the room at lightning speed, rushing into every room, every location, shouting the one word everyone would understand.

"War!"

With no sign of Gwendolyn, my fears were confirmed, and I found myself back in the cells.

Luke stood by the metal bars swearing a scowl...back to his normal self. Thank fuck for that.

"About damn time you're back. I need you. Hook stole Gwendolyn," I growled, unlocking the barred door and releasing him. "We need everyone ready because today, Hook dies."

"You'd better be fucking joking." Luke trembled, his eyes darkening with fury.

"I'm afraid not." I unfurled my fist, showing him the bolt covered in fairy magic that only Hook used.

"Goddammit," he muttered. "Okay, so today there's going to be a murder." He whipped around, racing up the steps, and I turned to chase after him, anger burning through my veins.

"Pan," Atlas growled from behind me in his dingy cell. "If he's got her, you have to let me fight with you."

"Fuck no," I snapped.

I turned away once more, but his growls grew louder, echoing around the cells.

"Don't be a fucking asshole. This isn't about you and me; it's about saving her. What have you got to lose by having an extra hand? Would you risk it? What if it came down to needing one more hand there that made all the difference?"

I ground my back teeth, unconvinced he didn't have his own agenda that involved taking my Darling away from me if he got the chance during the fight.

"I give you my word that this isn't my attempt to escape. That hungry need for retribution you feel in your chest is only a fraction of how severely I feel as her mate."

The chaos in my head thumped. I was wasting time by arguing with him. I guess I was going to be taking the chance he stabbed me in the back..

"Fine. But one wrong move, and I'll figure out a way to sever your mate bond, and I'll bury you somewhere Gwendolyn will never find."

"You vampires sure do like to hear the sound of your own voices. Are you going to let me out or keep rattling?"

I unleashed a growl and dashed along the long hall of cells to the last one where it was darkest, unlocking the wolf.

He emerged, cracking his neck.

"Keep up, don't get in my way, and don't think of crossing me," I warned.

"You got it. Now let's go."

I snatched him by the back of the neck and dragged him out of the castle faster than he'd ever be able to move on his own.

The moon was hidden, a storm of dark clouds rolling in. The perfect time to hunt.

The Lost Boys of my MC stood before me, vampires who'd ended up under my protection when they'd had no place to call home.

Most of my men stared at Atlas distrustfully, who remained by my side.

"Brothers, tonight, a great travesty has befallen us." I raised my voice so it carried effortlessly over the group who fell silent. "Hook has broken into our home and stolen our little Darling, Gwendolyn."

An explosion of shouts and chatter broke out, fury and snarling, fangs bared. "Today we kill him," Luke shouted, which led to more chatter. Whispers around me intensified and coalesced into a single voice that rose into the night.

"Kill Hook. Kill Hook."

"I gathered you all tonight for a call to battle! A dangerous one where we may not all return but where we have been wronged," I bellowed, and they silenced.

"And the wolf by your side?" someone called out.

"For tonight, he is an ally. He will help us fight the war, which means he's off limits, clear?"

My command was met with growls and hisses, but eventually, it gained a rumble of agreement.

We were suddenly on the move, not bothering with the bikes. Instead, we moved like a savage army, darting into the forest, carving a path for the cliff. Atlas in his wolf form moved just as quickly, surprising me with his agility.

We arrived at the edge of the cliff, staring out at Hook's pirate ship. It looked farther away today. What I noticed was that there was no wind tonight. Nothing moved, and in its place, a heaviness settled over my shoulders. The air was also thick, palpable.

I shut my eyes for a second, and instead of the dark pain that usually fueled my flights, I found myself thinking of only the most beautiful memories, which were all about Gwendolyn. Her lying in front of me, spreading those gorgeous legs for me, her pussy glistening with her desire. And me climbing over her, pushing into her without ceremony.

Already, my feet felt light, my body free.

Opening my eyes, I hovered in the air, my enforcement behind me doing just that. Atlas lingered by the edge, growling at me.

Before I could bark a command, Luke swooped down and snatched the wolf into his arms. I twisted around, projecting my body forward, flying with speed through the cool night's air, my men flanking behind me. I flew up front like the tip of an arrow, directing the path toward the bullseye target.

The pirate ship came into view, the skull and bones flag sitting limply on its pole in the windless night. Fairy lights across the beams revealed no sailors on the main deck or the crow's nest.

The thought that Hook expected us had crossed my mind, but I was hoping we'd still come in as a surprise.

As such, I pivoted to my left, swinging toward the stern of the boat at the rear, away from the cannons and where I saw no weaponry. With my group behind me, I swooped in and came in for a silent landing, hitting the wooden floor with soft feet.

My men had barely dropped around me when the shadows around us came to life. The enemy shifters flew at me, coming at me with teeth bared, claws out.

At first, I couldn't see the boat for how many came at us, but I always loved a challenge.

With a war cry, we charged forward like a great storm, rolling into our enemy with ferocity.

I threw myself into the wall of pirates, fangs bared, catching the first lackey who lunged at me, and seizing him by the throat. His mouth snapped at me, showing me two rows of shark-like teeth, a gruesome result most likely of Hook's experiments with fairy magic. I twisted his neck with ease and tossed him aside when someone else slammed into my back, thrusting me forward from the force.

Whipping around, I lashed out at my attacker--a fucking bear in his animal form, roaring and tossing spittle in every direction.

"You fucker," I growled and threw myself at him with such speed that I knocked him off his feet, then threw punch after punch into his face. I hurled myself into the battle that consumed the main deck of the ship. Bloodlust and the urge to kill beat into my skull as I moved.

Blood splashed across my face from the bear's throat I tore out, and with a roar, I reveled in it. Something heavy steamrolled into my back, sending me sprawling off the bear and onto the floor.

Gritting my teeth, I leaped to my feet and jerked around, my fist already swinging. It clipped a pirate with one eye right in the nose. Blood spurted from his nostrils like a faucet.

By the time I pushed through the fight, I had no doubt my men were on the winning side. But I'd come here to rescue my little Darling, not have fun.

I left behind the screams and massacre, moving with speed, down the steps and onto the main deck, finding two men slouched against one of the masts, snoring like beasts. Drinking, most likely, so I slipped past them and moved with urgency to the cabin of the captain's quarters. Where else would that asshole Hook take her?

On fast steps, I entered his quarters, noting there were no guards, and the hairs on my nape rose. Something didn't feel right in the slightest.

But I didn't give a shit. Not until I found Gwendolyn. I moved frantically, like a madman searching Hook's luxurious rooms. I could just picture him here, dining like he was a god. Disgusting. I was the only god in this place.

I snarled, my fist striking out and punching a hole in the wooden wall.

With each passing second of not finding her, my pent-up fury mounted three-fold.

Darting out of his quarters, I shoved through the chaos, slicing my way past the bodies locked in battle, lashing out at anyone standing in my way.

"Come on, asshole," Crocodile shouted at someone. "I'll make a fucking rug out of you."

I passed Luke who unleashed a primal howl, smashing a wooden bucket over someone's head, sending shards of wood flying in every direction.

"You think you're tough." A skinny thing blocked my path, fists raised, and an explosion of sharp spikes snapped outward from his body...Porcupine. "You're about to have your ass handed to you."

My pulse spiked, my fury was ready to detonate because I still hadn't found her. With no time to entertain this sonofabitch, I threw a round-house kick right to his throat, sending him flying right into Crocodile.

He twisted around, fury burning in his eyes. "Dickhead." He reached down and wrenched the shifter up and over his head, before tossing him into waters known for being infested with all kinds of deadly creatures... including the sharks Gwendolyn was so afraid of.

Throwing myself forward, I passed the chaos and reached the other rooms beneath the steps that lead up to the crow's nest.

That time, I didn't keep silent, but thundered into the rooms like a bull, breaking down any shut doors. There were four down here, to be exact.

On the fourth one, I kicked it open, the wood splintering.

My dead heart shattered into a million pieces at the sight.

Gwendolyn lay curled up in a bed, her ankles chained to metal restraints, attached to long chains that were bolted to the wall.

With huge eyes, she cried out when she saw me, tears sprawling down her cheeks. "Pan." Her voice was a painful shrill as she frantically shuffled to the end of the disheveled bed. Her clothes were ripped, the sleeve hanging off her shoulder. A purple bruise sat beneath an eye...something I knew would heal, but that wasn't the point, was it?

He'd dared to hurt her–this innocent angel who was mine.

I rushed to her side, reaching for her as she reached out for me.

"I'm here now. I've got you."

She curled up next to me, sobbing against my chest, and it completely destroyed me to see her this way.

"How badly did he hurt you?" I had to know before I lost my mind.

She glanced up at me with a haunted look in her eyes, with tears, and I wanted to burn down the whole fucking ship.

"I need to know."

"He forced himself on me, but I fought, Pan. I tried to bite his dick off when he shoved it in my face, and that was when he started to hit me. Apparently, my heat drew him to me." Tears slipped down her cheeks, and I caught them as they dropped from the edge of her jawline. "But I never once backed down. I didn't."

"Did he–" I couldn't quite form the words.

She shook her head. "No. I don't know why he stopped. But...he didn't get that far."

I embraced her, holding her tight, I wished I could push her into me so nothing in this world could ever hurt her again. "You did amazing. Bruises will heal quickly, and I promise you that Hook will pay with his life for what he did to you."

"Do you know where the coward is?" I whispered. "Tell me, sweetheart, is he hiding on the ship?"

She shook her head. "I don't know. But I've been alone for what feels like hours."

Something dark hammered in me, kicking me hard in the chest. I kept her close to me, scared to let her go. She'd suffered so much when she deserved everything she ever desired to come true.

Protect her, protect her... the words ran over my mind.

Her smell filled me once more, but with it came a darkness I wasn't prepared for. It had been a long time since I really cared for anyone to the point that I wanted to destroy the world for them.

"We're going to leave." I crouched down in front of her and curled my fingers into the shackle around her ankle to rip it apart. My mind boomed with hatred toward Hook for taking someone special to me once again.

It boiled my blood, so I snapped the restraint with my bare hands. I moved to the second shackle and tore it off.

Hurrying, I collected my little Darling into my arms. She wrapped herself around me, tucking her face into the curve of my neck. In seconds, I was outside with her where bodies littered the main deck. From what I'd seen, all were the enemy, but I didn't have time to check how many casualties we'd endured.

Climbing up to the crow's nest, I whistled, gaining Luke and Crocodile's attention. With one look my way, they saw she was in my arms and they understood we'd gotten what we came for. In moments, I was levitating, then I pushed forward, racing across the ocean.

She held onto me with a death grip, and it pained me to know that under my watch, Hook had taken her from me. It drove me fucking mad to think that he tried to rape her.

That part ruined me, and Hook was going to regret what he'd unleashed. I'd do whatever it took to get revenge for her.

Without pausing, I flew us right to the front steps of our castle, then hurried her directly to the doc's infirmary, figuring he'd need to check for injuries.

I lay her in bed, and there was no hesitation with me climbing in beside her. She curled up facing me, and I brought her closer, keeping her close to me.

"Nothing is ever going to touch you again. You're home now."

She didn't respond right away, so I stroked her head. She needed time, and I'd wait for a lifetime. Whatever she needed, I'd be there for her.

With a kiss on her brow, I whispered, "We all carry scars from our past, but they aren't a sign of weakness; they're a symbol of how powerful you really are."

CHAPTER 15

GWENDOLYN

Days had passed since my time with Hook. My bruises had long since faded, but the inside scars…those were taking time to go away. I wasn't quite sure why it was affecting me so much. Maybe it was because I had been spirited away while I was sleeping. Maybe it was because he'd made me beg. Maybe it was just because I could still feel Hook's malicious fingerprints against my skin…

The thing was…I couldn't remember how I'd gotten from his bed, to suddenly chained against the wall. I knew he hadn't actually penetrated me because I wasn't sore between my legs at all, and my clothes had still been in their proper place. But it was a mystery to me why he'd stopped, and why I couldn't remember the time between lying there on the bed, him hovering over me, and ending up chained.

Either way, I wasn't doing awesome. Luke, Pan, and Atlas

all took turns staying with me in my room, which was good since all I wanted to do was sleep, and I didn't think I could sleep without them watching over me. Atlas had been let out of his cell and given his own room since helping Pan rescue me. Or maybe it was because of Atlas's new status as my mate? We still needed to discuss the whole fated mate thing, but I didn't have the energy to delve into that, even if the thought of it made me extremely happy.

Two weeks had passed like that, with me barely eating, and mostly sleeping, before my door crashed open and Pan stood there, his jaw clenched as he saw I was still lounging in my bed, as I had every day since coming back.

"Get dressed," he ordered. "We're going out."

"I don't feel like it," I responded instantly, but he was already walking towards me. He scooped me out of bed and walked into the bathroom, heading immediately towards the shower and flipping it on.

"What are you doing?" I yelped, realizing that he had no intention of putting me back in my bed, or doing anything else I wanted.

"You smell, little omega, and not good. I'm not going to let Hook control your life, and that's exactly what's happening every day you spend in that fucking bed." He reached into the water and must've been satisfied with the temperature, because, without another word, he walked straight into the shower, both of us still in our clothes.

I yelped, but he was unrepentant as he ripped off my clothes and began to methodically wash me. He'd been wearing a black leather vest and tight black pants, and they were now sealed against his skin, soaked with water.

"You're being an asshole!" I screeched, even though I knew he was right. It wasn't like I usually spent my days in bed, which meant that I was letting Hook get to me, something no doubt he would take great delight in knowing.

But still…

"Men like Hook don't get to affect you. I'm going to do everything I can to rid him from this realm for what he's done, but in the meantime, I'm going to get you out of your head."

His words silenced me, and I remained quiet as he finished washing me. After I'd been thoroughly cleaned, he stripped off his clothes and began to wash himself. Licks of heat passed through me as I watched his hands run over his beautiful body, the first I'd felt since Hook had touched me

"See something you like?" he purred, and I gulped, my nipples hardening into points and the inside of my thighs growing wet as slick dripped from my core.

"Do you need a little reminder of who you belong to?" he murmured.

I nodded, deciding that was exactly what I needed.

I leaned forward and pressed my lips against his hard chest, letting my hands explore his broad expanse of muscle, the dips and contours of his abs which never failed to make me lose my mind. My fingers continued to trail down until I got to his long, hard dick. I gripped him hard with both hands, stroking him up and down and twisting at the top just like he liked.

He groaned and then his arms went around me, slipping down until they got to my ass. He picked me up abruptly and held me against the shower wall as I continued to work his dick between us. Keeping one arm under my ass to hold me steady, he moved the other to the front, quickly finding the perfect spot on my clit and beginning to build me up. We stayed there, just like that, until we both melted into simultaneous orgasms.

And then somehow, a few minutes later, he fucked me against the wall. And by the time we ended the shower, Hook's actions on that ship were just a little more in the past.

———

My hand was gripped in Pan's as we soared through the skies. He'd had me dress up for the night; I was in a black leather corset top that made my boobs and stomach look amazing, and a short red leather mini skirt. To complete the outfit, I was wearing lace-up black stiletto boots. I looked hot, and clearly, he thought so too because we almost didn't make it out of my room after he saw me.

Pan still wasn't telling me where we were going, only offering that we were going to have some fun.

We'd been flying for a few minutes when lights lit up the darkness in the distance. The closer we got, the more I could see there were small wooden buildings set up on a cove. One particular building caught my eye because it was yards off the shore, held up in the water on wooden stilts, connected to the shore by a long dock made of faded wooden planks.

"That's where we're going," he called to me, a glint of excitement in his gaze.

We landed on the deck, just outside the building, loud music pouring out from the front entrance. Peeking inside, I could see the place was packed.

Pan kept my hand in his as he led me inside to what I realized was a crowded bar, but not any kind of bar that I'd ever seen. Because half of it was in the water, the top of the bar was lying flush with the water. Males and females were swimming in front of it, fancy cocktails in their hands. The other half of the bar was similar to what I'd seen before-- everything above water with shelves of liquor bottles behind the thick wooden bar top.

I couldn't take my eyes off the underwater section.

"Are those..." My voice trailed off as I stared at them in the water...who had tails.

"Mermaids?" Pan finished for me, sounding amused.

The bar was completely packed, and it was interesting that no one seemed that impressed by Pan's entrance, which I assumed meant he was a frequent visitor here. Their attention was actually focused on me. More curious glances than anything else.

Pan led me straight towards the bar, where they did act normal in immediately clearing the space for him. A yummy-looking man, dressed in nothing but a pair of breeches and what looked like purple sparkles all over his chest and highlighting his cheekbones, came up to us immediately.

"The usual?" he asked as he and Pan exchanged some kind of complicated handshake.

"Yes, and some of the Sorceress for her," he answered, nodding his head at me. The bartender's mouth curled into a smile as his eyes lazily dragged from the top of my head down to my…breasts.

Pan gave out a low growl. The bartender's eyes immediately moved away, and he sent a questioning look to Pan.

"She's mine," Pan said simply.

"It's a shame. She's delicious looking."

Despite Pan's displeasure, the bartender gave me a wink before turning around and grabbing some bottles off the shelf.

"A friend of yours?" I asked, feeling like I was getting a peek at another side of Pan.

Pan's gaze was darting all over the room, most likely noting all the people that were staring at me.

"This is a bad idea," he commented, distracted.

The bartender set a glass filled with red liquid down in front of me. "My name's Sean, by the way," he called over the din of the crowd.

"Sean," Pan chided, clearly annoyed.

Sean held up his hands. "Hey, I'm just being friendly."

"Go be friendly somewhere else."

Sean rolled his eyes exaggeratedly and then shot me one last wink before going to help another customer at the bar.

"Sean's a fey," Pan explained casually. "They flirt with everything that moves. I'd forgotten about that." He frowned, like he was confused why it bothered him.

I was only half listening because I'd just taken a sip of the drink and the taste of the blood had exploded across my taste buds.

"What is this?" I murmured. "It's yummy, and…"

"It's going to get you drunk?" Pan teased as he sipped his own darker red drink. "It's sorceress blood. It's one of the only ways that a vampire can actually feel intoxicated. I thought you might want to let go tonight."

Evidently, I did want to "let go" because I was already throwing back more of it, enjoying the bubbly feeling spreading through my veins. I swung around on my barstool, taking a look at the occupants of the bar while I continued to take deep gulps of my drink.

"I can't believe I'm looking at mermaids."

They were gorgeous, every single one of them. Their hair was all various shades of green, with what looked like streaks of glowing paint across their cheekbones. Their tails were all different shades of green as well, matching whatever their hair color was, and they were wearing very little up top. I averted my eyes when I realized that the mermaid I'd been staring at was just wearing what looked like netting made out of seaweed as her top…and I could see her nipples clearly.

When she noticed me looking at her, she grinned, crooking her finger at me. I found myself sliding off my stool, wanting to go to her. Pan's hand gripped my arm. "Are you sure you want to go over there?" he asked, sounding amused once again.

My head was spinning a little. Everything was wonderful. I loved this place.

"I can make a new friend," I told him excitedly. I knew I

should probably be wondering why he looked so amused at that moment, and why I was acting so happy all of a sudden...but I was too excited about going over to where the mermaids were to think any deeper about it.

"I did say I wanted you to have fun," Pan muttered, releasing my arm and allowing me to walk over to the mermaid bar. I got to the end, where the wooden bar made way for what looked like concrete steps into the water, and I stared in distress from my black leather boots to my new mermaid friend. She slid off the stool she'd been floating on in the water and made her way over to me.

"Let me help you with those," she said in a musical, lilting voice that had me leaning toward her.

"Mariana," Pan said from behind me.

"She's beautiful, Pan," the mermaid—Mariana, I guess–purred.

My cheeks flushed as I took another sip of my drink, the warmth spreading even more through my body. I felt loose, free, better than I'd ever felt in my life.

Mariana pouted, her plump lips inviting, "I just want to meet her," she said innocently. She'd been intent on unlacing my boots, something I hadn't even noticed, and before I knew it, they were both undone and she was tapping my foot to help me slide them off before she reached out her hand towards me.

"Come here, sweetheart," she murmured, and even though a voice in my head told me that Luke was the one who called me "sweetheart", I found myself reaching out to her and allowing her to lead me into the water.

The water was chilly, but not freezing, and my drink was doing a great job of keeping me comfortable. I went in up to my waist, and she wrapped an arm around my waist, her fingers stroking against the skin between my now-soaked skirt and my corset top.

"You're beautiful, little one," she murmured.

"So are you," I answered, my voice coming out dreamy sounding.

I felt so good, so happy. Look at me making friends. I glanced up, my head snapping back when I saw that Pan was glowering down at the two of us, his heated gaze focused on where her fingers were touching my skin.

Someone chose that moment to come talk to Pan, and his jaw ticked as he listened to whatever they were saying.

"Sean," he snapped, his voice reverberating through the bar. A second later, my new bartender friend was there, holding another glass of my delicious drink.

"Watch her. Don't let her have too much fun," he growled, leveling a look at both Sean and Mariana in warning.

"I'll be right back," he tossed at me as he strode away with the male who'd been talking to him, exiting through a door where I could see what looked like someone tied to a chair through the entry.

That was strange.

I shrugged it off. Pan could go be all evil-kinglike, I was here to have fun.

"Why haven't I seen you before?" Mariana whispered in my ear, her fingers continuing to stroke my skin. Sean handed me my drink, giving Mariana a warning stare.

"You heard Pan. Please don't get him pissed off and ruin my bar," he cautioned sternly.

She giggled, the sound caressing my skin as I listened and drank my drink. The whole world was sparkling around me, and the water no longer even felt cold...it felt like a warm bath. I felt more hands caressing my skin, and I looked over to see some more of the pretty mermaids surrounding me, all of them cooing and ahhing over me.

There was a pulsing beat playing in the bar, a beat that felt like it was connected straight to my clit. I held my drink over my head and began to dance sloppily in the water as the mermaids rubbed against me.

I'd never partied...obviously. When I was old enough to do things like that, I wasn't able to because I was basically a servant in Sussana's house.

So it was nice to...let go.

"Watch that hand," Sean called, taking his job seriously as he eyed Mariana's hand on my ass. She removed it with a sweet, innocent-looking smile even as her other hand rubbed against my stomach. There were girls—and guys—that kept trying to flirt with him, but he brushed them off, keeping his focus on me.

Pan's reputation preceded him, obviously.

The mermaids and I danced and splashed around, and I continued to drink.

I drank until the world seemed to be literally made of sparkles and Hook seemed like nothing but a curse word or a bad dream.

Pan hadn't come out of the room yet, but I was having so much fun with my new friends that I didn't mind.

Suddenly, Mariana turned me towards her and plastered her body against me. Her skin was glowing, the sparkles I saw everywhere reflecting off her body like she was some kind of angel or something.

"Do you like girls?" she asked in a flirty, lilting voice, one of her hands twirling pieces of my hair and the other one dancing across the top of my breasts.

I thought I heard Sean's voice saying something, but I couldn't make out what it was. My gaze was focused on Mariana's face which was moving towards mine. Mariana's focus was on my lips, I realized...belatedly. And a second later, they were pressing softly against mine.

Suddenly, she was ripped away from me, a shocked cry falling from her lips, and then Pan was there, his chest heaving as he pulled me possessively against his body.

"I told you to watch her," he growled at Sean, who looked petrified...but still glittery as he stood there.

I turned in Pan's arms to face him. "Don't be mad. I'm having so much fun," I told him brightly. His anger wasn't even touching me thanks to the golden sunshine that seemed to be floating through my veins.

His face softened as he watched me, a small smile crossing my face. "I'm trying to let you have fun, little Darling. But I don't like very much when others touch you."

"You let Atlas and Luke touch me," I whispered, my hands going to his face and stroking lightly against his beautiful features.

"They're the only ones I'm making an exception for."

"What about Crocodile?" I continued, marveling at how his skin seemed to be made of glitter under my fingertips.

"I only let him continue because he was making you feel so good. He was punished greatly for what he did. He won't do it again."

Hmm. I guess that explained why I hadn't seen him for a while.

"I've never been free," I told him as he leaned forward and brushed his lips against mine.

"And you won't ever be free. You belong to me now. You'll always belong to me. But if you want to experience something, little omega, you can experience it by my side."

"But no kissing girls," I murmured with a smile.

"No kissing anyone but the three of us," he clarified darkly, kissing me hard enough to take my breath away.

"I'm really drunk," I murmured when his lips left mine.

"I noticed that," he smirked.

We moved against each other in the water. I could feel eyes on us, but I'd forgotten all about my mermaid friends now that Pan was back. The only thing that could make the night better was if Luke and Atlas were here. I missed them.

"Want to get out of the water?" Pan murmured, trailing kisses across the shell of my ear and down my neck, the sharp prick of his teeth occasionally nicking against the skin.

I moaned and Pan groaned in response. "Best get you out of here, little Darling. You're starting to smell good enough to eat."

I pouted. "But I'm having so much fun," I whined.

"How about I grab some sorceress blood to take with me?" he promised, and my eyes lit up.

He'd thrown back his head to laugh at me when, suddenly, a pair of elegant hands were encircling his waist, pushing in between us.

"Hi Pan," one of the pretty mermaids giggled, her lime green hair floating behind her in the water.

"Get off me, Lorena," Pan ordered, his tone promising violence if she didn't listen.

But his words weren't enough. Because at the sight of someone touching Pan, the glitter was quickly fading, and instead, something dark was building inside my gut. I could just tell she'd fucked him. She'd gotten to touch his perfect body.

I knew it didn't make sense, especially since one of the mermaids had kissed me, but I couldn't take her hands on his body.

Pan was eyeing me curiously as he pulled her arms away from him.

"Gwendolyn," he said cautiously. "Are you alright?"

Her face appeared next to his and she licked the side of his face.

And that was it.

I sprung forward...my teeth bared....changed into something desperate to tear her to shreds...

———

Atlas

I'd been watching from her balcony for hours, waiting for her to come back with Pan and feeling guilty that I hadn't been able to distract her better myself. I stared at the starry sky.

I didn't miss it as much as I would have thought, though.

Since the moment I'd let myself have her, Gwendolyn had become the sun for me, my centerpiece for existence.

As corny as that sounded in my head, it was the most fitting way to describe how I felt about her. She was the most important thing to me. She was the beginning and the end of my story. That's why I'd done everything to find her here, even when I was sure it meant sudden death. Because a life without her might as well have been death.

A figure appeared in the skies in the distance and I straightened up, just knowing that it was Pan. Except, why was he holding Gwendolyn like that? Almost like she was passed out. He hadn't told us where he was going, although Luke had assured me up and down that he wouldn't let any harm come to her. If she was so tired that she passed out, or she'd lost consciousness, I didn't call that "taking care of her".

A growl rumbled in my chest as they got closer, and I realized she was, indeed, comatose in his arms. He landed smoothly, and I reluctantly admitted to myself that he was cradling her as if she was the most important thing to him.

"Not now, wolf," he spat, striding into the room with her in his arms. She was dressed in quite the outfit, and I only let myself admire how sexy she looked for one second before going back to being worried about her.

He walked to the door and threw it open. "Luke!" he

yelled. "Get your ass in here." I guess it said a lot for vampiric hearing, because this was quite the castle, and Luke appeared not a minute later, anxiety streaming across his features when he saw Gwendolyn's prone form.

"Can you at least explain it to him?" I asked sarcastically, trying to withstand the urge to rip her out of his arms.

Pan ignored me.

"We were at La Isla," he began, and Luke raised an eyebrow.

"I bet the mermaids loved that," he interjected.

Mermaids? Those existed? I didn't know why I was so surprised; I'd learned everything existed, but for some reason, that tale being true was blowing my mind.

Pan huffed. "Oh, they did. They were all about her...until they weren't."

"Just spit it out. What's wrong with her?" I growled, and he shot me a dirty look.

"We were about to leave, and one of the mermaids put her arms around me, and right as I was pushing her away... Gwendolyn just..." His voice trailed off like he was seeing it in his head again and was still just as astonished.

"She...what?" pressed Luke.

"She transformed into a giant violet-colored wolf. She was walking on two legs and she just went rabid. Before I could do anything, she destroyed the entire bar. We're going to have to rebuild it for Sean, if he ever talks to us...if he wakes up."

"If he wakes up?" repeated Luke, his face scrunched up in confusion. I was still caught up on the whole purple wolf monster thing that he was claiming Gwendolyn had transformed into.

She was definitely in girl form right now.

I tried to remember if I'd ever heard what she shifted into before. Certainly not a giant purple monster. As an omega, she would have been small in her wolf form—dainty, even.

"She destroyed everything, Luke. I've never seen anything like it. I was just lucky that she didn't kill anyone, just severely maimed them. The mermaid who had her arm around me is going to have to grow back a new one. She and her girls weren't very pleased about that." Pan smirked. "It was incredible. At least now I know that she's got some major feelings for me."

I huffed and he shot me a wide grin, loving to rub in the fact that my fated mate had it just as bad for him as she did for me. It was going to take a minute for that to sit right.

Luke was in front of Pan now, his hand gently moving her disheveled hair from her face. I didn't miss the look of longing written across his features.

He had it just as bad as the rest of us.

I was trying to get over that as well, but at least Luke was a million times more likable than his king.

"Set her down on the bed," Luke ordered, and Pan immediately did what he said, gently laying her down, his gaze dancing across her face, the unmistakable look of…obsession in his eyes.

I was well versed in that feeling when it came to Gwendolyn.

"How did you get her to change back?" Luke asked, as he

felt her pulse and took out a stethoscope from a bag I hadn't noticed him carrying.

Pan stiffened, not looking proud of himself. "I had to knock her out," he said after a long silence. We both stared at him incredulously.

"Don't look at me like that. It was only a matter of time before she did something we couldn't go back from, and then we'd be at war with the whole supernatural population, and not just Hook. I just used pressure points to get her down; it's not like I punched her," he snapped defensively.

Again, I just couldn't imagine it in my head, her transforming into a beast that attacked everyone.

"Something happened when she was turned? Did something go wrong?" I asked worriedly.

Pan glared at me. "Of course not. I know how to turn someone into a vampire."

Luke was biting his bottom lip, like he knew something he wasn't saying.

"Spit it out," I snarled, and Luke's eyes flashed at my tone.

"It is strange that she still perfumes, and that she had a heat." He paused, like he was trying to think of the right words to say that wouldn't piss off his asshole king.

"I just wonder if something is different about her. I never heard of an omega being changed; maybe there's something to that. Omegas are such biologically interesting creatures to begin with; maybe they make interesting vampires."

The way he spoke made it seem like he didn't actually believe that theory, and it didn't sound quite right to me. I wasn't sure that an omega would warp into a monster; it went against their very natures. Something told me there was more going on to this than met the eye.

"Has she been changing like that since you brought her here?" I asked, trying to not sound too bitter talking about the fact he'd taken my fated mate from me.

Pan and Luke both shook their heads. "I probably wouldn't have taken her to a bar if I'd known she was going to try and kill everyone," drawled Pan sarcastically, and my hands fisted as I took a deep breath to restrain myself from shifting and attacking him.

I'd love to show him who was the biggest monster in the room.

Just then, a sigh slipped from Gwendolyn's sweet lips, and all three of us turned so our attention was immediately glued to her face.

Luke had a stethoscope over her heart, although what he was listening for...I wasn't sure. Since she didn't have a heartbeat anymore.

He shook his head as he pulled it away. "Everything seems normal. Her skin isn't flushed. I'm going to have to do some more research about this," he muttered, and then he was practically running out the door.

"He's going to the library," explained Pan, exasperatedly. "If this has ever happened to anyone else, he'll find out about it. It will be in those books." I nodded and moved towards the bed, settling on the other side of her.

"I have to go do some damage control about what happened tonight," Pan said regretfully, stroking her cheek with the back of his hand. "I don't want to leave her, but I don't want it spreading all over Darkland about what happened."

"Well, I won't leave her side," I offered, thinking this was the perfect opportunity to get to spend time with her, even if she did sleep through it.

He nodded, looking conflicted as he continued to stare at her. Finally, he shook his head and stood up. "Yell for Luke if anything seems off," he snapped, waiting for my nod before he prowled out of the room, shutting the door behind him.

I sighed happily, glad that I was alone with her at last.

Before her heat, I probably would've been trying to spirit her away from this place. But now I knew that she was connected to them, connected to this place. It would only hurt her to take her away. The only thing I could do was stay here with her, and that wasn't a great burden. I would do whatever it took to make her happy.

She sighed again, and her fingers were moving, tapping on the bed like she was listening to music in her dreams. It took a couple more minutes, but finally, she opened her eyes and I was met with her brilliant amber gaze. She smiled when she saw me, lighting up my whole world when she did so.

"Atlas?" she murmured, confused. She glanced around the room. "Wasn't I at a bar before this?" She groaned and squeezed her eyes closed for a second. "I shouldn't have drank that sorceress blood. I must've blacked out."

I frowned, realizing that she didn't remember shifting; she didn't remember what had happened.

Which was definitely abnormal, because regular shifters

were still aware of everything that was going on around them when they turned.

"What's the last thing you recall?" I asked cautiously.

She pursed her lips, her forehead wrinkling as she tried to remember.

"I think I was dancing with Pan?" she mused. "I think a girl was flirting with him!" She sat up, looking around the room suspiciously, like she expected the mermaid to pop out at any moment. "Where's Pan?" she growled, sounding almost as possessive as the three of us were towards her. I hoped she sounded like that about me.

"He just went to deal with some things," I said vaguely, deciding not to mention the whole shifting into a giant wolf monster right now until we figured it out more. No need to frighten her when she was still getting the hang of the first monster she'd been turned into.

I really needed to stop calling vampires monsters since my fated mate happened to be one of them now.

Satisfied with my answer, she rolled over on her side.

"Do you feel okay?" I asked, stroking her hair as we watched each other.

"Better than I should with how much I drank," she murmured with a laugh.

"Did you at least have fun?"

She grinned softly. "It was nice... Not to be me for a minute tonight."

"What do you mean?" I asked, confused.

"It was nice to feel free, and to not feel weighted down by all the stupid thoughts I constantly have in my head about myself." Her nose was scrunched up, and I could tell she was embarrassed by what she'd just admitted to me.

"I'm sure with a group effort, we'll be able to get rid of those dark thoughts. I have no problem working to get an 'A' on that particular assignment."

She blushed at my words.

A thought hit me then. I'd been talking about how much I loved this girl in my head for what seemed like forever, but had I ever actually said it…to her beyond that moment in the cells? A rush of shame flowed over me.

"You know you mean everything to me," I said haltingly, watching as her eyes gleamed and welled with moisture.

She didn't say anything; she just continued to look at me like she couldn't believe the words that were coming out of my mouth.

"I should've told you that I loved you a long time ago, because that's how long it's been--so long that I can't remember not loving you," I whispered, loving how the words sounded on my tongue. "I love you, Gwendolyn. I'll always love you."

Tears were streaming down her face now, a look of wonder in her beautiful gaze.

"Say it again," she murmured.

I grinned at her. "I. Love. You."

Her body was shaking as she threw herself towards my chest, burying her face in my neck.

"I love you too," she cried in a muffled voice, her lips moving against my skin as she spoke, the sensation, and her words, giving me shivers.

We lay there for the next little while, and I whispered the words to her over and over again, hoping I could replace whatever thoughts she had about herself with the knowledge that she was my entire existence.

Who cared if I was a bastard son? Who cared if I was the alpha that my father had never wanted? Who cared about anything? Everything dimmed in the knowledge that she loved me back. I'd found the other half of my soul.

And as she clung to me on the bed that night, I vowed to protect her. We'd figure out what had happened to her. And then I'd make it alright.

I promised.

CHAPTER 16

GWENDOLYN

A knock sounded on my door. Atlas had just left to grab some food for us. There were two guards out on the balcony though, their gazes sharp as they searched the skies for any sign of Hook. I shivered just thinking of him invading my space again. I would have asked to switch rooms, but fortunately, I had no memory of him stealing me away. And I was never alone. That helped to assuage my fears as well.

I slid off my bed and walked to the door, frowning when I saw who it was…

Crocodile.

"What are you doing here?" I sniffed, beginning to close the door on him. He put his palm on the door and stopped it from closing.

"I know I'm the last person you feel like talking to right now… but I'd really like to apologize."

My gaze widened. "You—want to apologize?" I stuttered.

I'd certainly never expected an apology from him. I wasn't sure he was even capable of it. I eyed him suspiciously, definitely not trusting him.

"Look, you can stab me with this knife if I fuck-up," he said with a sigh, pulling a knife from his belt and pushing the hilt forward for me to take.

"Something tells me you'd probably get off on that." I took the knife from his hand anyway, and against my better judgment, opened the door farther and let him in.

"All right, say what you have to say," I snapped, not feeling particularly generous at that moment. My mind drifted back to that night when he'd impersonated Pan. It had been hot, but a lot of what I felt that night had been because of the experience I'd just had with Pan and the feelings he'd evoked. When Crocodile was himself, I didn't get the same fluttery, star-crossed yearning inside of me that I did with Pan, Atlas…and Luke.

"I'm sorry about that night," he began, and his face actually looked pained, like he was sorry.

"It started off as one thing, and then I just took it too far. The chance to be with you like that…" His voice trailed off and he looked at the ground, a slight blush to his cheeks.

I realized then that he had feelings for me. Feelings…that I didn't return. My anger dissipated, just a little bit, in the face of that truth.

"I'm sorry I don't feel like that about you," I finally said quietly, and his shoulders drooped.

"I know you don't feel that way towards me. I could feel it

even when I was inside you, that all of your emotion was for my brother, and I guess the wolf as well." He shrugged his shoulders sheepishly, and I didn't bother bringing up that I had feelings for a third guy as well. I would probably just be rubbing salt in the wound at that point.

"Something's always been wrong with me. My entire life. I just felt like something was missing inside, and I've been searching for it in all the wrong ways. I'm finally realizing now that I'm not going to find it by hating my brother, and I'm certainly not going to find it trying to steal his girl." He chewed on his lip, while I stared at him, still amazed that all of this was happening.

"Why have you hated Pan all these years?" I asked softly.

He crossed his arms in front of himself, almost defensively, but when he spoke, it was calm and quiet. "I begged Pan to change me after he was transformed. And I guess I hated him afterward for actually listening to me and doing it."

He sighed and brushed an exasperated hand through his hair, a move that was very similar to his brother's mannerisms.

"It's stupid. I've been stupid," he continued. "You'd think that it wouldn't have taken me a couple thousand years to realize that."

I wasn't sure what to say; he'd thrown a lot at me just then, but despite everything he'd done, I was finding myself believing him. And I hoped for his sake, and Pan's, that he would actually follow through with changing.

"I think she's out there..."

I cocked my head. "Who's out there?" I asked.

"The piece of me that's missing. From the second I saw you...I was hoping you were her." His smile was bittersweet. "But I'm getting better at wrapping my head around the fact that you're not."

He tipped his head at me and then began to walk back towards the door, before stopping in the entryway.

"I'm going to be leaving soon," he said quietly. "I think it'll be best for everyone that we get some distance, and maybe it's about time that I start writing my own story instead of living in Pan's and trying to wreck it."

An image came to my head, of two dark-haired boys running through the meadow, their laughter filling the air. Something told me they'd once been like that. I just hoped that they someday could be like that again.

"I forgive you," I murmured, and I watched as his body trembled from my words. "And I hope with everything in me that you find what you're missing."

He was still for a long moment, and then he turned and glanced at me over his shoulder. "Thanks, Gwendolyn," he said... And then he was gone.

I stood there for a few minutes, feeling distraught over our conversation, but realizing I felt hopeful too. I finally walked over to the door that he'd left through and closed it, feeling like I was closing a chapter of my life as I did so.

And then I went back and sat on my bed, wondering if Crocodile would ever find what he was looking for and who he would be after he found it.

***

The next time a knock sounded on the door, it was a far more welcome face behind the door. I grinned widely when I saw it was Luke standing there.

"Hello, sweetheart," he purred warmly, giving me a sexy wink for good measure. I couldn't help but blush even though I knew he used it as a weapon. I was defenseless against it.

He looked especially good today, his golden-red hair offsetting nicely with his tight, royal blue shirt.

"I was wondering if I could steal you away for a bit?" he asked.

Luke's voice was eager and hopeful, and my insides fluttered like they always did around him.

"I'd love that," I answered shyly, and his beautiful grin widened.

"Great!" There was so much exuberance in his voice, and my blush deepened. Luke...really liked me. I was getting that now. It was hard to believe that such a perfect creature thought I was something worth liking, that any of them felt that way.

It was going to take a while to get years of being told I was worthless out of my head. But the way he was looking at me certainly helped the effort.

I extended my hand to him, watching his eyes fill with momentary shock before he eagerly took my hand and led me out of the room.

"Where are we going?" I asked as he walked me through the dimly lit hallways, out into the night.

"It's a surprise," he answered, giving me another wink.

"But I think you're really going to like it."

We'd just gotten outside when Luke surprised me with a peck on the lips.

"Oh," I squeaked, my free hand brushing against my lips. They were burning where he'd pressed against them, and everything inside of me was hoping he'd do it again.

There was a pleased look on his face as he squeezed my hand. "Soon, sweetheart."

He pulled me a few steps from the castle. "Put your arms around my neck." As soon as I wrapped my arms around him, he pushed off from the ground, and we were flying. The warm night air was especially balmy tonight, feeling like a soft caress as we soared through the sky. We flew away from the sea, the forest stretched out like a dark tapestry beneath us. I laid my chin on Luke's shoulder, absorbing the beauty around me.

I'd never really liked the night. I'd always been so exhausted from working around the house all day that I wanted nothing more than to sleep. I was appreciating more and more the dark beauty of the midnight hours. I thought that I'd miss the sunsets, but I hadn't yet. I felt more at home underneath the dark stars of Darkland than I ever had in my old life.

I wasn't sure what that said about me.

We began to descend then, pulling me out of my reverie. We were heading for an open glen in the woods. Nothing looked out of the ordinary about it, but I was just happy to be spending time with Luke.

He landed us softly but continued to hold me loosely.

"You do know that I can fly myself," I teased, as his fingers twitched around my waist, like he was holding himself back.

"Mmmh, I have heard that somewhere." His gaze was dancing across my features. He looked so handsome in that moment, even more than usual, with the breeze blowing his hair gently and the moon's glow turning it darker than normal.

"You're crazy beautiful," I spat out, the words just erupting out of me. Immediately, I felt like an idiot, but he seemed charmed by my words.

"I'm glad you feel that way, sweetheart. Because you're going to have to love my face for a very, very long time."

He groaned when he saw the look of panic on my face when he'd used the word "love". It felt like I was heading that way, but the idea of falling in love with him was terrifying. The idea that I was having feelings for three different males...one of who was very much an asshole, was terrifying.

"I'll work on that, sweetheart," he murmured, patient as always.

He led me into the middle of the clearing and pulled me with him to the ground until I was sitting in his lap.

"Look up," he ordered, and my jaw dropped when I saw shooting stars rocketing all over the sky.

"It's amazing." I gasped.

"I know," he answered, but there was an ache in his voice that had me turning from the beautiful sight above me to his beautiful face.

"What's wrong?"

He closed his eyes for a second, as if my question pained him.

"They just remind me of my mother. Shooting stars were her favorite. She dragged us outside even if she just heard a rumor there was going to be one. She had little knickknacks all over the house, and my dad carved her a new one every year." There was a glossiness to his gaze that had me entranced. What did it say about me that I was finding myself attracted to his pain?

"You always think that eventually, the ache of missing someone will go away, but I don't think it ever leaves. I think we just get better at pretending."

I agreed with him about that. I didn't think that the pain of losing my parents was ever going to go away.

"Were your parents still alive when you were turned?" I asked, tears gathering in my eyes because his pain was so tangible.

He laughed bitterly, and like usual, the sound was all wrong coming from his lips which were usually curved in a smile.

"They were alive when I was turned. And I never let them see me again. I didn't want to scare them, not with how long it took me to get control of myself." His breath hitched as he relived the painful memories. "I used to go spy on them at night. I'd look in the window and see them gathered with my two sisters, living their lives. And I had to watch them mourn me and then grow old, and then pass away." He brushed his hair off his face, trying to get ahold of his emotions. "I regret it now, you know? I regret not trying to see them at least one more time, and I regret not being able to say goodbye. But after what happened with Celia...I just didn't want to risk it."

"Celia was your fiancée?" I asked quietly, hating myself for how irrationally jealous I felt of a woman long since gone.

He just nodded and turned his attention back to the sky, still filled with shimmering, shooting stars.

"I think I get so upset when I think about her because I feel guilty that after I hurt her, I realized I never really loved her. She never was the same after that attack. She never recovered. I tried to check up on her without her knowing; she never married, she dropped out of school...I ruined her life. And I didn't even love her."

"You didn't mean to hurt her," I whispered reassuringly, taking one of his hands and wrapping both of mine around it.

"Her love for me ruined her, and I was just able to move on."

I wasn't quite sure what to say to that. It wasn't right, how he was thinking, but I think he knew that. Just like I knew I wasn't a complete waste of space, better off gone. Sometimes it was hard to get rid of ingrained traumas.

"Sorry for killing the mood. Talking about my fucked up head wasn't exactly what I brought you out here for."

"Relationships aren't just sunshine, Luke," I chided gently, before realizing what I'd just said.

A smile broke out on his face at my words, far more brilliant than any shooting stars.

"You don't know how much I love that you just said that," he purred, and I couldn't help but giggle at how outrageous he was. He pulled me closer to him.

"Now, enough sad stuff. It's about to happen," he said.

"What's about to —" my words trailed off when I saw that the ground was beginning to glow around us. What I thought were wildflowers, or some other ordinary flower, because they had been closed when we landed...they'd transformed, unfurling since we'd been talking, and the white petaled flowers were now glowing, shimmering golden dust floating up from their centers. And I knew, this time, when I saw the world was sparkling, it wasn't because I was drunk--it was really happening around me.

It was spectacular.

"We call them wish flowers," Luke exclaimed in a hushed voice. "Because they only open up when there are shooting stars in the sky, and a lot of them at that."

"And the gold dust?" I asked, watching as the sparkles danced in the breeze, settling on our skin and hair. Luke pulled a vial out of his pocket.

"The gold dust actually has healing properties. It promotes a sense of wellness, and when people feel better about themselves, the actual internal part of them usually follows suit."

I watched in awe as he collected some of the dust into the vial and then stopped it up, placing it back in his pocket.

"You're incredible," I blurted out again. He was so interesting. So knowledgeable. I loved that he cared about healing people even if it was practically the antithesis of a vampire to keep someone alive.

I loved...everything I found out about him.

We stared at each other, a small smile on both of our lips

as the sky continued to dance above us and the flowers continued to glow around us.

"Kiss me," I demanded, loving the heat and happiness in his gaze as his mouth descended on mine in the sweetest kiss I'd ever been given.

I wanted more. I wanted all of him. I deepened the kiss, and he got the hint quickly as his tongue began to thrust in my mouth. I whimpered as his lips closed around my tongue, sucking eagerly. He groaned in response, his hands pulling up on my blouse. It was all I could do to move away from his hungry kiss as he pulled the shirt over my head, baring my skin to the cool air around us.

"Is this alright?" he asked, a tremble in his voice.

"Yes, it's perfect."

Evidently, that was all he needed to hear, because I found myself on my back, the flowers scattering gold sparkles all over us as his lips met mine once again. I'd been wearing a skirt, and Luke made quick work of dragging it off of me, his lips leaving mine to make a path down my skin. My muscles were trembling and my core was clenched at the sensations of his tongue and his lips taking my body. His fingers slipped under my panties, stroking through my folds until they were sliding into me, fucking me.

"Can you give me one tonight, sweetheart? I want you squeezing my fingers."

My whole body clenched at his command. Fuck, he was hot. He continued to move his fingers in and out, and then I came for him, shocking myself with the ferocity of it.

"Yes, that's so good," he growled. I shivered at his words,

staring up into his gaze. He was losing control, his eyes becoming desperate and needy....and possessive.

"I want you," I whispered, and his answering grin lit up the night.

"Whenever you want," he whispered, pressing another kiss against my lips softly. "Breakfast, lunch, and dinner," he reminded me, and I giggled.

I somehow knew that lovemaking would be like this with him. Like a burst of light; not heavy but still filled with all the meaning and emotion you could want. He fumbled with his clothes, his eagerness evident in his movements. Ripping off my underwear, I gasped as he moved between my legs, his weight pressing me down against the chilled ground as the world glowed around us. He rubbed his cock in between my folds, and I froze as I felt something cold and hard lining the bottom of his dick.

"Did I not mention it, sweetheart?" he growled. "I got it pierced a few years back, and you're going to love how it feels," he purred. My eyes widened at finding out that my delicious, sweet doctor had a pierced cock. He knocked my legs wide then as I grabbed onto his thick biceps, and then he was pushing in slowly, carefully. And I could feel how precious I was to him, how much he cared for me. He was huge, and I could feel every bump of the piercing as he stretched my walls. His body was trembling above me, and there was this awestruck look on his face, like he couldn't believe his good luck. As soon as he was in all the way, his mouth was against mine, our tongues dancing together as I whimpered against him. He stayed still for a moment, letting me adjust to his size before I tilted my hips, desperate for him to move.

He began to pull out slowly before slamming into me hard, my cry ricocheting through the air.

"You take me so good, sweet girl."

The way he was staring down at me, I had to close my eyes, because there was so much there. He kissed me softly again, his lips languidly moving against mine.

"You're beautiful, sweetheart," he murmured. "I can scarcely believe you're real." He began moving faster then, angling his hips until they were hitting the most delicious spots inside of me. And the piercing... fuck, I was going to demand that all of them get one because it felt incredible. No matter if he was going at a slow pace or a fast pace, it rubbed against all the important parts inside of me until I was writhing underneath him, my pleas melting in the air as he thrust into me over and over again. My senses were on overload. I was consumed by him, my perfume thick in the air. He pushed one of my legs up towards my chest, opening me more to his thrusting hips.

He looked at me hungrily as his cock pounded into me relentlessly.

"Tell me I can have you," he begged into my mouth. "I love you so fucking much."

An orgasm was building inside of me; all of my muscles were tensed. I closed my eyes, my head pushing back into the ground as pleasure surged through my spine, his words pushing me violently into pleasure. And then I was convulsing, almost violently. I turned my head and sunk my teeth into his chest, gulping his blood down as he growled and moaned in ecstasy, never slowing his pace.

"So fucking good," he growled, and I came again, his gorgeous taste and the feel of him too much for my body.

"You're making me come, sweetheart," he purred as his movements became erratic.

Right as I felt his warm heat pulsing into me, his lips were against my throat and his teeth were sinking into my skin. And then...

————

Luke

One second I was having the most profound and incredible sexual experience of my life with the girl I was determined to make mine...

And the next second, there was a beast underneath me, growling and trying to rip my jugular out. I sprang off of her, my hand covering my dick as she rose from the ground and swiped at me with long claws.

Fuck.

Obviously, I'd believed Pan when he'd described what happened when she'd shifted, but seeing it was a whole other thing.

She growled fiercely, and then she took off into the forest, heading in the direction of the castle. Fuck, she was fast.

I quickly pulled on my pants, and sprung into the air, knowing I could keep a closer eye as I flew above her, which was easier than trying to run behind her.

I'd thought I'd have to figure out a way to get her back home, but she seemed driven by something, running in an almost direct path to the castle.

"Pan!" I called out as soon as we got onto the castle ground. She was making no move to slow down.

"Get out of her way," I yelled at Thomas, one of the new pledges who was sitting around a bonfire, right in her path.

Unfortunately for Thomas, he didn't move quick enough, and she barreled through him, knocking him to the ground and slicing him with her claws as she moved.

His shriek rang through the night, but I didn't stop to help him. He was at least still alive, judging by his screams.

I continued to fly after Gwendolyn, my hand reaching into my pocket and grasping the syringe that Pan always had me carry around, just in case I needed to subdue someone or knock them out for emergency surgery.

I did not fucking want to use it on her.

Pan appeared on the edge of one of the balconies just then, and I breathed a sigh of relief. He could subdue her, and I wouldn't have to.

After she almost ripped another lost boy in half, Pan jumped easily down in front of her, holding up a hand in front of him.

"Easy, girl," he murmured, and she came to a screeching halt, scenting the air in front of her.

They eyed each other, and just as I saw her lean back on her haunches, prepared to spring at him, he jabbed his hand at one of the pressure points on her neck, and she immediately began to fall to the ground, changing back into Gwendolyn as I watched in shock and horror.

Pan caught her in his arms before she could hit the ground, and we both stared at each other.

"This is a problem," I stammered, stating the obvious. There was a hard glint in Pan's gaze as he began moving towards the doorway, taking her inside.

"That's an understatement, brother. That is an understatement."

CHAPTER 17

PAN

A female scream rang in the air so loud, it pierced the night.

My stomach dropped. *Gwendolyn!*

It came from inside the castle. I turned and darted inside because, of late, things had been tense in Darkland. Gwendolyn had come back from Hook...not completely herself. She'd been struggling to deal with what the bastard did to her, but the big concern was the physical toll it was taking on her body.

I'd do anything to alleviate her pain, to take away the fear. Luke has been working relentlessly on a game plan to find a cure for her sudden transformations into a wild creature... one I had never seen before. Half vampire, half wolf–it amazed me that even after her death, which turned her into one of us, she'd retained her omega side. It explained why she turned into a mutated version of both, but we had no clue what Hook had done to her to make her shift so abruptly.

Luke insisted that Hook had cursed her, while Atlas suggested it was her wolf side trying to gain dominance.

I didn't know, but I needed her fixed. She had no idea how powerful she was… And we had to find a way to help her.

The destruction, the devastation was too much for her to keep enduring.

I finally tracked down the scream to a communal room up on the top floor and came to an abrupt halt in the doorway to make sense of what I was seeing.

One of our maids sat curled in the corner, crying out. The room lay in complete disarray, furniture tossed and broken, the light fixtures torn out of their sockets in the ceilings, Luke and Atlas slumped across the room from where it'd been clear they were tossed against the punched up wall.

And in the middle of the room stood Gwendolyn in her beast form…again.

She rose up on her back legs, her body covered in a violet fur, which was absolutely beautiful…but the long claws on each paw and the deadly long fangs dripping with saliva were a bit unnerving. Vampire fangs on steroids. Her face was that of a wolf, eyes bright as fire. She was a sight to behold and unique in every aspect. But also fucking dangerous and unpredictable.

Whatever was going on here, it had gotten out of control.

"Gwendolyn," I barked to grab her attention away from the maid.

Atlas and Luke were on their feet, seemingly none the worse for the wear.

"Submit," I commanded. "Stand down." I threw the words laced with commanding power, stepping into the room.

She studied me, those amber eyes unflinching.

The tension snapped in the air like electricity.

"She's somehow stronger," Atlas stated.

"Luke, anything on a cure?" I snapped in his direction.

"Everything I've tried has failed. I'm tearing my hair out at this stage."

A flicker of movement, and she was lunging at me, claws extended, fangs bared. I darted out of her path with a millisecond to spare... or so I thought.

The scorching bite of her claws caught me across my shoulder, flesh tearing, the wound deep. I ripped out of her clutches and whipped around, coming at her from behind.

Slamming into her back, I drove her up against the wall, her grunt vibrating through her body. She was fucking strong, and when she swung back around, the elbow of her front leg caught me in the ribs, while her head smacked right into mine.

I flew backward, reeling to catch my balance.

Luke and Atlas were suddenly joining in, flanking me on either side.

"How the fuck do we stop her without hurting her?" Atlas muttered.

But there was no time for a response.

She charged at us, absolutely terrifying. I fucking loved her.

The three of us scrambled out of her path and leaped onto her because we had to get her off her feet. She smacked the ground, face first, but not before she bucked and tossed Luke right into the fireplace. Thank the gods of hell it wasn't lit. Soot and ash blew outward from his impact, staining everything.

Atlas and I wrangled a thrashing Gwendolyn, her growls thunderous. "Luke, get me something to tie her up."

I hated the notion, but she was becoming stronger, harder to contain without using force.

With my hands pressing down on the back of her head, forcing her cheek flat to the floor, I shouted, "Gwendolyn, settle the fuck down. Listen to my voice."

For a smidgen of a second, I believed it worked, but then she went feral, thrashing and snarling to get us off her back.

"Your command is clearly not working," Atlas pointed out with a snarky remark, and I wanted to smash my fist into his face.

He had a knee in the middle of her back, then purred his words. "Gwendolyn, my sweet omega, listen to my voice. Come back to us. You can control your beast side. It doesn't own you."

I shifted my attention to Luke who got to his feet, soot floating around him. But it was also when we lost control of her...

She bucked her body, sending Atlas and me flying in different directions. I slammed into a chair, breaking it on impact. Like everything else in this room--the furniture, the walls--what was one more broken thing.

But it was also the moment the maid decided to run out of the room, and while I was certain the beast would leap after her, she went for Luke instead.

Luke might have made a shrieking sound; she bowled him over, but not before he'd managed to snatch an iron rod for stoking the fire from the hearth in defense.

I scrambled to my feet, but not before Luke broke into a death roll with her across the floor. She got Luke finally pinned to the floor beneath her, an explosive growl spraying all over her face. I hurled myself forward, Atlas finally getting up too.

But in the span of a second, Luke shoved the iron poker in his hands up against her chest lengthwise to keep her from biting his face off. My hands fisted, knowing I needed to knock her out again.

She abruptly unleashed an unexpected shriek.

In a flash, she scrambled backward, whimpering, the front of her chest marred by a burn mark…exactly where the poker rod had touched her.

"What did you do to her?" Atlas barked.

"She's reacting to the poker," Luke answered, while I flanked my violet beast so she didn't escape the room.

Instead, she was dropping to all fours, her body convulsing. Her whimpers were a blade to my chest. It wasn't long before the beast vanished, and in front of us was Gwendolyn, who collapsed to the floor, pressing her hand to the burn mark on her chest, groaning.

I ran to her side and fell to my knees, Atlas right there too. Both of us held her as she looked up at us, confused and with tears welling in her eyes.

"It happened again, didn't it?" she whined.

"Yes, but it seemed you got hurt this time," I stated, lowering my gaze to the red welt mark running from one shoulder to the other across her collarbone.

"I think I know what happened to you, gorgeous," Luke stated, coming across the room, still carrying the poker rod.

"And?" I asked instantly, a growl hanging off the word.

"This poker is made of pure iron. And what's allergic to iron?" He raised an eyebrow.

"Fucking fairies," I spat, my insides curling with fury. I loathed Hook more than I thought was possible.

"And we both know that Hook hunts and traps fairies for their magic. Ground-up fairy wings are potent, and mixed with blood, it could create all kinds of curses."

"Are you kidding me? What fucked up part of the world are we in? Is this even Earth anymore?" Atlas was shaking his head, but the asshole had a lot to learn if he intended to stay alive and remain in Darkland.

I also rolled my eyes at his stupid questions, but Luke exercised greater patience than me as he went on to explain that we were indeed on earth but this piece of territory was infused with an ancient magic from an ancient time when it had once been ruled over by the fey.

"So, what happens now?" Gwendolyn asked. "You can fix me, right?"

All three of us turned our attention to Luke who had his lips pursed into a tight grin. "Yes, but it will be painful."

"Hell, can't anything be easy?" she murmured, and I held her shaking body against me while Atlas kissed her fingers, both of us letting her know she was loved.

"Can you make it hurt less?" I demanded of Luke.

He swallowed hard. "There's only one way I know of to remove a curse that uses fairy wings, and there's nothing I can do to lessen the hurt. I'm sorry. I wish I could bear all of this for you." His heartfelt eyes and the shiver in his voice told me he meant every single word.

And it also told me this was going to be really bad.

The wind whistled outside the barn, sending the doors into a shuddering groan. We'd followed Luke's advice on eliminating Hook's curse, which evidently entailed coming down here and having Gwendolyn sitting on a chair with her feet in a bucket of water.

She looked petrified—wide eyes, swallowing constantly, and watching everything Luke did with intensity.

Atlas was kneeling by her side, whispering sweet words to calm her, but her demeanor wasn't changing. She was terrified.

I moved over to Luke who was hooking up booster cables to a battery on one of our bikes. Then he clipped the alligator clips on the other end to the iron poker.

"Are you sure this is going to work? I swear to hell, if you burn her to a crisp or kill her for real, I'm going to *kill* you."

"Can you cool your fucking jets? You're stressing me out. I'm barely holding it together," he muttered under his breath. "There is literally no other way to remove such a curse without flushing it out of her system."

I groaned, leaning in closer. "By electrocuting her?" I was already on the verge of losing my shit, but the dramatic risk Luke proposed was doing my head in. On the inside, I was in full panic mode, my mind yelling that this was going to kill her, that I had to stop it.

But Luke had never let me down. His knowledge of supes was unprecedented. Trusting him was instinctual to me, yet my muscles tensed, bracing for a disaster that would devastate us.

"She won't die because she's already dead, but the shock in her body will eliminate the curse. Fairy wings are made up of tiny living particles that, even when consumed in a curse, never die. They'll wreak havoc with her until she completely loses her control and her beast takes over forever. Is that what you fucking want?" he growled, the nerves in his temples pulsing, the anger behind his voice fueled by distress.

I respected Luke for standing up to me, but it didn't ease my own trepidation. "So you're sure this will work?"

He stared at me, looking ready to burst into another rant, the bridge of his nose creasing. "Nothing is ever guaranteed. But I don't see another option, do you?"

Tensing, I knew he was right. To hunt down a fairy might

bring war with the fey to our doorsteps, but there was no guarantee they'd know how to remove the curse either.

Begrudgingly, I nodded, while hissing through clenched teeth. "Do it then."

Luke moved about quickly, drawing the iron rod attached to the cable leads to Gwendolyn. She stared at him, then me, then Atlas, her chin trembling.

I felt crushed on the inside, like nothing could ever be right again if anything happened to her under my command.

At her side, I crouched in front of her, taking her hands. "Everything will be okay. And just think, a bit of pain now for complete freedom from turning into a savage beast that wants to kill everyone."

She eyed the iron poker and cables. "This doesn't look like a bit of pain at all. Am I going to die for real?" Her face grew paler than normal, and she trembled harshly in her seat, going into shock.

I swept the hair from her face. "My little Darling, you're a powerful vampire, already dead if you don't remember," I tried to joke. Cupping the sides of her face, I tried my best to hold my own emotions back, to not show her the dread that clung to me, or that unfamiliar emotions were brimming behind me gaze. Everything we were doing went against my instinct, but I also understood the logic behind Luke's decision. It was sound.

I kissed her; it was short and sweet, though I wished I could steal her away from all of this. Luke stood over us without the cables, and I stepped back for him to kiss her, followed by Atlas.

Being electrocuted wouldn't normally affect vampires, but we were talking about an unknown curse.

Finally, we all pulled back. She had to just hold onto the rod.

"Okay, I'm ready to do this," she said bravely, and I loved her in that moment more than she'd ever know.

Luke handed it over and she accepted it with two hands.

Immediately, the sparks of power snapped outward from the rod, racing up her arms. She screamed, her body convulsing. Her back bent, then she started to transform. In flashes, she became her creature, then flipped back to her human form; the chaos of her flickering back and forth so fast made my head spin.

My stomach hurt, and every instinct screamed for me to go save her.

A burnt smell misted the air, and the three of us lingered especially close, my fingers itching to tear her out of there. To hold her, to make it all better.

Finally, she slumped in her seat in her human form only. Her eyes rolled back into her head, and she was frothing at the mouth. Her arms fell to her sides and the iron slipped out of her grasp, hitting the concrete floor.

It all happened so fast, and yet it felt like a lifetime of torture crashing into me to watch her come out of that, unresponsive.

Luke frantically kicked the iron away, then pried the alligator clips from the battery.

I threw myself at her, and the moment I touched her, a zap

of electricity slammed into my arm, the sharp pinch of its bite surprising me.

Regardless of the pain, I grabbed her by her arms and lifted her out so her feet were no longer in the bucket of water. I cradled her against me, my emotions wound tight. I wanted to scream, to tear the world apart for her pain.

Luke was there too, pulling back the eyelids of her now closed eyes, while Atlas was pacing like a caged wolf, growling, his hands fisted, murmuring shit like, "She's dead. You fucking killed her."

He was getting on my damn nerves. As usual.

I barked, "Shut the fuck up and stop panicking."

Sure, on the inside, I was a clusterfuck of a mess. But for centuries, I lived in Darkland, just going through the motions. Hunting. Collecting my sacrifice, who always ended up dead, and sleeping. She'd changed everything. I couldn't go back to an existence without her in it. I wouldn't.

"Gwendolyn," I said, my lips on hers. "Wake up for me, beautiful. Please wake up."

But when she didn't respond, her body slumped against me, terror swallowed every inch of me, and I did the only thing that I could control.

"Hold her," I commanded Luke, who took her into his arms. Atlas had finally calmed down and joined us.

Lifting my wrist to my mouth, I unsheathed my fangs and tore into my veins, ripping them open. Then I placed my hand over her mouth as Atlas pulled down on her chin to open her mouth.

Blood dripped into her mouth, some on her lips, the sight striking against her pale skin.

No one made a sound.

The silence grew deafening.

Desperation wound up within me, a madness I didn't think I could ever come out of starting to pass over me.

But I focused my attention on Gwendolyn. *Please, my little Darling. Don't you dare leave me after you made me find love in a dead life.*

With a sudden gasp, her eyes flipped open, and she coughed, convulsing in my arms.

Atlas shouted with joy, while Luke gasped. But me... I just smiled down at my girl who finally settled down in Luke's arms, glancing up at us all.

"I'm guessing I survived then," she croaked.

"Welcome back, my beauty," I murmured. "How do you feel?"

"Surprisingly energetic." She licked the last drops of blood from her lips. "And hungry."

"I have every assurance that you will be stronger than before."

Even with her words, Luke refused to lower her from his arms. Instead, he peppered her face with kisses. Atlas peered down at her. "Hello, little omega. You gave us a huge scare. I never want to experience that again."

She broke into a laugh, and it was the most delicious sound to my ears.

"I love you," I whispered to her, watching as her eyes widened in shock.

"I love you more," Atlas countered, and instead of glaring at him, I smiled. I…liked seeing how much she meant to each one of us, more than we'd ever expected.

A loud knock came from the side door leading to the barn before Finn burst inside, blood splashed across his face, looking terror-stricken. He stumbled forward, and my hackles instantly bristled.

"What happened?" I asked.

"We're under attack," he rasped, and I didn't need him to tell me who had invaded the castle. I knew instantly.

Hook.

CHAPTER 18
GWENDOLYN

Just when I thought I could finally catch a break, it turned out that fate had no intention of leaving me alone. You'd think being electrocuted would be the icing on the cake. Nope. Apparently, things were about to get worse.

Pan darted out of the barn, the rest of us following on his heels.

And I wasn't sure anyone could have prepared me for the sight unfolding in front of us. My muscles tensed, and my mouth fell open.

Pirates swarmed the woods behind the castle, rushing forward like an army, and I felt every bit like a deer caught in the headlights of an oncoming car. A handful of vampires darted toward them to stop the invasion.

Can't you just give us a break, I murmured internally to the universe.

A sudden siren rang out, and I flinched at how loudly it carried across the land.

Pan was cursing under his breath before he turned to me, fear twisting his expression. "You need to go and hide inside. Go now," he ordered me, but I couldn't move my feet; everything was happening too fast.

Pan quickly turned his attention to Atlas while I noticed Luke throwing himself into battle. It was in that same moment that a river of vampires poured out from either side of the castle and darted toward the action.

"Atlas, if you wish to call this your home, you must defend it with us."

The corners of his mouth curled upward, and something sparked in his eyes. "I thought you'd never ask. Count me in." And then he glanced at me, frantically nudging me. "Baby, you gotta get out of here now."

But that opportunity sailed away when, behind them, half a dozen pirates descended upon us.

My stomach clenched, bile hitting the back of my throat.

Then chaos broke out.

Pan and Atlas swung around, throwing themselves at the attackers who brandished axes and clubs.

I backpedaled, needing a weapon, something.

But when a huge pirate, wearing a black eye patch, came charging directly for me, panic slammed into me.

I turned and ran for my life right back into the barn, then spun and slammed the door shut, hitting the lock.

The pirate crashed into the door, shaking the whole thing on its hinges.

I backed away, rushing over to pick up a wrench off the floor, my fingers gripping it hard. I reminded myself that I was a fucking vampire and I should act like one. Yet I trembled all the same.

When the brute finally broke through the door, sending shards of wood in every direction, I stiffened.

He jerked in my direction, wearing a saccharine smile. "Come here, pretty girl. My captain hasn't finished with you yet. But maybe beforehand, I'll do to you what he never did." He groped his cock over his pants, the sight sickening me.

But with it came a flare of anger. I was so damn tired of all these assholes treating me like just a piece of ass.

"Fuck off," I shot back. "Unless, of course, you're ready to meet your maker."

He laughed like a hyena, and just hearing the sound had me burning up with anger. It came at me in waves, my body shuddering, and something deep inside me started to growl.

The asshole came at me, but I swung the wrench in my hand and clocked him right in the face. Then I threw the damn thing at his head.

He howled, clasping his head as blood sprouted from his mouth. And instantly, the metallic smell floated on the air. With it, a desperate hunger punched me in the gut, and where earlier fear shivered up my spine, something new stirred within me. An inferno that burned over my body with only one thing on my mind.

To feed.

I flew at him before he even saw me coming. He smacked

into the doors, with me pinning him in place, and I wrenched his head aside.

Then I bit into his neck, my fangs sinking into the soft flesh, and his blood filled my mouth. Warm, it felt like it almost pulsed with its own heartbeat.

He screamed, shoving his fists into my sides, ripping at my body to toss me aside. But I felt nothing except for the exhilarating hunger I was satisfying.

Blood rushed down my throat, and I couldn't get enough, couldn't drink fast enough. When he went slack and slipped out from under me, I broke my hold of him and pulled back. He slumped on the floor, his breathing shallow while more blood trickled from the two puncture wounds in his neck.

The temptation to bend over and lick it all up grew, but Pan's words came to mind about how he created vampires... drinking them dry until they died.

That thought alone had me stumbling away from the man who would die in his own time. I sure as hell didn't need him coming back as a vampire.

Instead, I lunged for the doorway, running so fast that it was only once I charged over the grassland did I realize that I ran on all fours. My mind startled and I paused, glancing down at my huge paws, at the violet fur running up my legs.

Panic might have been my go-to emotion, except this felt different. I was in the driver's seat of my own body, not this monster.

I might have done a little dance of happiness that I had control over her, that I might be a vampire, but I also held onto my wolf side.

A thunderous growl broke my celebration, and I once again focused on the manic battle escalating around me. At the pirates and vampires fighting to the death. The stench of blood growing heavier in the air, calling to me. And for once, I was happy to follow my primal instinct.

I lunged forward, charging into the woods, prepared to do whatever it took to protect my new family.

Roars blended with the screams.

Rushing forward, I eyed a beefy pirate clubbing Finn, who lay on the ground, bleeding severely. With all my force, I drove into him, head first, which sent him head over heels right into another of his buddies, sending him off his feet too.

But I didn't miss a beat and charged after them, biting into one man's arm, thrashing him aside to get out of my way. With a sloshing sound, his whole arm ripped out of its socket. Blood and sinew went everywhere, and the guy wailed.

Well, I guessed I didn't know my own strength. Who would have known?

Spitting out his arm, I lunged over the man and landed on top of him. He crumbled beneath me, and one swipe of my paw to the back of his neck had me half lopping his head off.

I liked my strength a lot.

"Gwendolyn," Luke called from behind me, and I swung around to his huge eyes, partly in shock at seeing me like this again.

My attempt to talk came out as gargled growls, so instead, I charged over to him, bowling over two pirates in the process. Luke came to my side in a flash and disposed of one pirate with a fast twist of his head. I, on the other hand, had stood on my pirate, squishing him while he cried out and threw punches into my legs. But when something sharp bit into my leg from a blade, I stomped my back paw onto his face, claws piercing his skull.

He fell silent after that. I turned to Luke and pushed my head into his shoulder, rubbing myself against him.

"You can control your beast? That's incredible." His smile was contagious as I nodded, even if I was grinning on the inside. Then he reached over and scratched behind my ear, sending my tail into a mad swing, which I learned was completely out of my control. Damn, that was freaky.

Around us, the pirates were falling, and it felt like it would be over before it started, which filled me with warmth after everything. Maybe this wouldn't be so bad.

A loud cry suddenly bellowed across the night sky.

I flinched around to where the woods in the distance were swarming with torch lights. And dozens upon dozens were coming this way, and by their jeers and whistles, I could only imagine they were pirates.

Of course.

The vampires around me snarled, and with Luke, we ran toward our enemy. I caught Atlas' stare from across the field where he did a double take my way, almost tripping over his own feet.

Pan led the charge ahead of me, and I focused on what was coming our way.

My paws hit the ground and I traveled as quickly as the vampires around me.

We reached the pirates, both parties clashing in an epic clap of bodies.

Fighting seemed to come naturally to me in this form, and I never paused, taking out as many of them as possible. And yet, the wave kept coming. I didn't understand how they could all fit on that boat, but I guess, Hook could have had them living on shore someplace.

Speaking of the asshole, I started looking out for him, desperate to make him pay for what he'd done to me.

It wasn't long before I finally did find him. With a thunderous growl, I charged for him, shoving others aside.

Dead...that's the word that kept flaring over my mind when it came to Hook.

He towered over everyone, using his hook as his weapon, slicing the throat of a vampire feet from me.

I snapped, fury tightened around me, and I lunged at him, striking before he got the chance to react.

But we barely hit the ground when hands...so many of them...wrenched me off of Hook.

The roaches suddenly threw themselves onto me until my legs buckled out from under me from the weight. I snarled, thrashing and snapping to throw them off, but only more came back.

Hook suddenly stood before me, snatching my ear. I shook my head vigorously, but not before the sharp bite of a blade sliced over the top of my ear. It stung tremendously, and I whined, fighting harder to escape the bastard.

"I'm going to enjoy this," he sneered. "For each of my men who died today, I'm going to slice a piece of you."

A newfound fear howled in my head, the dread intensifying that I'd made a terrible mistake...gotten a little too confident.

But not once did I stop fighting, even as the pirates keeping me pinned to the ground kicked and punched me.

But then a familiar tingling sensation rushed down my spine, and in seconds, I felt my beast withdraw.

No, don't you dare, not now.

But in moments, I lay sprawled on the ground beneath pirates in my human form, and the assholes didn't seem to care. They kept beating me.

Hook abruptly snatched my hair and tugged me away from the mob. I kicked and scratched at his hand, throwing myself up to my feet.

Just when I thought I'd catch a break, the glint of the hook hand came swinging directly for me. I leaped back just in time, the sharpness slicing across my thigh. My ear and leg now stung like someone poured acid over the wounds.

I winced, glaring at him with death.

From the corner of my eye, it became clear that his men encircled us with a kind of shield, while the rest of his crew distracted the vampires.

"I've come back for you, omega. Didn't I make myself clear back on the ship? Pan doesn't deserve you. I can give you the world, you can be my bride as I rule Darkland."

"Not in this fucking lifetime," I sneered.

"That can be arranged," he said with a cocky grin. Hatred was bitter in my mouth as I glared at him.

Hook snatched at my throat, but not before I lashed out

and scratched him on the face. It was enough for him to release me, and I seized upon the opportunity.

I hurled myself at him, using my vampire agility, my fangs latching onto his neck. I tore into his flesh, gouging at his veins. His blood tasted bitter, but I wasn't doing this to feed on him. He shoved me aside, and I stumbled free.

Good. Because I pivoted on my heel and catapulted myself through the barrier of pirates, knocking them over like dominos. I realized then their presence had nothing to do with protecting Hook, but everything to do with hiding me.

Hook was on my heels, the huge asshole moving faster than I could imagine. He'd been around a lot longer than me, which obviously made him stronger. He snatched me by the hair and yanked me backward.

My feet tangled and I flew, hitting the ground hard.

I groaned, staring up at Hook who set his booted foot onto my chest, pressing down. He weighed a fucking ton. He smirked down at me, holding a blade.

Glancing around us, I noted most of the fighting had moved closer to the house, and somehow, we'd ended up as far from the masses as possible. I was in alot of trouble.

"I'd stop fighting. It will only make me hurt you more. It's not like it would be the first time I took something from Pan. He'll get over it."

"You fucking psychopath, let me go." I writhed and clawed at his leg, his words about Pan leaving me confused.

"My, what a filthy mouth for a new bride. We'll have to do something about that tongue of yours, won't we? Better we do it now and leave Pan a parting gift."

Panic strangled me, and I thrashed wildly as he crouched next to me. The cold touch of the blade on my cheek left me shaking.

"Please don't."

He laughed one second, and the next he flew right off me. I had no idea what happened, but I scrambled to my feet to see a savage brawl happening between Pan and Hook.

They sounded like wild animals, and I moved forward, needing to help him. Just then half a dozen pirates jumped into the fight.

I focused deep down on my beast because if she was to come out it would make a world of difference. Just as I felt the softness of her fur on the inside, Atlas was at my side, puffing for air.

"Get back," he bellowed.

His clothes were stained in blood, torn, his hair a mess and his face scratched up badly.

"Atlas," I gasped, but he joined the battle, as did Luke. Even Crocodile jumped in. It had grown into a battle for survival, and with so many people fighting, I couldn't tell who was who.

All of a sudden, Hook was thrown out, his body grazing across the forest floor, coming to a stop right at my feet.

He snarled, cut up and bleeding, his lip busted. There was an awful open wound on his leg where his tibia had snapped in half, the bone sticking out through torn flesh, and it made me slightly nauseous. Another deadly gash had his side split open, with so much blood pouring out of him that he'd take a long time to heal.

But the moment he groaned and attempted to get up, I stomped a foot down on his chest, and just as quickly snatched the blade from his belt.

"You piece of shit. You aren't going anywhere." Moving with speed, I bent forward and sliced his ear completely off.

He howled like a fucking baby.

That was when I lifted my gaze to find I had an audience. My men, plus Crocodile, standing there, grinning despite looking like they'd been thrown down a cliff with how badly beaten up and bruised they were. Behind them lay a mountain of dead pirates.

"Eye for an eye, or in this case, ear for an ear," I teased. I tilted my head to the side to show them where the bastard had sliced off the top part of mine. "He deserves so much worse." I then kicked Hook in the side of his ribs where he had his wound.

He wailed. "Fucking bitch."

"Feel free to slice anything from this prick," Pan chuffed, while Hook groaned and clutched his bleeding ear.

"Want me to yank down his pants for you?" Crocodile asked with a bit too much enthusiasm.

"All I want is to stop feeling like I'm constantly running for my life," I admitted truthfully, suddenly feeling a wave of exhaustion going down to my bones.

"If you're done with him, little Darling, it's my turn with this fucker." Pan seized Hook by the throat and dragged him to sit up against a tree. "It's been too long, Hook. I should have come and finished you years ago. But this ends now between us."

Hook raised his chin defiantly. "If you're going to do it, then finish the job. But my death won't bring her back, will it?"

I tensed, knowing immediately he was talking about Pan's lost love, Lillian.

Pan's jawline tensed. "Most of your men are dead. The rest we'll hunt down. You have nothing left, Hook. So why don't you tell me, since you have nothing left to lose...Why did you take Lillian from me?"

Hook twisted his head, scanning the woods littered with dead bodies...mostly his men. I could see his internal struggle..to accept it was over. Despair burned in his gaze. And then he finally sighed heavily, defeat settling onto his features.

Gone was the fire in his eyes, the permanent scowl. Instead, what remained was a man who'd lost his way.

"It was never meant to be this way, you know," Hook murmured. "But sometimes one decision can have a ripple effect that changes the course of your life and all those around you."

I had no idea what he was talking about, but like the others, I hung onto every one of his words.

"Why can't I remember my past clearly? What did you do to me?" His voice was dark, but his tone was even.

"I'll tell you everything, not that it will change anything...," Hook muttered, and I tensed, wondering what he was going to say.

"I'm listening," Pan countered through clenched teeth.

Hook licked his lips, blood crusted around the edges of his mouth. "I was in love with her."

Crocodile groaned behind Pan, gaining Hook's attention. But he continued regardless. "I'd been in love with her, long before you noticed her. And just when I was going to declare my intentions...you waltzed in, sweeping her off her feet. So she never saw me. Having to watch you and her both so happy...it was hell."

Pan didn't move, didn't blink. He was terrifying in his anger, just glaring at Hook with a predatory stare.

"And when you're desperate, you fuck up," Hook murmured, as blood began to dribble from his mouth as his injuries worsened.

"What the hell did you do?" Crocodile snapped.

"Soon after, I found out I was sick...dying most certainly. And because I was scared, I visited a crossroads and summoned a demon to ask for eternal life. I wasn't ready to die," he whispered. "So I made a deal."

A demon. I hadn't expected that. But I guessed if fairies and mermaids existed, why not demons, right?

When no one said anything, he continued. "As soon as the deal was struck, the demon lunged at me and bit me in the neck. Of course, I thought at the time he was having a snack and that I was just going to die right then. Until I woke up the next day no longer a human. I had no idea what a vampire was, obviously...but I was suddenly hungry. Apparently the demon had a fucking sense of humor in his definition of eternal life." He paused and licked his lips once more, his hand coming up to wipe the blood dripping from his mouth, smearing it all over his face in the process. "That night, I was searching for something to help stop the hunger. I ran into Lillian at the village fair." He closed his eyes and his body shuddered, as if he was reliving it right then. "Something came over me, and I just lost my mind over how delicious she smelled. I attacked her. And fuck, I had no idea what I was doing or why I had to drink her blood, so I accidently killed her."

"You fucking bastard," Crocodile snarled and threw himself at Hook, driving a fist to his face. No one stopped him, and it was a miracle in itself that he drew himself back.

I kept studying Pan, watching how he trembled, how his hands fisted by his side, like he was reliving his past love's death right alongside Hook. Did he still pine for her, or think of her when he was with me?

Atlas had his hand on my lower back, drawing me against him as if he somehow sensed my unease in the conversation about Pan's ex-lover.

"You obviously don't remember, but you walked in on me feeding on her, and then you came at me. We fought and I was still lost to the hunger, so I threw you down hard to the ground and fed on you, only later realizing that I'd cracked your skull from the force. I drained you completely, and hitting your head while I did that made you forget your memories. When you woke up the next day, you had no recollection of anything from the previous night."

"And you never told me either," Pan spit.

"There was no benefit for you to know what happened. I'd made a mistake going to the demon out of fear, and I've had a long time to live with these memories and my regret over what happened." He coughed then, the sound of it rattling around his lungs.

"And do you regret killing Lillian? Do you hold any remorse for that? Your family has been paying for your mistake for generations."

I'd guessed right, apparently. Hook Silver was related to Alpha Silver! That explained so much. Why Pan took a regular sacrifice from their family–to get revenge against Hook.

By the looks of it though, Hook could have cared less.

"Pan, you were once like a brother. We'll never be that way again, but if it means anything, I'm sorry."

We'd all gone dead silent, and I couldn't speak for anyone else, but fuck. Talk about tragedy, love lost, and secrets. And so many innocents dying because of one bad decision.

Still, I half expected Pan to accept Hook's apologies. Maybe even let him live.

"I could have forgiven you, if you hadn't shown what a snake you were and taken what's mine once again," Pan spit, suddenly snatching a dead branch from the ground by his feet. Without pause, he drove the wooden branch right into Hook's chest, shoving it deep into his heart.

Hook shuddered, and his eyes widened at the realization of what was happening. I watched as his body started to break apart into tiny fragments of ash, flying away on the breeze.

Strangely, he smiled genuinely at that moment. And I

couldn't help but feel as though he was just relieved...for it all to finally be over.

I was relieved, to be honest. Hook's jealousy had completely ruined Pan's life, and if I had a working heart, it'd be breaking for him. I stepped up to him, sliding my hand into his, our fingers interlacing.

There were no words, just the knowledge that the shadow hanging over his life was finally gone. He couldn't change the past, but the future was ours to carve whichever way we wanted.

We all crowded close. Pan, Atlas, Luke, and even Crocodile joined us in a hug.

"It's going to be okay," I murmured to them. "We have each other. Our newfound family."

As much as I came into Darkland absolutely terrified, what I found was something I hadn't had for a very long time.

A family and love.

Our backyard might be littered with dead pirates, but I'd take Darkland over any version of my past.

I was home.

CHAPTER 19
GWENDOLYN

The castle was badly in need of repair, and we'd been working at clearing some of the rubble for a few hours. There were bodies that needed to be taken care of, but other Lost Boys were already working on throwing Hook's crew into wheelbarrows. I didn't know what they were going to do with the bodies, but I also didn't really care.

I was just looking forward to some rest, without having to look over my shoulder for Hook to appear.

Luke and Atlas were discussing something with Crocodile, but I didn't see Pan. Turning around with a frown, I finally saw him in the distance, standing on one of the higher balconies and looking off at the sea.

There was a melancholy air about him, even from here, and I decided to go make sure he was alright. It was almost second nature to fly now, and I barely had to think of any specific memory to start soaring toward him. He didn't turn when I landed, and when I slid my hand into his, he didn't seem at all surprised I was there.

"What's wrong?" I asked softly, enjoying the night breeze licking across my face, carrying the salty scent of the ocean with it. "I thought you would be happy it was over…after so long."

He smiled, and it was a little bittersweet. "Letting go of memories, I guess," he murmured.

"Of Lillian?"

He shrugged. "I think I'm letting go of being mortal more than anything. I'm letting go of what once was, something I thought I'd done long ago." He squeezed my hand. "I stopped missing her the moment she was gone. What we had…it was a love born from proximity, from growing up together. But there was no weight to it." He finally turned to look down at me. "Not like what I feel for you."

I froze. Despite his actions, there was a part of me that wondered if he could ever love me. Obsession was one thing. Feeling possessive was something else. But love…He'd said it that one time…but I still hadn't believed…

My chest felt like it would explode from what he was saying.

"I think I felt responsible for her death, because I couldn't remember exactly how it happened, other than Hook was a part of it. I guess I've carried that guilt all this time."

He and Luke could probably have a few heart-to-hearts about guilt, judging by what I was hearing.

"Hook was my best friend for years…and then my worst enemy for far longer. But a part of me still remembers who he was. I hated him because of who he was. It's a strange sensation that he doesn't exist to hate anymore."

I leaned my head against his shoulder. "Maybe you'll be less of an asshole, now," I remarked casually, rejoicing when I felt his body shake as he chuckled.

"I wouldn't count on that, little Darling," he murmured, a smile on his face now instead of the strain that had been there before.

Silence embraced us once more, when a question came to me. "With Hook now out of the picture and the truth out, will you stop taking sacrifices from the Silver family?"

Pan took his time responding when he answered with, "Would you like me to?"

While the notion of bringing terror into Sussana's life did sound appealing, she would always make someone who didn't deserve it be the sacrifice. "I think now's a good time to stop them."

He nodded, and I yawned then, my immortal body still feeling the strain of the day.

"Let's go take a nap, little Darling." He turned and wrapped me in his arms, taking off around the other side of the castle before I could even answer. I waved at Luke and Atlas who were watching Pan fly us, annoyance on their features that Pan was spiriting me away. I had no doubt they'd find their way to my room soon.

To my surprise, Pan went around the back of the castle, instead of up to my balcony, going through an entrance with staircases that descended into the ground…a path I remembered clearly from the fateful night he'd found me in his room.

"What are you doing?" I asked hesitantly as he stopped in front of his doorway.

"We're taking a nap," he answered evenly as he threw open his door and carried me across the threshold, so to speak.

"I thought you didn't like people in your room…or more specifically…me in your room."

He walked over to his bed, still carrying me, before setting me down gently in the middle of the silky black sheets.

"I'm old," he said.

I watched him, lust building as he unbuttoned his black silk shirt, showcasing the abs that definitely didn't look old. It was still amazing how ancient he was, but how young he appeared.

"I'm aware of that," I answered, confused.

"No, sweets. I'm very old. And I'm the vampire king. My lair is kind of a big deal. I'm this low in the ground because it grounds me. The soil recharges me, so to speak. It's a sacred space, a vulnerable space…not somewhere I let just anyone come in."

"So you've decided I'm not just anyone," I whispered as he stalked towards me, looking like a dark dream.

"I've decided you are the *only* one." He pushed me back onto the bed and hovered over me, his teeth sharpening with a click as his silver eyes gleamed hungrily. Pan gripped my chin. "Tell me you love me," he ordered, leaning down and grazing his teeth down my neck. I shivered, my breath coming out in gasps, my perfume thickening in the air. "Tell me, my omega. Tell me you love me just as much as I love you."

"And how much is that?" I asked breathlessly.

"All consuming, Gwendolyn. The love I feel for you is all-consuming." His teeth pressed into me more. "Now tell me what I want to hear."

"I love you," I finally whimpered back as his teeth blissfully cut into my skin and he carried me away into hours of orgasms where *sleep* was the last thing on my mind.

***

My cheek was resting on Pan's chest and I was idly tracing patterns on his skin. I should have been exhausted from the hours of pleasure he'd wrung from my body, but for some reason, I was still feeling achy inside, still perfuming, and my thighs were still covered in my slick.

To try and distract myself, since I wasn't sure that Pan had any more orgasms in him after what we'd just done, I was examining Pan's scary artwork.

"It's interesting you chose to hang demon and hell paintings on your walls when you didn't even know that demons created vampires until Hook explained what he'd done."

"I've always been fascinated by the concept of hell. I guess since I'll never make it there," Pan answered lazily.

"What do you mean?" I asked, glancing up at him.

"As vampires, we just cease to exist if we're killed, my sweet."

My arms tightened around him. "We just cease to exist?"

"Hmmm, since you still seem to have some omega traits, I doubt that's your fate, little omega. Even though I would never allow you to be killed to find out."

That didn't make me feel much better, but I figured the risk was worth the tradeoff of having a chance at immortality with my lovers.

"Let's just all never allow any one of us to be killed," I said sternly, and he chuckled under my head, not concerned at all about it.

I moved my legs together, the ache building. Fuck, what was wrong with me? A second later, I was flipped onto my back and Pan was once again hovering over my body, his erection pushing between my legs.

"Have something you want to tell me, little omega?" he growled, beginning to thrust against me.

The ache was beginning to turn unbearable, and I found myself whining and moaning as slick trickled down my thighs.

"Please, fuck me."

"Trying to start the fun without us?" Atlas purred from the doorway. I glanced over feverishly and saw that Luke and Atlas were standing there, huge erections tenting both of their pants.

I reached for them, all rationality beginning to fade away...there was just the urge to be fucked...now.

I was in heat.

Again.

Pan glanced towards them, annoyed, his body still

thrusting steadily against me, torturing me because he was just sliding his dick through my folds, not giving me what I needed.

I was so empty…And I wanted all of them.

"Please," I begged breathlessly, worried he wouldn't allow them in his room after what he'd said before.

"Get in here and lock the door," he ordered, assuaging my fears…right before he slammed his cock into my sopping wet core.

I came instantly, my scream echoing around the room.

"I want to play," purred Luke from somewhere nearby, and Pan somehow managed the feat of flipping me over until I was suddenly astride his hips, with him underneath me. His hands were on my hips and he was lifting me up and down on his dick as I mewled and pleaded for more.

"Fuck, yes. Milk my dick, omega," Pan growled, his gaze heavy-lidded with pleasure as Atlas came into view next to me, already unclothed. I eyed his long, perfect dick hungrily, and my golden boy laughed.

"You're welcome to it, baby." He shifted until he was up by Pan's head, and I leaned forward more as he fed me inch by inch until it was hitting the back of my throat.

Atlas began to slide in and out with a groan. "Fucking perfect, baby."

This was so good. But I needed more.

Right as I had that thought, Luke rubbed against my asshole, taking some of the slick dripping from my thighs and massaging it around the rim until his finger was popping in easily. I could already imagine how good his piercing was going to feel there, and my heat had me so ready for him that I wasn't even nervous about having his huge cock stuffing my ass.

"Such a pleasant surprise, sweetheart," Luke breathed from behind me as he moved his thick finger in and out of my ass, finding a perfect rhythm with Pan's thrusts. I could only moan in response as he bent me forward until my breasts were dangling in front of Pan's face.

"I want your eyes," snapped Pan. "And keep your balls from hitting my face," he warned Atlas, who was now slamming into my mouth, tears falling down my face as I struggled to get more of his length between my lips.

Without warning, Pan struck, slicing his teeth into my breasts, blood dribbling down my body. I came, tightening around his cock, right as Luke nudged my asshole with the blunt tip of his dick.

"Ready for me, sweetheart?" he asked, but I could only whine in response as he popped past my outer ring and began to move in and out of me with shallow thrusts.

"Forgive me, sweetheart," Luke muttered, and then his teeth were sinking into my throat.

"Filthy bloodsuckers," I thought I heard Atlas mutter as I sucked his cock down my throat, blood coating my body as the four of us moved together. Pan and Luke sipped at my blood as I came, again and again.

I wasn't sure how my life had become such a dark dream…

All I could say was that I loved it.

Through death, I had found a new life…

The End.

BONUS EPILOGUE

S ign up for our newsletter list to get a bonus epilogue and see what Pan, Luke, Atlas, and Gwendolyn are up to now...
Sign up here.

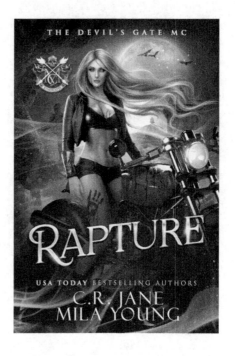

And keep reading for a sneak peak at our monster romance…Monster's Temptation…

MONSTER'S TEMPTATION
BOOK 1

The Monster King wants to play...

It's been 1097 days and 14 hours since I've been locked in this place.

And they've come to me every night.

The monsters in my dreams worship my body.

And when I wake up, I'm desperate for more...

But they're never there to finish me off.

Dr. Adams says I can leave the asylum if I start to take my meds, but I've always hated how they made me feel...and I'm not sure that I agree with them that I'm actually crazy.

Because dreams don't make you crazy, right?

I've got to start living someday though...so I finally take the plunge and obey so I can get out.

My dreams stop, and the monsters disappear. I'm finally starting a new life.

And that's when he comes...the monster king.

Evidently my little dreams, weren't just dreams. And he and his demon horde were feeding off my lust.

Their glowing eyes, sharp teeth, and big…

They're all real.

The Monster King wants me back. I'm their favorite plaything after all.

And I just might want to play.

Get your copy of Monster's Temptation today!

CHAPTER 1

3 YEARS LATER

BLAKE

"Don't you dare cover up, Pet," he growled as he pulled on my dress. My breath was coming out in gasps as my eyes moved across his muscled chest. He was wearing tight, black pants, and I watched as he slowly slid them down his sculpted thighs, revealing a huge red dick with two heads that were designed to give me as much pleasure as possible. As I watched, his clawed hand circled his thick base, and he bit his bottom lip with a half-lidded gaze, his sharp fangs peeking out over his full lips.

"Slide those panties down so I can make you come."

I had no choice but to obey. As usual, he had me soaked and ready even though he hadn't so much as touched my skin yet. I slid down my panties obediently, and he grabbed me, pulling me into his lap and rubbing my soaking wet core over his hard length.

"*Fuck, you're sexy.*" *He yanked me forward, and my hands automatically moved to his broad shoulders for balance as he moved me into place—my legs spread wide straddling him, my breasts flush with his chest, his huge cock flexing under me.*

Despite the fact that he towered over me, in this position we were eye to eye. He was beautiful, my monster. His glowing red eyes flecked with gold sparks, his chiseled nose, his sculpted mouth that would've made Michelangelo weep. I loved the hunger in his gaze. After an entire life of never being wanted, I couldn't get enough of him...and his friends.

His lips crashed against mine in a deep kiss, and I instinctively opened my mouth, allowing his forked tongue to slide in and tangle with mine. He devoured me. His licks were aggressive and filthy, and I could feel it all the way to my core.

There was an ache inside of me that I knew only he could fill. I moaned as I returned his kiss eagerly. My hands moved from his shoulders, up his face, until I was fisting his two long black horns. I held onto them as I moved, trying to get friction on my aching clit. I was mindless with desire.

But my king wasn't in a hurry, and instead of giving me what I wanted, he simply deepened the kiss, sliding his fingers through my hair so he could hold me in place as he continued his hot, wet licks in my mouth. His other hand softly stroked my lower back, the sharp tips of his claws teasing my skin.

Tension was building inside of me, and I knew from experience that I could come just from this. His hands on my back slid down, and he squeezed my ass before grabbing his dick and positioning it right where I wanted.

"*You gonna give me what I want?*" *he growled, and all I could* do was whimper in response as he pulled me down and pushed into me. I gasped at the tight stretch. He was so big, the two heads of his crown massaging different places inside of me.

"Fuck," he groaned, a guttural growl laced in his words. "Relax, Pet. You're going to be my good girl, aren't you?" he purred.

A soft scream slipped out of me as my thighs moved flush against his and he slid all the way in. My breath came out in gasps as I tried to get a hold of myself. I was so full, it was hard to think outside of the sensations.

"Good fucking girl," he rumbled as he moved both hands to my hips and lifted me up slightly before thrusting up hard.

I whimpered again, and his grip tightened at the sound. He started fucking me desperately, his movements rough and powerful, and all I could do was go along for the ride.

His cut abdomen bunched as he moved his hips, and his gaze was hungry and determined as he watched me closely.

One of his hands moved off my hip, and he sliced down the center of my dress with his claws, showcasing my straining breasts.

He began to suckle on one of my nipples, and I gasped as my body arched backwards.

"Yes," I breathed, caught in the sensation of his mouth torturing my nipple and his long, thick cock spearing in and out of me. I continued to hold onto his long horns as we moved desperately together. His sharp fangs pricked against my skin, setting me off in an agonizingly good orgasm that threatened to destroy me.

Something slid softly against my ass, and I gasped as I peeked backwards only to see his long pointed tail sliding in between my cheeks and caressing my rosebud softly.

"Tightest fucking pussy I've ever felt," he growled as he moved to my other nipple, his hips thrusting desperately against mine.

"Going to keep you forever, Pet. My good girl," he breathed as he stretched me.

And then…

I woke with a gasp, sweaty, and with my core aching as my breath left me in gasps. My whole body was a live wire, and I was on the edge of orgasm; one touch and I'd go off.

Just like every morning, I had to center myself and force my brain to start working again after a night of…dreams.

Not nightmares. Obviously. They made me feel way too good for it to be that.

Although it was always a monster ravishing my body.

I peeked up at the camera situated in the wall in front of me, the red light signaling that someone on the other end was watching me. Always watching me.

I'm sure they were getting off to the sight of me panting in my sleep, my nipples peeking out from my thin pajamas. At least I hadn't woken up with my hands rubbing furiously at my core. That happened quite a bit.

Although, at least those times my body had cum before I'd woken up. Now that I was awake, it was going to be hours before my body would settle down and I wouldn't be desperate for…a dick.

I fell back into my pillow, wanting to scream. It was this place. It was what was making me go crazy.

It had started slowly. A few dreams here and there of sexy scenes with…well, the psychiatrist here actually, but then one night it had morphed.

And *they* had begun to fill my dreams.

Every night, no matter what I tried, or how much I tried to stay awake, I was sucked into an erotic dreamscape. A dreamscape where...monsters ravaged my body over and over again.

It was the same four monsters. At this point, they really did feel like my lovers because I could tell you about every one of their features. I also could describe in detail all of their weird dicks. And all the ways they liked to play.

Considering I was definitely still a virgin, these dreams were quite alarming—and uncomfortable, and they'd only ratcheted up in intensity as the months and years had gone by. Last night's dream was relatively tame; I'd been gang banged the night before. A monster in my ass and pussy as I gave blow jobs back and forth to the other two.

I shifted uncomfortably in my bed as my core clenched again, begging to have some fucking relief.

If it weren't for the cameras, I would have. But with someone always watching...

My father had convinced everyone that I was crazy, and the sex dreams, the ones where my moans and screams of desire were so loud they rattled down the entire hallway... they were what cemented it.

There was no hiding what I dreamed about every night.

I'd tried the sleeping pills the doctors had given me, but those only trapped me in the dreams longer...much to the delight of Bright Meadows' other residents. Who needed porn when you had a soundtrack starring me, right?

So I didn't use the sleeping pills anymore.

The other medicine they tried to give me zombified me. The one time I'd taken them, a whole day had passed and I'd been mauled by another of the patients here, unable to do anything. I'd come to life in my room, the moon peeking through the tiny window above my head, terrified when I couldn't recall anything.

I'd refused to take the pills after that. No way was I going to be comatose at a place like Bright Meadows, where anything could happen to you.

And at least my screams weren't the scary kind. Not like all the other screams you heard in this place at night.

The screams from the other residents were always worse at night. Before I inevitably was dragged into my dreams, I would lay on my tiny cot that I was pretty sure was made of cardboard, staring up at the ceiling, and then the screams would start. It was much quieter during the day, but at night it was a cruel symphony. Maybe all the patients here found it impossible to sit with their thoughts at night too.

It's not like we were tired from the day's activities. Meal-times, medicine time, group therapy, and art therapy—they weren't exactly activities that required a lot of energy. Maybe for some people, it would've been exhausting to share their feelings, but I'd stopped sharing any of my real emotions the first week.

Since my father had threatened to kill me if I ever opened my mouth, there wasn't much that I could say except that I wasn't crazy. And apparently, that sort of thing was frowned upon in this institution. Who would've thought?

Unlike the asylums you saw in movies, the rooms in this

place weren't perfectly white; instead, they were black, which felt suffocating when you could walk across the room in two steps, and your window was only as big as your head. Mornings began with a bell that sounded more like a shrill siren. It woke us up at the same time every morning at seven a.m. Evidently, they were big believers in that adage, 'rise early and go to sleep early', because I now had the sleeping hours of an 80-year-old woman.

The bell rang just then, and I sighed as I dragged myself out of bed and went to change. You were expected to switch from your dishwater gray sleeping uniform to your dishwater gray day uniform in the minutes after the bell rang. There were no mirrors in the room, and the brushes they gave you were soft and completely ineffective so you didn't try and off yourself with them, thus everyone looked like a mess all day, every day.

If you weren't out of your room within ten minutes, one of the staff would barge in and force you out. I'd had that happen once, and I'd never let it happen again. Andrew, one of the resident assholes of the institution, had made sure to do a boob and an ass grab as he yanked me out of the room, so I'd learned quickly.

After dressing, I made my way out of the living room, along with most of the others that had rooms around me. We all walked slowly to the dining area filled with circle tables to facilitate a sense of "community", where we would be served a sugar-free, gluten-free, dairy-free breakfast that basically tasted like sawdust and paint thinner, but was apparently good for our brains.

There was one prisoner—I mean patient, who sat across from me every day, and today was no different. He must have felt the same way about the breakfast as I did, because every day he would use his fingers to smear it across his entire face. It didn't matter what they gave him. Seeing him try and slather himself with vegan bacon had been a particularly interesting experience.

Props to him for livening up the place. Even if he did it with drool dripping down from his mouth.

After breakfast, we were shuffled to the nurse's station, where they forced pills down our throats and stuck their fingers in our mouths to make sure the pills were gone. Luckily I was just on a mood stabilizer after I'd refused the other pill—not that I had anything against taking medicine for mental health. But considering I didn't have any of the disorders I'd been diagnosed with while under the influence of the drug I'd been injected with on that fateful day, taking anything stronger probably wouldn't have been great.

Evidently, my father was fearful of the effect that stronger meds could have on me and had ordered that I not be given any. He recognized that stronger drugs might have the detrimental effect of "loosening" my tongue, and he wouldn't want that.

Not that anyone was ever going to believe my story. It was so outlandish that I would sound crazy to anyone who heard it. That was the beauty of my father's plan. Have everyone on the outside doubt my sanity, and everyone on the inside doubt it as well. I would never have anyone believe me again.

We had an "A" schedule and a "B" schedule, just like school, and our routine was followed strictly. Except, instead of Calculus and English, we were learning how to paint our feelings, use recorders to "play our emotions out", and talk in small groups.

That was one of the hardest things about my new reality. Not only had I been thrown in here before the end of school, but I wasn't even allowed to take any tests to get my diploma, or even a GED, despite the fact that I'd been number two in my entire class. Stanford seemed like a fantasy that I'd made up in my mind at this point.

Most of the therapists were completely intolerable. They treated us more like toddlers than adults, and I cringed every time they spoke to me in their slow, sympathetic voices.

Since I knew I didn't have a chance to get out, and the therapists weren't interested in hearing about my innocence, I'd begun telling fairy tales during group therapy. But I'd make them so convoluted that it would take at least ten minutes for the therapist to figure out what story I was telling. It was a game I played, with only myself, of course, to see how long I could go before they caught on.

Anything to make the day go by quicker.

There was only one bright spot in Bright Meadows Asylum. Steele Adams.

Dr. Steele Adams, I should say.

Seeing him twice a week was most likely the only thing that kept me from falling off the deep end and becoming as crazy as my parents claimed I was.

Dr. Adams was the most beautiful man I'd ever seen. He

looked like he'd just stepped off the catwalk, and he was completely out of place in the drab, gross atmosphere I existed in now. During our sessions, I honestly wasn't even sure what we talked about, because I would get lost just looking at him and listening to the cadence of his voice. It's like someone out there had scooped out any fantasies of male attractiveness I had lurking in my brain and created him just for me.

When I was in sixth grade, I'd been to Iceland and we'd visited the Blue Lagoon. That's what his eyes reminded me of —they were a glowing blue color I'd never seen on another human being. Combined with his raven-colored hair, the effect was stunning. It was no wonder I was having dreams about him.

It was a Thursday today, which meant that I would be seeing him after breakfast.

I was pushed out of my lustful daydream by a tray clattering to the floor nearby. I looked over and saw that Candace was brandishing her spoon at a girl I'd never seen before. The poor girl was covered in the sweet potatoes the kitchen staff was trying to pass off as breakfast, and there were big tears rolling down her cheeks.

Maybe in another life, I would've stepped up to defend her since I was pretty sure that Candace was one of the resident murderers in this place. But apathy...and self-preservation was about all I was capable of feeling right now. Plus, I had a scar on my leg where Candace had somehow whittled a spoon into a knife and stabbed me in the leg a year ago. I'd bled so much that I'd passed out.

So someone else could handle Candace.

Candace started cackling wildly as orderlies rushed in. As soon as they got to her, she began to flail her arms, hitting and scratching every person that she could. "I'll kill all of you mother truckers," she screeched, making the word 'trucker' much more menacing than you would think. For some reason, Candace had a thing against swearing. She didn't care about murdering and mutilating people, but swearing crossed the line of her moral compass. "Let go of me, you butt munchers!"

She managed to cut one of the nurse's cheeks with her spoon before someone plunged a needle into her neck.

Almost immediately, her eyes took on that glazed, faraway look I was used to seeing here, and she stopped struggling. Two of the orderlies led her out of the room and then we were all instructed to go back to eating like nothing had happened. Just a typical day in Bright Meadows.

I wished I could say that Candace was the worst resident in this place, but there were far scarier people than her. And a bunch of them at that. I did my best to try and stay away from them. But every couple of months I'd slip up, and I'd be caught somewhere where the staff wasn't present. Slammed against the wall, a piece of my hair hacked off, burned with a lighter they'd come across…they were always quite inventive.

The only time that I could let my guard down was about to happen. My session with Steele.

I put my tray down, keeping my head tucked just in case any of the psychos thought I was looking at them wrong, and then hustled out of the dining area towards his office.

Butterflies ricocheted through my veins the closer I got to his door.

My dreams might've been filled with him, but he'd never given me any notion he felt similarly.

But then again, why would he? Here I was, a 20-year-old locked away in an insane asylum, while he was an accomplished doctor, able to live his life out in the real world. I wondered if he had a girlfriend out there. I didn't think he had a wife. He didn't wear a ring; not that his lack of one really meant anything.

I knocked on the door of his office, and a minute later, he opened it, a warm smile on his beautiful, beautiful lips.

"Hi," I murmured, inwardly wincing as I realized how breathy my voice sounded.

"Blake," he said with a nod, a piece of his hair falling into his face. I bit my lip in an effort to prevent myself from being weird and reaching out and brushing the curl out of his face. I'm sure that would go over well.

He was dressed in his typical uniform—a perfectly pressed, buttoned-up white collared shirt and navy black dress pants—and looked like he was about to conquer a corporate boardroom instead of spending an hour asking me how I was feeling.

I passed by him with a nod and entered the room, and he followed me inside. In my daydreams—not my night dreams, since those were solely filled with creatures—he was checking out my ass as I walked right now. But our uniform pants were shapeless, so that probably wouldn't happen even if he was interested in me like that.

The room was cozy. He'd obviously done his best to make it feel welcoming. It had to have been him who decorated the place because there was no way that anyone else in Bright Meadows would care about something like comfort. There were tall shelves on every wall stuffed full of books. Most of them were boring psychology books, but there were some classics scattered in there as well. He had his patients sit on a comfortable leather couch that had an assortment of squishy pillows and throw blankets he encouraged me to use every time. There was a red and black oriental rug on the floor, potted plants here and there, and a massive fireplace on the far wall that he had lit most days. Which was heaven since Bright Meadows believed that its residents should feel like human popsicles judging by the freezing temperatures we were kept in.

I settled into the couch, immediately grabbing a fuzzy blanket and wrapping it around me. Dr. Adams walked over to the fireplace and threw another log in before opening his small fridge that sat next to it and pulling out a can of my favorite orange soda.

My mouth started watering just looking at it, and it was honestly all I could do to not jump up and grab it out of his hands like I was Gollum from Lord of the Rings. *My Precious*, my inner voice cooed.

That was creepy.

"You obviously were listening last week," I said with a blush as he handed me the drink.

He smiled at me, and the butterflies in my stomach started

doing freaking cartwheels and flips like they'd made it to the Olympics.

"I always listen to you," he murmured as he settled into the warm armchair across from the couch. "It just took a minute to track it down. Evidently, they stopped making it last year."

While I was definitely twitter-pated...and interested in the fact that he'd tracked down the soda I'd mentioned was my favorite, I was also thinking that I'd been trapped in here long enough that they discontinued my favorite drink. I mean, I may have been the only person in the world who drank it, so that was probably why, but it still represented the stark passage of time and all that I'd lost.

"I made you upset," he commented, leaning forward in dismay. I threw him a tremulous smile and popped the tab on my drink before taking a large gulp of the drink, moaning a bit as the fizzy orange beverage hit my tastebuds.

"Finally, something that doesn't taste like old leather," I said as I glanced at him, almost spitting my drink out when I saw the expression on his face.

He looked—almost hungry. Starving, in fact.

For me.

Dr. Adams blinked and the look disappeared. His face was blank again, only the kind, caring psychiatrist to be found.

But I swore that I'd seen it.

Unless the dreams were driving me to see sexual desire everywhere.

I didn't think that was happening. I hadn't thought Mr. Drools-a-lot was into me at lunch.

Focus, I chastised myself as I took another sip of my drink.

"So, have you thought at all about what we talked about last session?" he asked, his bright blue eyes boring into me.

I shifted in my seat. "I've told you that it won't make a difference."

He'd been bringing up the medication he wanted me to try for weeks now. One of the main focuses of our sessions was my…intense dreams. He knew in general that they were sexual—the staff had told him that. But he'd never pressed me on specific details—thank god. Dr. Adams seemed to be under the impression I wasn't going to be trapped in this place for the rest of my life if I could get my dreams under control.

He seemed to think that was the main concern and not the fact that I was being held hostage here because of my father.

Dr. Adams leaned forward. "If you could just stay on it for a while, enough to convince them you're ready to be released—"

I squeezed my can so hard that orange soda went everywhere.

"Shit," I gasped, attempting to use my shirt to blot at the soda now all over the leather couch. Frustrated tears built in my eyes as I wiped. I knew what would happen—I would go on those pills but would still be trapped here, of course, and I'd lose even more when I began to walk around in a daze.

Suddenly, his hand was on mine, and I looked to see that

he was crouched in front of me. This close to him, it was almost unbearable. He was so fucking beautiful.

"Blake," he murmured, his gaze searching my face. "I'm sorry. You can tell me if there's something else going on."

My lip trembled, and I was very much aware that his fingers were softly caressing my hand. I wanted to tell him about my father, and how I'd ended up here. I wanted to so fucking bad.

I opened my mouth, the story on the tip of my tongue, but then I remembered my father's warning the day I'd been dropped off. I remembered the way the staff had reacted when I'd even dared to say that I wasn't crazy.

Dr. Adams was my only safe space here. I didn't want to ruin that on a pipe dream.

"I'm fine, Dr. Adams. I'm so sorry I've made such a mess," I finally said stiffly, watching as disappointment leached into his features.

"Steele," he said as he pulled his hand away and stood up.

"Steele?" I asked, confused, and hating that I missed his touch.

"You should call me Steele." I watched as he went and grabbed some paper towels from a shelf in the back corner of the room and then walked back over and methodically cleaned up the rest of my spilled drink.

"Oh. Okay." I had to have cracked. That was the only way to explain what was happening. I mean, maybe to a normal girl it wouldn't have seemed like much—the special drink, the hand touch, the first name. But for me, it was a lot. A hell of a lot.

After throwing away the towels, he sat back down in his chair, and he asked his normal questions.

I responded with my usual answers, but everything felt different. I could feel it in the air. I could see it in his eyes. Something had changed.

And as his hand brushed the small of my back as he opened the door at the end of our session, I wondered what I'd done to make the universe hate me so much.

Because in this life, I could never have Steele or anything else that I wanted. Even if he wanted me.

I walked down the hall away from him, feeling the heat of his stare caressing my back, but I didn't look his way.

The only comfort I was ever going to get in this forsaken place was in my dreams.

With my monsters.

I had to live with that.

ACKNOWLEDGMENTS

We would not bring out all the incredible books we do without our amazing support team who never let us down and work tirelessly.

Leah, for your meticulous attention to detail. We love your work so much. Your cheerleading gets us through each day of writing.

Caitlin for your dedication and catching all the small things that slip through the cracks.

To Jasmine, our editor who we'd be lost without, and always being supportive even with our insane deadlines.

And to our beautiful readers for all your support and all the wonderful comments and messages you sent us about how much you love our books.

We love having you on our journey and adore you from the depths of our hearts for helping us reach our dreams.

XOXO,

Mila & C.R.

BOOKS BY C.R. JANE

www.crjanebooks.com

The Fated Wings Series

First Impressions

Forgotten Specters

The Fallen One (a Fated Wings Novella)

Forbidden Queens

Frightful Beginnings (a Fated Wings Short Story)

Faded Realms

Faithless Dreams

Fabled Kingdoms

Fated Wings 8

The Rock God (a Fated Wings Novella)

The Darkest Curse Series

Forget Me

Lost Passions

The Sounds of Us Contemporary Series (complete series)

Remember Us This Way

Remember You This Way

Remember Me This Way

Siren Condemned

Siren Sacrificed

Siren Awakened

Siren Redeemed

Kingdom of Wolves Co-write with Mila Young

Wild Moon

Wild Heart

Wild Girl

Wild Love

Stupid Boys Series Co-write with Rebecca Royce

Stupid Boys

Dumb Girl

Crazy Love

Breathe Me Duet Co-write with Ivy Fox (complete)

Breathe Me

Breathe You

Rich Demons of Darkwood Series Co-write with May Dawson

Make Me Lie

BOOKS BY MILA YOUNG

www.milayoungbooks.com

Savage

Lost Wolf

Broken Wolf

Fated Wolf

Shadowlands

Shadowlands Sector, One

Shadowlands Sector, Two

Shadowlands Sector, Three

Shadows & Wolves Complete Collection

Chosen Vampire Slayer

Night Kissed

Moon Kissed

Blood Kissed

Monster & Me Duet Co-write with C.R. Jane

Monster's Temptation

Monster's Obsession

The Alpha-Hole Duet

Real Alphas Bite

Kingdom of Wolves

Wild Moon

Wild Heart

Wild Girl

Wild Love

Wild Soul

Winter's Thorn

To Seduce A Fae

To Tame A Fae

To Claim A Fae

Shadow Hunters Series

Boxed Set 1

Sin Demons

Playing With Hellfire

Hell In A Handbasket

All Shot To Hell

To Hell And Back

When Hell Freezes Over

Hell On Earth

Snowball's Chance In Hell

Kings of Eden

At the Mercy of Monsters

Kings of Eden

Stolen Paradise

Ruthless Lies

Wicked Heat Series

Wicked Heat #1

Wicked Heat #2

Wicked Heat #3

Elemental Series

Taking Breath #1

Taking Breath #2

Gods and Monsters

Apollo Is Mine

Poseidon Is Mine

Ares Is Mine

Hades Is Mine

Sin Demons Co-write with Harper A. Brooks

Playing With Hellfire

Hell In A Handbasket

All Shot To Hell

To Hell And Back

When Hell Freezes Over

Hell On Earth

Haven Realm Series

Hunted (Little Red Riding Hood Retelling)

Cursed (Beauty and the Beast Retelling)

Entangled (Rapunzel Retelling)

Princess of Frost (Snow Queen)

Thief of Hearts Series Co-write with C.R. Jane

Siren Condemned

Siren Sacrificed

Siren Awakened

Broken Souls Series Co-write with C.R. Jane

School of Broken Souls

School of Broken Hearts

School of Broken Dreams

School of Broken Wings

Fallen World Series Co-write with C.R. Jane

Bound

Broken

Betrayed

Belong

Beautiful Beasts Academy

Manicures and Mayhem

Diamonds and Demons

Hexes and Hounds

Secrets and Shadows

Passions and Protectors

Ancients and Anarchy

———

Subscribe to Mila Young's Newsletter to receive exclusive content, latest updates, and giveaways. Join here.

ABOUT C.R. JANE

A Texas girl living in Utah now, I'm a wife, mother, lawyer, and now author. My stories have been floating around in my head for years, and it has been a relief to finally get them down on paper. I'm a huge Dallas Cowboys fan and I primarily listen to Beyonce and Taylor Swift...don't lie and say you don't too.

My love of reading started probably when I was three and with a faster than normal ability to read, I've devoured hundreds of thousands of books in my life. It only made sense that I would start to create my own worlds since I was always getting lost in others'.

I like heroines who have to grow in order to become badasses, happy endings, and swoon-worthy, devoted, (and hot) male characters. If this sounds like you, I'm pretty sure we'll be friends.

I'm so glad to have you on my team...check out the links below for ways to hang out with me and more of my books you can read!

Visit my **Facebook** page to get updates.

Visit my **Amazon Author** page.

Visit myWebsite.

Sign up for mynewsletter to stay updated on new releases, find out random facts about me, and get access to different points of view from my characters.

ABOUT MILA YOUNG

Best-selling author, Mila Young tackles everything with the zeal and bravado of the fairytale heroes she grew up reading about. She slays monsters, real and imaginary, like there's no tomorrow. By day she rocks a keyboard as a marketing extraordinaire. At night she battles with her mighty pen-sword, creating fairytale retellings, and sexy ever after tales.

Ready to read more and more from Mila Young? Subscribe today here.

Join Mila's **Wicked Readers group** for exclusive content, latest news, and giveaway. Click here.

For more information…
milayoungauthor@gmail.com

Printed in Great Britain
by Amazon

23950691R00225